STRIKEOUT

MILLIE PEREZ

For the islands that made me and raised me.
Manhattan
Puerto Rico
Dominican Republic
This is my love letter to you.

Tesoro

AUTHOR'S NOTE

Hello lovely readers, and welcome to the world of the New York Monarchs.

This is the first book in an interconnected series and I am so excited and cannot wait for you to dive into these new characters. No, truly, I can't. That's why I have added a special treat at the end of the epilogue for those interested in what comes next.

Below are some content warnings. Please take them into account before reading this story to ensure an enjoyable experience.

Happy Reading!

xo,
Millie

CONTENT WARNINGS

Mention of natural disaster (hurricane relief)

Brief mention of death of a parent (off page)

Discussions around online bullying and revenge porn

Open door spice with explicit sex scenes

ISABELLA

NINETIES MARC ANTHONY VOCALS filter through my flimsy bedroom door, alerting me that at least one of my parents is up and cleaning our modest Upper West Side apartment. And by cleaning, I mean beating the baseboards with a Swiffer.

And by *our* apartment, I mean *their* apartment. The one I am currently squatting in... indefinitely. Because nothing screams thriving twenty-five-year-old quite like still living with one's parents. But what can I say? I have an aversion to New York City rent prices and the idea of adulting in general. Sue me.

Lies.

You know why you're still here, the voice in my head reminds me. As if I couldn't google my name and remember all the ways my past still haunts me. How the actions of another keep me tethered to the only people who make me feel safe and unjudged.

I huff out a frustrated breath.

Not this shit again.

I lift my head and scour my bedding to find where my Kindle landed after I dozed off last night. Because, like most nights, I fell asleep way too late feeding myself that "just one more chapter before I go to bed" lie.

Reading seems to be the only thing that can take me out of my head and transport me into another world. One where I'm not Isabella Morales, the girl whose fall from grace was everyone's water cooler chatter, each headline slowly bleeding me dry of my sanity, and quite frankly, my desire to ever fall in love again.

Which is why romance books are my haven. A place where I can be a spectator, because the romance genre isn't just about two people falling in love. It's a safe space to learn about how people of diverse backgrounds go through transformations that happen to align with meeting the loves of their lives. Something I never plan to let happen to me, because while I can't rewrite the pages of my past, I can absolutely keep the reins to my heart tighter than the heroine in the cowboy romance I binged last night.

Because I, under no circumstances, will ever fall for a man's false promises again.

Mark my words.

CHAPTER ONE

ISABELLA

"Buenos días, Mami." I press a quick kiss on my mother's cheek and dart out of her reach before she has the chance to poke me with whatever cleaning weapon she has at her disposal. Dominican mothers, especially Claribel Morales, have a way of getting creative with the greetings they give their children. I would drop dead if my mother hugged me and said, "Good morning, sweetie." I'm much more accustomed to the disgruntled mumblings about how back in her heyday, she would have to walk seven miles to a convenience store or ride a *burro* to school.

I'm pretty sure only one of those is a lie.

Essentially, I'm usually greeted with a dash of grump and a heavy serving of attitude. All in love, of course. Because my immigrant parents tend to show their love through acts of service, not words of affirmation. At least that's what my many years of therapy have taught me to understand.

So color me surprised when my mother simply smiles at me, and says, "Hola, mija. Any plans for today?"

I halt midway to grab an apple from the kitchen and spin on my heel, eyes narrowed. "What's going on? Are you sick? Did Abuela die?" My voice hitches as I run through the potential scenarios that would cause my mom to give me such a calm greeting.

My mom's shoulders drop as she rolls her eyes. "¿Viste? This generation talks about wanting gentle parenting, pero when I do it..." She waves the rest of her comment away in mock annoyance.

Suspicion laces my voice as I say, "So, you were trying to 'gentle parent' me, a woman in her mid-twenties?"

"Mira, I didn't read the whole article you sent me the other day, okay? So I didn't know there was an age cutoff. I just wanted to talk to you about something." I gesture for her to go on, which is unusual in and of itself, since the woman can carry a whole conversation on her own. "So, Mateo is still looking for a nanny, and Anna is starting school soon—"

"*Mami*." I groan. Not this again.

My mother has been trying to get me to nanny full time for her best friend's son ever since I stepped in to nanny for a few days during a New Year's Eve trip down in the Dominican Republic. Mateo's mom had to cancel at the last minute due to a medical procedure. But Anna had been looking forward to quality time with her dad before things got busy, so calling off the trip was a no-go. Mateo still had vital work calls scheduled, therefore he needed part-time child care. Which was me, in a pool chair lounger, tanning while judging a five-year-old's underwater handstands. Truly living the dream.

But that was a onetime gig.

I have my own job to think about. Even though it's a far cry from my dream job.

Because I'll be honest, working as an assistant librarian at the New York Public Library isn't exactly lining my pockets. It's more like a pity volunteer position with a tiny stipend. But it allows me to be surrounded by books. And more importantly, book covers.

Ever since I fell down the rabbit hole of collecting paperback copies of my favorite books, I've rediscovered my love for graphic design. When I have a free moment in the library, I can be found creating an alternative cover for my latest read. And while some may consider my hobby glorified doodling, I think of it as a potential career path. If I can finally get my online book cover design business off the ground, I would be the happiest human on the planet.

I work under a pseudonym and use an illustrated profile pic for privacy reasons. Unfortunately, the pipeline of book cover requests is mighty dry at the moment over at Bella Covers. Which is probably why my mom keeps needling me to take the job as a nanny for Mateo.

The problem is that *Mateo* is Mateo Martinez, a.k.a. the starting pitcher of the New York Monarchs and probably one of the most talented and famous athletes of our generation.

So yeah, big fucking deal.

Our moms have been best friends for almost a decade, yet besides the New Year's Eve trip, I can probably count on one hand the number of times I've met him in person. Mostly by my own design, but that's partly due to the tiny bit of self-preservation in me that's still activated.

Because, you see, Mateo isn't just impressive on the baseball field.

Nope, God clearly has favorites.

He's also insanely attractive. Like wipe the drool off your chin hot. And it only gets worse when you see him interact with his daughter. The man has heart eyes when it comes to her, and it turns the entire human population into putty in his hands.

And that's great if you're into really tall men with muscles designed to throw balls close to one hundred miles per hour. Men with short, brown hair and light hazel eyes. Along with a plump bottom lip and straight white teeth designed for toothpaste commercials. And while we're at it, let's not forget the perfectly trimmed beard that must be tended to by the people who keep the Versailles garden impeccable. I have seen that man up close and in HD, and not a single hair is out of place, not even an ingrown in sight.

Ugh, I can't believe I've stooped low enough to wish an ingrown hair on someone's face.

But truth be told, even if he didn't have a reserved exterior when it came to everyone besides his mother and his daughter, and if he were certifiable enough to bypass all the stunning women on the planet who would gladly throw themselves at his feet, then decide that I, Isabella, were someone he would be interested in... yeah it would still be a hard no for me.

Because not only have I sworn off men, but even more so a specific breed.

Baseball players.

"Isabella Marie Morales. Por favor, no seas tan dramática." My mother disrupts my thoughts. "Just give it a chance, for Anna's sake. You know that Bethzaida can no longer run after her after she got that hip replacement that made her miss the New Year's Eve trip. And Anna is starting school for the very first time. La pobrecita, she must be so excited and nervous."

The mention of Anna makes me smile, because she is quite possibly the funniest kid I've ever met. I swear, if we were the same age, we'd be best friends.

The thought quickly sours in my stomach and makes me feel pathetic, since a kindergartener is the coolest person I've hung out with in a while.

"And all the perks, Isa. You know that man will be paying a pretty penny for whoever takes care of his little girl."

"Mami, it's not always about the money," I grumble as I take a bite out of an organic apple, one that I most certainly did not pay for when I went grocery shopping with my mom earlier this week.

Mami stares at my apple as if she's recalling that fact as well, then continues. "Are you listening to me? That little girl will be going to school, so for eight hours a day, you will be getting paid for doing absolutely nothing. Plus, we're already in August. The season ends in October, and that's only if they make it to the World Series."

I slow my chewing as I think that nugget over. Eight hours of uninterrupted paid alone time means I'd have time to dedicate to my book cover design business and work on marketing myself better, as well as work on premade covers.

I try to keep my face impassive as my mom stares me down. I know she's capable of sniffing out any scent of interest, and I'm not ready to show her my cards quite yet.

She finally turns her head and gives a sigh worthy of a telenovela award. "Okay, well, I tried." My mom starts spraying down the counter in front of her. "I guess you really must love living here with your Papi and me. I mean, I really can't blame you. We are fun to be around." She begins to wipe down the counter like she doesn't have a single care in the world until she spins quickly, facing me. "Although, if I were you, I would jump at the chance to live in a beautiful high-rise apartment that overlooks Central Park and is within walking distance of all your favorite restaurants..." She dreamily looks up at the ceiling.

I look up as well, wondering if there's a mystery stain up there I should be worried about, until I realize I have no idea what she was referring to. "Why would I suddenly be living in a fancy apartment by Central Park?"

My mother's smile unfurls slowly as she tilts her head. "Oh, did I forget to mention that the job comes with your own room in their apartment? Well, practically a whole floor since their rooms are on the second floor and the guest room is on the first." She nods to herself. "And Mateo would be away half the time anyway. So the lucky person who manages to snag that dream job will not only get paid spectacularly for a few hours of work, but she'll also get to live in the lap of luxury."

A tiny squeak escapes my tight-lipped mouth.

Shit.

I'd be lying if I said still waking up in my childhood bedroom while listening to my mother unmercifully blast old-school bachata while vacuuming at an ungodly hour wasn't making a good argument for me to get off my ass and finally put on my big girl panties.

My resolve is slowly crumbling, but there's still something holding me back.

My mom moves closer to me, placing a gentle hand on my shoulder as her eyes soften.

She knows what's holding me back.

"This isn't the same thing, Isa. The world has moved on, and you deserve to as well. You need to start putting yourself first and stop focusing on what others may think about you."

My eyes threaten to fill with tears, so I quickly hug my mom around her middle while she's still holding her cleaning supplies.

I release her, then take a step back, nodding. "Okay. I think I can do this."

She smiles brightly. "Yes, you can do this, mija."

I continue my bobblehead impersonation as I say, "I can do this. No, better yet, I deserve this. I deserve to give my dreams a chance. And this is an opportunity of a lifetime. I can't keep letting the trolls win."

"¿Qué diablos are trolls?"

"Never mind. I'm having a moment here, Ma," I say, sounding a bit out of breath even though I haven't taken a single step. "I'm gonna reach out to Mateo and let him know that I'm interested in the position. Hopefully, since he knows me, and you, and, well, basically everyone else who knows me, that'll do for references. Yeah? Cool? No? Please tell me when to stop, Mami."

"Stop," she deadpans.

"Okay, thanks, because for a second there, it kinda felt like I was on a runaway train, and you were gonna let me keep on—"

"Isa, cállate la boca and listen to me."

"Mm-hmm." I bite down on my lips.

"You're gonna take a shower, then you're gonna get dressed. While you're doing that, I will call Bethzaida and have her put you on Mateo's visitor list."

"Wait, visitor list? Why?"

"Because, hija mía. You will go to his apartment today. Now, actually, and ask for that job his mother and I have tirelessly been working on you two to agree on. These kinds of matters are best handled face to face." She puts her hands on my shoulders and guides me to our small bathroom. "And besides, I have a whole pan of Beth's flan you can take to him. That man will never turn down his mother's cooking or sweets."

I quickly give my mother another squeeze before stepping into the bathroom. "Thank you so much for supporting me, Mami. You're the best."

I faintly hear her huff out a "por fin" while I take the world's fastest shower. I don't have time to straighten my hair, so I use a bit of my mom's nice hair product to comb the sides and throw my hair into a high ponytail, letting my curls go wild as I sway my head.

I dress as quickly as a deranged Tasmanian Devil through the apartment, hopping into yesterday's jeans and accepting the floral blouse my mom hangs in front of my face. I slip my feet into chunky-heeled sandals. The two inches won't do anything for my five-three frame when I come face to face with Mateo, but a girl needs a little armor when going into battle.

I grab my purse, and I'm almost out the door when my mom shoves a heavy pan of flan into my arms. "I already ordered you an Uber and texted you their details. They'll be downstairs in two minutes." Right. Thank God for my mom, because I don't even know Mateo's address. She reaches out and wraps a loose curl around my hair tie. "You got this, Isa. I have a feeling that this will be good for you." She places a gentle hand on my cheek.

"Thanks, Mami." I beam. "I love you. Thanks so much for the not-so-subtle push." I laugh. "And don't worry. I'm getting this job. I can feel it in my bones." I raise the flan to my head and smile widely. "Besides, who can say no to this face?"

Chapter Two

MATEO

"NO."

"No?"

"No."

"But... but I have flan," Isabella pouts.

I sigh. This is one of those moments where I wish I had a front door and not an elevator as an entrance to my home. Can't exactly herd her back into the elevator with as much finality as a slammed door. So I let my manners kick in for the first time since I laid eyes on Isabella Morales standing in my home, taking the flan from her iron grip and waving her farther into my apartment.

"I'm sorry you came all the way downtown. I'm sure my mother put you up to this, but like I told *her*, I'll figure out the nanny situation on my own." I set the delicious-looking flan, my mother's, I'm sure, and turn to face Isabella.

But she's not behind me. She's still standing by the round table in the foyer, wide eyed and slack-jawed.

I never have guests over, so I tend to forget how intimidating my place can be for someone who's never been here before. Especially for someone like Isabella, who grew up in the same neighborhood as me on the Upper West Side.

This lifestyle is a far cry from my childhood, when I used to sit on bodega crates as street furniture while hanging out with my friends or playing baseball until the streetlights came on.

Now, that neighborhood is filled with skyrocketing rent prices and fancy restaurants. But back when I was a kid, there was nothing like playing in the streets until the neighborhood abuelita yelled at us to get home to our families.

And while I love the life I've built, I sometimes find myself craving the simpler times. When I could walk out of my house and run a simple errand without informing my security detail. Or take my mother out to dinner without having to factor in an added hour for fan pictures and autographs.

Sometimes I wish I could go back to my old neighborhood and reconnect with those childhood friends. Because even though I'm a thirty-three-year-old baseball player living in one of the most expensive buildings in Manhattan, there's no shaking the feeling of heading past 96th street and basking in the sense of home.

And that's what Isabella reminds me of.

Home.

Which makes her the most dangerous woman in my life.

Yes, even more so than my overbearing mother. Because Isabella Morales has managed to do what no other woman has done since my daughter was born.

She's carved out a special place for herself in my head.

And, I fear, my heart.

Ever since she joined Anna and me on our New Year's vacation, I haven't been able to shake the image of her in a tiny red bikini that was designed for sin.

Or her fresh, makeup-free morning face and the wild curls crowning her head like a queen as she sat for breakfast.

And possibly the worst of it all was the jaw-dropping New Year's Eve dress that reminded me of all the places I wanted to put my hands on at the stroke of midnight.

She was no longer *Izzy*, my mother's best friend's daughter. The young girl with braces in the photos in my mother's apartment who was skinny in an unintentional way, as if puberty had all but forgotten her.

No. The grown-ass woman who met me at the tarmac beside my private jet now went by *Isa*. A woman I swear God handcrafted to bring me to my knees with the way she grew into her body and confidence.

The sway of her hips, like a pendulum, could hypnotize me into giving into all the sexual energy I've kept locked up tight.

And if I'm being honest, her physical appearance is only the bow on the real gift that is Isabella.

Even though I tried to keep my distance, anyone within a ten-mile radius of our resort could see that Isabella was sunshine personified. Within a day, she had become best buddies with most of the hotel staff, asking everyone where they were from and being genuinely interested in their stories.

By midday, she would usually be holding court by the pool, coming up with the most ridiculous aquatic competitions to keep my adorable yet lightning bolt of a daughter entertained for hours on end.

At dinner, she would teach my daughter how to pronounce local dishes in Spanish and agree to whatever princess movie was on the agenda for the night.

It could have ended there. I could have thanked her for her help and moved on with my predictable life.

But on our final night, the last string that tethered me to my self-restraint almost snapped clean at the sight of Isabella teaching my daughter how to dance salsa in front of a live band.

I sat back and nursed my one and only beer as I watched the light of my life, the tiny human who had changed my world for the better, inch closer to her Puerto Rican roots by learning our music, our dances.

The way she shimmied and shook her hips in an uncoordinated manner that only her DNA could save her from brought an ease to my soul.

Only for it to be set alight the second my focus moved to Isabella. It wasn't the way she demanded everyone's attention on the dance floor or even her incredible moves that made my resolve falter.

No.

It was the way she laughed. Especially with my daughter, without a care in the world, as if Anna were the only person in that crowded room. I was tempted to break my no dating rule and ask her out right then and there.

But I have never let myself go that far.

Imagined myself bringing someone new into our lives.

It's too risky. I won't put Anna in a situation where she gets too close to someone just to have them leave us.

And my decision has never bothered me, not one bit.

That is, until Isa.

Dangerous, dangerous woman.

Which is why I need to get her out of my home before I do something stupid.

Like hire her to be my fucking nanny.

CHAPTER THREE

ISABELLA

Holy shit.

This is not a normal New York City apartment.

Hell, this makes *Million Dollar Listing* apartments look like cheap dorm rooms.

I'm not even hung up on the fact that there is no front door with at least four locks, a New York staple, because the lobby to this place runs like a mini Fort Knox, with a private elevator bringing me right up to the top floor.

Or should I say *floors*, since my eyes keep going up, up, up to the second floor that overlooks the living room, kitchen, and dining room.

But that's all I can see from the spot I've been rooted to since I arrived and yelled "Nanny's here!" in my best Snooki voice.

In hindsight, that probably wasn't the right move, given the fact that Mateo's face immediately went from shocked to annoyed.

Followed by his one-word dismissal.

No.

I shake my head and step out of my shoes. God forbid I bring filth from the city sidewalks onto these pristine floors.

I can't believe he said no.

I need to fix this. Quickly. I can't let this opportunity pass me by because my reality-TV drenched brain couldn't come up with a normal person greeting.

Mateo stares at me from his kitchen island, arms crossed over his wide chest. His simple white T-shirt is working overtime to contain muscles I'm sure are extremely important for throwing baseballs at super speeds. And I'm pretty sure I saw him wearing those jeans on a billboard on the way here. I got a good view of the way they mold around his hips and ass when he walked away from me with my flan offering in hand. I quickly lowered my gaze, because the last thing I want is to be caught staring at my potential new boss's butt. It was clearly the wrong move. Because he was barefoot, and the size of those things should be studied. I quickly closed my eyes and shook my head, because staring at the man's feet seemed more violating than ogling his ass.

I'm not sure why. Maybe it's because I keep seeing "no free toes" on social media and believe all naked feet this day and age are entitled to compensation.

Mateo's eyebrow quirks, as if to say *you done having that conversation in your head yet?*

I give him my brightest smile in an attempt to disarm him of any argument he may have to not hire me. I clearly have my work cut out for myself.

"Mateo, your place is beautiful," I say as I walk over to stand across from him, the kitchen island separating us.

"Thanks," he gruffs. "Listen, Isabella—"

"Okay, hear me out," I start. No need to beat around the bush when it's apparent this man wants me around as much as he wants his next root canal. I put my arms up in a placating manner. "I know that our moms have been circling us for months, hoping I'd be your nanny—"

"Anna's nanny," he corrects.

"Right, of course. Because you're a grown man. One who doesn't need me to take care of, err—"

"Isa." He exhales.

"My point," I exclaim, more to myself so I stay on track, "is that Anna needs a nanny, and who better than someone who's already done the gig? Plus, you know me, so you can trust that I'm not a crazy person off the street." I chuckle nervously. "*Right*?" I straighten when he doesn't answer. "Right?"

Mateo places his hands on the island and bows his head. I've never seen someone concentrate so hard on taking deep breaths, but clearly, my presence will do it to him.

"Isabella." He says my name in its Spanish pronunciation. "Like I was saying, I'm sorry you came all the way down here, but my mother really shouldn't have overstepped this time. Yes, I need childcare for Anna, but I don't think I'll be able to have a live-in nanny." He pushes off the counter and slowly starts making his way back to the foyer, expecting me to follow.

"Wait! I can provide references, and I can be available twenty-four seven." That's a lie, because this girl likes her sleep. But desperate times and all.

Mateo halts his movements, then unexpectedly changes trajectories.

Back toward me.

It takes all my willpower to keep my eyes on his and not roam over his delectable body. Feels like I have to remind my brain that this man is supposed to be my boss, and I don't think giving him a once-over is going to seal the deal for me. We're standing toe to toe, and no matter how hard I try to stop it, my chest keeps rising and falling due to Mateo's intoxicating scent.

"I'm sorry, Isa, but I don't think I could get used to having staff in my home."

I take an obvious look around the place, craning my neck around him to stare at every inch of the pristine apartment we're standing in.

Mateo Martinez is clearly skilled on the baseball field, but I have a hard time imagining him wiping Windex on all these floor-to-ceiling windows by himself.

As if he can hear my thoughts, he continues. "My cleaning team comes twice a week while the apartment is empty. My chef cooks my meals and stores them in the refrigerator for me while I'm at practice, and any other household errands are taken care of by the downstairs concierge." He runs a hand through his hair, making his T-shirt sleeve stretch around his bicep in a way that should be deemed sexually inappropriate. "I've tried the live-in nanny gig twice already. First guy used my kitchen like an all-you-can-eat buffet while lounging around in his adult-size onesie. An adult-size onesie, by the way, should not be considered appropriate sleepwear, at least not in my home. And the second nanny made a mess of this place. She was chaos incarnate, keen on baking goods that were barely edible, all while almost burning down my kitchen. A kitchen that was built to withstand more than most, yet a batch of sprinkle cookies almost had us condemned." He sighs. "And these are the candidates that were sent to me by an agency that has a very high fee for vetting people for these kinds of placements. So believe me when I say that I'd prefer to decline going through this experience for the third time now."

Valid points.

But not in my favor, so I ignore and pivot.

I take a large step back, hoping my wits will follow and start making my way over to my dream couch. A large U shape that looks like a cloud, perfect for reading on my Kindle or an afternoon nap. I slowly lower myself onto it and bite back a moan once the cushions envelop me, welcoming me as one of their own. "Look, I get it. Not wanting to have *staff* around. But it's me, Isabella. We're practically family." I lean back and put my bare feet on the coffee table.

"Feet down," he demands.

I bolt back up and stand. "Okay, yeah, totally. I took it too far there. My bad." I nervously rub my sweaty hands up and down the front of my jeans as I feel my cheeks blush ferociously at the tone he just took with me. And the fact that it made me feel *things* I shouldn't at a time like this.

I'll unpack that another time. Like the day after never.

He moves to stand in front of a massive built-in TV above the fireplace while facing me, hands on his hips. "When I said I don't want to live with others, I meant that when I get home, it's usually only Anna and me. Sometimes my mother if it's late and Anna bribes her into staying over. But inside these walls is where I have some peace. A place where I don't need to smile and nod or worry that I'm not giving someone the best Mateo Martinez experience. Here, I get to be myself. And unfortunately, I don't think I could give that up," he offers softly.

His unexpected vulnerability has me wavering.

And dammit, he's right. A man like Mateo has his movements tracked every second of the day. As soon as he steps out of his home, he's surrounded by people who want something from him. Or worse, people who want to get their fifteen minutes of fame by getting him to break from his picture-perfect persona. It's never actually happened, but I've seen enough people on the street heckle him on social media, complaining about a game loss or yelling lewd comments.

I can only imagine that makes him even more protective of his home life and his mental well-being. And while I cannot put myself in his exact shoes, I know firsthand how important it is to have a safe place to call home, especially when you need it the most.

I clear my throat and take a step forward, the coffee table standing guard between us. "Listen, I get it. I have no idea the pressure you are under, but I know a thing or two about having all eyes on me."

Realization sets in his gaze, and he wipes a hand over his bearded jaw. "Fuck, Isa. I'm sorry. I knew about—I didn't mean—"

I put my hand up to silence him. "I'm not asking for your pity, Mateo. That's not why I brought it up. I'm simply here to say that I understand. And if it means me hiding out in the guest room when I'm not needed, to respect your boundaries and desire for peace, then I promise you it's a better setup than what I currently have going on." His face looks pained, like it physically hurts him to have to turn me down. But if I'm going to walk out of here without the job, I need to make sure I put it all out there. That way I'm not banging my head against the tiled wall while I replay this conversation, acting out all the things I should have said. "I need this job. I need a place to stay. Not because I don't currently have those things, but because today, for the first time in a long time, I told myself I deserve better. I deserve more. And who knows, maybe tonight, I'll laugh it off while I go to bed and go back to thinking that I'm right where I deserve to be due to my past, but not right now." I steel my spine, because this is the part where I usually get the condescending smiles. "Right now, I can tell you that I have hopes to be more. To become a respected book cover designer. I've always loved creating, and paired with my love of reading, it has become a new passion of mine. And I know it may sound silly—"

"It doesn't. Not to me," he interrupts.

I nod in agreement, because I'm on a roll, and partially because I can't let myself get sucked in by the intensity of his sincerity. "Exactly. And this job would be the perfect environment for me to grow my brand and focus on my craft. While Anna is in school, of course," I quickly add, since I don't want him to think that I haven't factored in my actual job duties. "Because while she's with me, she will be my number one priority. I will go above and beyond for her. I promise you that." I release a deep breath as my arms fall to my sides. As if to say *that's all she's got, folks. Take it or leave it.*

Preferably take it, of course.

His eyes bore into mine, as if he's trying to work out a problem he can't find the solution to, yet hoping I somehow have the answer.

After a few torturous moments of silence, he shakes his head and laughs humorlessly.

His voice comes out gravelly. "Isabella... go home."

My last bit of hope leaves my body, and it takes everything in me not to show how utterly crushed I am by his words. I tuck a loose curl that must have escaped the confines of my ponytail while I delivered my meek monologue, then I start my way out of the U-shaped couch, which means I have to walk right past him in order to get to the elevator and leave.

I keep my head down, because I'm too embarrassed to look him in the eye after I laid my woes out there for him to see.

Just as we're shoulder to shoulder, his hand shoots out and softly wraps around my wrist. A small gasp leaves my mouth as I stare up into his molten gaze.

"I wasn't finished." His thumb gently caresses the inside of my wrist as he says, "Go home *and pack*. Then come right back to me... I mean here. And come right back *here*." He clears his throat and gives his head a slight shake. "I'm giving you a one-week trial. If this arrangement works for the both of us, then I'll send for the rest of your stuff."

My eyes widen as my brain catches on to his words. "So, I got the job?" I whisper, afraid that he may come to his senses if I speak too loudly.

"One week, Isabella. That's all I'm promising for now." He looks down at his gentle hold on me and slowly releases my wrist.

"I-I promise I won't let you down." I cough and laugh at the same time. I didn't know his touch would wreak havoc on my nervous system, so I quickly back up toward the foyer and put on my sandals. Because I know I'm probably one inappropriate joke away from changing his mind. "I promise, Mateo." I laugh nervously as I walk into the elevator and press the button for the lobby. He stands on the other side of the open elevator doors, watching. "And hey, you can even use a *three strikes and you're out* rule with me. Ya know, *strikeout*, to keep it on brand with your baseball world and all."

I'm met with silence and an unflinching stare.

He doesn't laugh.

Shit.

That's probably the dumb joke that killed my chance.

But Mateo says nothing. Until the doors almost come to a close and he mutters, "I plan on it."

MATEO

I CAN'T BELIEVE I just—

I'm so fucked.

ISABELLA

MY BEDROOM LOOKED LIKE a disaster zone by the time I was done packing the largest piece of luggage I could get my hands on. I needed options on how to dress for the upper crust of Manhattan while also being comfortable enough to run after a kindergartener.

My mom watched the spectacle as she sipped her third cup of coffee with a smug look on her face, boasting about the ways society would advance if everyone listened to their mothers.

My father, bless his heart, looked as confused as ever as I gathered my laptop and ancient iPad from the living room. When he finally asked what was going on, my mom answered. "This is what it looks like when I'm right, mi amor."

If I wasn't properly freaking out about making this one-week trial go smoothly and without a hitch, I would have probably reminded my mother about the fact that this was only a temporary agreement.

But I guess if I had a twenty-five-year-old daughter who had yet to leave the nest, I might have been drinking wine in that coffee mug. So I let her have her small win for the time being.

I decided to skip out on the typical Latine goodbye where you stand by the door for forty-five minutes chatting and instead gave both of my parents a quick peck on the cheek before heading out.

I felt like if I spent a second without moving, the gravity of what was about to happen would sink in.

I was moving in with Mateo Martinez.

A sports legend whose name is more revered than those of Brady and James. A celebrity in his own right. Dubbed America's Sweetheart. Even though he is much more reserved than flirtatious. At least in the media. I have no idea how he is in his personal life.

Or even the story of Anna's birth mom.

The internet exploded the day paparazzi caught an exhausted-looking Mateo pushing a stroller through his neighborhood. The look was completed with a diaper bag slung over his shoulder.

He then made an official announcement that he had, in fact, welcomed a daughter into the world but would be providing no further details and asked the media to please respect his privacy as he learned to navigate his new role as a single father.

The media did not respect his request, and instead created a frenzy around him. It got so bad that my mom told me he had to move out of his previous home when security cameras caught a reporter trying to break into the nursery window.

The search for Mateo Martinez's baby mama became late-night show fodder. And more than a handful of socialites began wearing baggier clothes in attempts to have the internet believe that they could be the secret mother in hiding.

In the end, no one ever got the answer, and eventually, they moved on to the next big story. But I've always wondered.

Even my mom doesn't have the full story, which means Mateo must have sworn his mom to keep the details surrounding his daughter's conception under lock and key.

And now my nosy self is going to be living with him and will have to be on my best behavior if I want this to pan out.

I breeze out of my parents' building, but freeze when I see an older man in a full suit and tie leaning against an SUV, smiling at me warmly.

No one smiles warmly in New York unless they're related to you or plan on distracting you while stealing your purse. So to say that I'm instantly on high alert is an understatement.

"Ms. Morales, I presume?" he yells out over the noisy street.

"Uh..."

He steps forward, slowly bringing his phone close enough for me to see his screen.

It's a text thread between him and a contact named BOSS.

BOSS:

> Hey Hank, before you're off for the day, I need you to pick someone up for me. Her name is Isabella Morales. She's Anna's new nanny, and she should be coming over with some luggage. I have to run out and get her a few things, but I promise to be back for when you drop her off at my place. Thanks.

The text is followed up with my address and a selfie of Anna and me in the Dominican Republic.

I completely forgot we had taken it. We're sporting wide smiles and slightly burned cheeks and noses.

Anna must have taken this picture on her father's phone instead of mine, because I've never seen it before. An odd sensation washes over me, knowing that this picture has lived in Mateo's phone for months. Pathetically, I wonder if he's looked at it since the end of the trip.

I laugh to myself. Yeah, that's probably going to be a hard no.

The driver tries to make a move for my luggage, but my survival instincts kick in, and I stop him. "Hold on a sec. How can I be sure that *BOSS* is who I think it is?" I squint at his amused chuckle.

"Well, I can't exactly be listing every famous person I've driven for with their real name. Would make it too easy for their information to get in the wrong hands." He taps his phone a few times, then turns it over to me again, showing the contact details.

I pull out my phone and confirm that it's the same number I have for Mateo. The one whose text chain consists of messages from when I vacationed with them in the Dominican Republic, mostly me telling him I'm at lunch or the pool with Anna, while he responds with *ok*.

"Smart girl. You've got good instincts. I'm sure Anna will be safe in your hands." He smiles as he gestures toward my bag, and I nod my consent.

"Sorry. I'm not used to this kind of... um, treatment. You know." I point at the shiny SUV double parked on my street as if it has every right to be there.

He opens my door, and I hop in and sink into the comfortable leather interior while he goes back to loading the trunk.

"I'm Hank, by the way." He smiles into the rearview mirror as he slides into his seat and buckles his seat belt.

"Hi, Hank. Nice to meet you. Sorry for the third degree back there. Just trying to make sure I never land myself on an episode of *Dateline*." I chuckle bashfully as I take in the man who resembles a caring grandfather far more than a serial kidnapper.

Hank's face instantly drops. He clears his throat while he struggles to meet my eyes again. "My, uh, sweet wife, Linda, was featured on one of those episodes." He hesitates. "The Brooklyn Butcher, they called him."

I gasp as my hand covers my mouth in mortification. This poor man's wife was *murdered,* and I made a terrible joke about the television program that covered her story. I've been known to put my foot in my mouth, but after this instance, I know for sure I'll have to quit this job before I even get started. I need to figure out how to enter the witness protection program or find a way to buy a new identity.

"I-I'm so, so sorry, Han—"

His boisterous laugh interrupts my apology. I'm still trying to find the right words, but he beats me to it.

"My wife is alive and well, Ms. Morales. She's a crime scene unit tech, so she was asked to be featured on the show. To give her first-hand account, so technically, I didn't lie to you. I was just pulling your leg."

My jaw drops. I was already running scenarios through my head, calculating how I could make it to JFK airport in time to board a flight to Timbuktu.

"Pulling my leg?" I squeal. "You pulled my heart out of my ass, Hank," I say, my filter obliterated by being the unsuspecting victim of the world's most morbid joke.

He's still wiping his laugh-induced tears as he pulls into traffic to make our way downtown. "Oh, Ms. Morales."

"Listen, Hank, you made me shit my pants less than five minutes after we met. I think we can drop the last name shtick. Call me Isa," I playfully snark.

"Isa." He tries to take a breath between chuckles. "I don't think I've ever laughed this hard while on the job. Thank you for that."

I shake my head while suppressing a smile. "Yeah, yeah. I'll be here all week. Unless Mr. Big Shot fires me before then."

He glances my way, his face mischievous. "Oh, Ms. M—Isa," he amends. "I have a good feeling that you'll be around for the long haul."

By the time I return to Mateo's building, we've exchanged CliffsNotes versions of our life stories. I learn about his very *alive* wife, Linda, and how they've been together for almost forty years. He has two daughters and a son, all in their thirties, and gushed about all five of his grandchildren.

While I tried to focus on every detail, I was a bit distracted by my phone. I'd already been contacted twice by Mateo's assistant, Josh. Once to give me a personalized entry code for the building and apartment. And a second time to give me Anna's school and extracurricular activities schedule.

That email had an eleven-page PDF file.

The school itinerary was simple enough. Pick up and drop off information, what days she needed PE clothes and whatnot.

But the after-school activities are absolutely mental. There's no way this girl is signed up for ballet, gymnastics, swimming lessons, karate, piano, and soccer, plus Spanish and French tutoring. She's five, for crying out loud.

But according to the meticulous calendar that is now saved to my phone, she is.

When we enter the underground parking garage, Hank unloads my luggage from the SUV and into the waiting elevator labeled PH and wishes me good luck on my first day tomorrow. He also mentions that he'll be driving me to and from Anna's school, as well as all of her after-school activities. I feel a little more at ease knowing that there will be a friendly face with me.

When I enter the code provided for me earlier, the elevator closes and starts its ascent.

I try to take a few calming breaths before I'm faced with Mateo again. I need to make sure I stay focused on being professional and not letting my mouth get me into trouble before I pass this one-week test.

The elevator doors open faster than I anticipate, and I step out into the foyer. It seems like it's been days, not hours, since I was here last.

I quickly kick off my sandals and start rolling my luggage toward the exuberant female voice singing in the kitchen.

The sound instantly puts a smile on my face.

Chapter Six

ISABELLA

"Mi Isabella, tan bella." Mateo's mom beams as she welcomes me with the same greeting I've been getting from her for years. I walk up to the kitchen stool she's sitting at so she doesn't need to stand for me.

She's fully healed, but since she had a hip replacement, I've made a conscious effort to keep her off her feet when she's around me.

"Bendición Bethzaida." I give her a kiss on the cheek as she cups mine. We're obviously not related, but Latinos rarely let blood determine the closeness of family. So out of respect, I always bless her when I see her, like I would to my aunts, grandmothers, or other family elders. We're not even religious, besides maybe a prayer at Christmas dinner or a baptism here and there, but it is still customary.

Mateo appears at the mouth of the hallway beyond the living room. "Ah, you made it. Perfect timing. I just finished setting up the guest room," he says as he leans in close to me.

I'm on autopilot when it comes to greetings and don't even think twice about greeting him with a kiss on the cheek like I did for his mother moments ago. Only when I take a step back, I realize too late that he was merely leaning down to retrieve my luggage from beside me.

He coughs awkwardly, and I swear I'm imagining a blush forming beneath his short, impeccably kept beard. "Yeah, um, welcome again. I'll, uh, be taking this to your room. Be right back." His long strides take him out of sight within seconds.

Note to self: do not kiss your boss again, unless explicitly asked to do so.

Not that he would. But yes, noted, nonetheless.

Bethzaida tries to get my attention while I keep staring down the hallway where Mateo made his swift escape, praying my heated cheeks aren't giving away my embarrassment. But before she can goad me with what I know will be a teasing remark, I hear my name being shouted from the second floor.

I don't even need to look up, because that little voice of excitement can only come from one of my favorite humans. I start moving toward the staircase to meet her halfway, but it's in vain, since Anna Martinez sprints down the stairs and makes a beeline straight for me. I underestimated her strength and energy, because by the time I open my arms to welcome her with a hug, she tackles me, and we go tumbling over the back of the couch. Thank God this thing is massive and extremely comfortable, because I don't think it would be ideal to request workers' comp on day one.

"Isa, you're actually here!" she yells, even though she is perfectly perched on my chest and stomach, with our legs intertwined. "I couldn't believe it when Papi said that you were going to hang out with me for a whole week, like we did in the Dominican Republic, remember?" I brush the hair out of her face while I watch in amusement as she tries to catch her breath.

"Yeah, I even get to take you to school tomorrow. Are you ready for that?"

She nods vigorously, just as I sense him looming over us.

"Anna, tell me I must be getting old and that my hearing is failing me, because I seem to believe that I heard you flying down the stairs, followed by a grunt that I assume came from you winding Isabella and tackling her to the couch." He raises a stern brow.

She smiles sweetly as she says, "You're getting old, and your hearing is failing you, Papi." She giggles as he reaches down and easily throws her over his shoulder to tickle her as he spins her around the room.

The moment is so sweet that no one hears me whisper as I say to myself, "I didn't grunt. It was more of a heavy exhale due to the element of surprise."

After he puts her down, he looks back at me where I'm still sprawled out on the couch in the same position Anna put me in.

"Good. It seems like you're already making yourself at home here." His words carry a slight bite to them, and I quickly stand, remembering I'm supposed to respect his space and need for peace once he's home.

Not reading the room, Bethzaida says, "Mateo, it makes me so happy seeing the three of you together." Her eyes bounce over the three of us, all standing in different parts of the room.

He says nothing as he moves toward the kitchen, then starts unloading Tupperware from the fridge.

"So you'll really be taking me to school tomorrow, Isa?" Anna asks as she pulls my hand and leads me to the kitchen island, where her grandmother still sits.

"Yes, kiddo. Hank and I will be ready to celebrate your first day with you tomorrow morning. Any requests for breakfast?" I ask as I twirl the end of her ponytail.

Mateo interrupts us. "Actually, I'll be coming along as well tomorrow, since it's Anna's first day. I also need to register you with campus security so you can do pickups without me."

I nod, keeping my face blank of emotion, hoping that's what a professional nanny face is supposed to look like.

"And as for breakfast, when I don't have morning practice or an away game, it's kind of our thing to make breakfast together. Anna and me."

Well, then. Point taken.

"Sounds good. Can you tell me where her uniform is so I can—"

"A week's worth of uniforms are dry cleaned and hanging in her closet, and her after-school activity gear has been sorted by day and is stored in the laundry room closet."

Shit. He's basically done everything I was planning to do to keep myself busy tonight and prepare for her first day. Now it feels like I'm lingering in his home, with no actual nanny duties to complete.

As if sensing my looming panic, he decides to throw me a bone. "Listen, Isabella. Your first day officially starts tomorrow. Why don't you get settled in for the night, and tomorrow, I can have my assistant email you any things that need attention for the week?"

"But it's only six o'clock," his mother complains as he subtly shakes his head and makes his way back to the refrigerator. "It's dinnertime, and I spent all morning cooking a feast. Mateo is going to heat it up for us. There is more than enough for everyone." She smiles salaciously. "Besides, you can't go off to bed without eating some good Puerto Rican food. We've got to feed those beautiful new curves of yours. Right, Mateo?"

His knuckles look white from where one hand grips the refrigerator door as he releases a deep groan near the gallon of milk.

I'm used to my mom and Bethzaida poking innocent fun at my delayed body development. Because truly, who grows tits and ass after they turn twenty-three? Now at twenty-five, I feel more confident in my curves, and I'm owning them.

Luckily, I grew up in a home where every bite of food was meant to be enjoyed and bodies were meant to be appreciated for all that they do for us. And I guess it's also been par for the course to have family friends ask which devil I made a deal with in order to get a free ass in this economy, since I used to be flat as a pancake.

But while I'm used to these comments, constantly being around hilarious Latinas, I know it must be making Mateo uncomfortable, which was the number one thing I was trying to avoid during this trial period.

So I lean in and give Bethzaida another kiss and take a large step back.

"Actually, I think I'm going to settle in for the night. Get my things organized and ready for the big day."

Mateo turns, his expression stoic.

"Nonsense, you can't skip dinner—" Bethzaida starts.

"I already ate," I interrupt. "A really big early dinner at my mami's house. You know, as a sendoff and whatnot. So I'm truly very stuffed." I pat my empty stomach twice to really seal the deal.

"I'll show you to your room," Mateo says as he starts leading the way past me. Seems like I made the right call, since he covered an impressive distance in such a short amount of time.

"Buenas noches," I call over my shoulder. "See you in the morning, kiddo!"

"Buenas noches," they both respond, Anna carefully blowing on a hot piece of plátano maduro. My stomach almost weeps.

I turn back around and stop abruptly. Mateo is standing by an open door, which I assume belongs to me for now, with his arms crossed, studying me.

I keep a smile on my face as I walk past him and into the room. I don't know what I was expecting, but it wasn't this. Like the living room, an entire wall is a floor-to-ceiling window that overlooks Central Park. The rest of the room is decorated in soft tones, meant to complement the city skyline. Plush carpets, an ivory desk on the wall to my right with a table lamp adding a gentle glow to the sunset displayed behind the massive king-size bed.

"Wow."

Mateo clears his throat to get my attention but doesn't enter the room. "The door on the left is your ensuite bathroom. I went ahead and got a few things for you."

I fully turn to look at him. His hands now rest in the back pockets of his jeans. "You got me stuff? You didn't need to do that."

He waves it off. "I don't have many guests, except my mother, but she has her own unofficial guest room upstairs next to Anna's room, and it's fully stocked with her things. Just wanted to make sure you had what you needed to settle in for the night. It's probably all the wrong stuff, so you can probably—"

"I'm sure it's perfect. Thank you." I bite my lip, and his eyes immediately track the movement.

"Money." His voice rises an octave. "Uh—here." He pulls his wallet from his back pocket and hands me a black American Express card. My eyes widen, and my eyebrows shoot up. "I don't want you using your money when you're out with Anna. If you guys stop to eat or need to buy something, you use this card." I nod, studying the heavy piece of metal in my hand. "For you as well." My eyes reach his once more. "When you're on the clock, your meals are on me. If Anna needs school supplies or... you know... girl stuff." He rubs the back of his neck awkwardly.

I smirk. "What exactly constitutes as 'girl stuff,' Mateo?"

"Use your discretion, Isabella," he grumbles.

There he goes again, only saying my full name in its Spanish pronunciation. I guess I've become so familiar with my peers using the English version that the Spanish version now makes me feel... unsteady.

So I resort to my usual go to. I make a joke.

"Got it, boss. So do Hermès bags fall under 'girl stuff,' or..."

He releases a deep breath, as if he's been holding it in this whole time.

I raise my hand to stop him before he can get a word in. "That was a joke, Mateo. I know this is not your ideal situation, but I promise to make the best out of it. Yes, I might make a joke here or there, because that's who I am. But I promise you, there will only be extreme professionalism coming from me. You can rest easy knowing that it truly is my pleasure to be a part of Anna's life right now, especially at a time that must be so exciting yet nerve-racking for her."

His face softens at the mention of his daughter. It's a great reminder that I should keep all conversations limited to her in order to make sure this working relationship progresses without a hitch.

He nods as he takes a step back. "I didn't really get the chance to give you the full house tour, but I'll be sure to do it tomorrow. Our bedrooms are upstairs, in case you need anything. The pantry and fridge are stocked. But, um, try to not eat the grilled chicken and broccoli stuffed Tupperware. Those are the lunches I take to practice."

"I'll use all my willpower to keep my hands off your carbless meals," I tease.

A ghost of a smile flashes across his face before he dips his head.

"Now go enjoy your dinner with your family. I'll be ready by seven a.m."

He knocks on the doorframe twice. "All right. Good night, Isabella."

"Good night, Mateo."

Chapter Seven

ISABELLA

A good night, it is not.

Because it's midnight, and I am about ready to chew my left arm off due to hunger. I knew calling it an early night would be risky after only eating a bodega sandwich when I went home to pack.

But now my stomach has progressed to making whale noises that I fear will echo around the apartment.

The last bit of movement I heard was around eight p.m. when Anna loudly said goodbye to her grandmother. After that, they probably went through Anna's bedtime routine.

It's been almost four hours since I've heard even a pin drop, and I truly don't think I can hold out anymore.

I kinda wish Mateo would have gotten me a robe to match the hotel like slippers I found beside the bathroom vanity to help cover up my mismatched pajama tank top and sleep shorts.

Not that I'm complaining, since that vanity was filled with a toothpaste brand so fancy, I've never heard of it, a cool-looking electric toothbrush, a stack of the world's softest towels, and an absurd amount of cherry ChapStick.

That last one made me laugh. I always carried one with me while vacationing with them, and I'm pretty sure I got

Anna hooked on them. She was always trying to mimic my morning routine alongside me, and she quickly learned that I go nowhere without my ChapStick and maybe even a backup.

So I'm sure he probably grabbed these from Anna's stash.

Without anything to help cover up my fashion faux pas, I decide to bite the bullet and make this the quickest kitchen raid in history and hope it doesn't look like a rabid raccoon was let loose inside their home.

I crack open my bedroom door to make sure the coast is clear. Once I'm certain it's safe to make my escape, I book it. But not before holding on to my boobs, because even though I'm sure jiggly tits don't make too much noise, you can never be too careful.

I'm about to head straight to the pantry, when I decide it's best to grab a water first, since I'm also thirsty. Once the bright light of the massive refrigerator greets me, I'm half-stunned. Because even though everything is perfectly sealed, I can still smell the sofrito goodness within these Tupperware containers. I lean in farther to confirm that I'm right, and there is some carne guisada, along with arroz con habichuelas in here.

And my favorite type of plantain taunts me as the plátano maduro stares at me longingly from the back of the fridge. I quickly decide it's too late to try to microwave anything and risk alerting anyone to the fact that I've turned into the rabid raccoon I feared I would become and instead lean almost my entire upper body into the fridge so I can grab the sparkling lemon water in the back corner.

I can feel my shorts riding up as I continue to reach for the bubbly goodness, to the point where the cool air brushes along my exposed ass cheeks.

And that's when I hear the unmistakable sound of a glass landing harshly against the island counter behind me.

Chapter Eight

ISABELLA

I immediately straighten, but not before banging my head on one of the fridge shelves.

"Mateo," I gasp. Not because I didn't assume he would be the person lurking behind me, but rather because he is standing behind the island across from me, and he looks like he's naked. And mad. Mad and naked.

My eyes lose the battle of subtlety and slowly take in his massive chest. His muscles seem to flex in every place my eyes land while I follow the smattering of light chest hair that leads to his happy trail.

As if granting me permission for my perusal, he rounds the island so I can confirm that he is not, in fact, naked.

It's much worse.

Call me old-fashioned, but I'd like to believe that a rogue penis would cause me to immediately avert my gaze.

But low-hanging gray sweatpants?

Ones that only add emphasis to the deep, grooved V lines that seem to point to where the Holy Grail truly lies keep me frozen in place. And these must be some thin sleep pants, because I can clearly see the outline of his, Jesus Christ, is that thing—

"Isabella." His gruff voice causes my head to snap up so I meet his eyes. Only then do I realize how badly I've stepped in it.

He looks royally pissed. At my nipples, I assume, since his line of sight seems to be focused on my chest. I quickly glance down to make sure I'm not having a nip slip, only to realize that my tank top isn't currently leaving much to the imagination, since I'm pretty sure my light brown nipples are visible through this white top. The nipples who, not five seconds ago, were fully hanging out inside a very cold refrigerator, seem like they're trying to poke their way out of confinement.

I open my mouth to say something, anything, but my stomach beats me to it.

With an unmistakable noise of distress that seems to last eons, I cover my stomach and whisper, "Sorry. I—"

"Sit," he commands, and I don't even give it a second thought before I quickly seat myself on an island stool.

He walks past me and opens the fridge. I can hear him rummaging through it, but I don't dare to look back. Clearly, my eyes can't be trusted.

I can hear him plating food, followed by the sound of a few buttons beeping on the microwave. I want to tell him that he doesn't have to do that, but I'm too afraid that I'll say the wrong thing.

I hear more plates and utensils being pulled out, as well as ice filling a glass. I try to control my breathing, because knowing that we're both half-naked in the kitchen together at midnight will probably lead to some inappropriate playtime with my vibrating toys.

I know I shouldn't, but I probably will.

After a few moments, one muscled arm enters my line of vision and sets a plate large enough to feed a small army, full of all the foods I was salivating over a few moments ago, in front of me. Then his other arm sets a glass of sparkling water to my right. I'm about to thank him and apologize, but he's back with a massive slice of flan. The same one I brought over this morning to help soften him up to the idea of hiring me.

I'm sure this interaction has only taken a few minutes, but it feels like the silence has stretched on for hours. So, without looking back at him, I take a deep breath and finally say, "Thank you. You didn't have to do all of this. And, uh, I'm sorry about—"

The words die in my throat as his large hands grip the counter on either side of me, and I feel the heat of his bare chest on my back. I'm taken by surprise, but not enough that my body doesn't immediately lean back into his slightly.

I can feel his breath on my cheek, his scruff tickles my ear.

I think I'm about to spontaneously combust. Or make a mess on the very expensive stool I'm sitting on at the rate I feel moisture gathering between my legs.

That is, until he finally speaks.

"Strike one."

CHAPTER NINE

MATEO

"WHO PISSED IN YOUR Café Bustelo?"

I look up at Anthony Torres, my catcher and sometimes best friend—when he isn't working my last nerve—and watch him shake his hand out of his catcher's glove.

"What?" I grunt. "Can't catch a fastball anymore? Sorry to say, but you might be losing your touch, man."

His easy smile slips off his face as he walks toward me. "Yo, you okay, bro? You've been edgy all morning, biting everyone's head off." He looks back at the dugout, and I can see a few of our teammates staring at us. Knowing Torres, he probably told them he'd volunteer to tell me to cool it.

But I can't.

Because every time I close my eyes and try to focus on practice, all I can see is Isabella. *All* of Isabella.

Bent over, shorts barely containing the ass that's become my personal kryptonite. Only to turn around and show me something I most definitely should never have seen.

Not because I'm a good man. My thoughts are far from good when it comes to Isa, but rather because I now know what she hid behind those tiny bikini tops she unknowingly tortured me with while we were on vacation.

And now, all I can do is rewrite the events of last night.

Where instead of almost shattering my glass of water, I walked around the counter and easily ripped that sorry excuse for a tank top clean off her body and filled my hands with her luscious breasts. Backing her into the refrigerator so I could lean down and suck one of her pebbled nipples into my mouth.

Scenario after scenario flood my mind, making it impossible to reel in my frustrations.

This morning's school drop-off was awkward enough.

She tried apologizing multiple times. Although I never let the words leave her mouth, since I kept this morning about Anna and all the necessary security approvals Isa needed from the school.

But what would she be apologizing for? That I'm not certain of. Since I'm sure she's not apologizing for making me escape to my room moments after I left her warm meal waiting in front of her.

I made sure to bite my tongue to guarantee her name didn't escape my lips as I quickly finished myself off in the shower.

Strike one.

What the fuck was I thinking, caging her in my arms and whispering "strike one"?

It's as if my mind short-circuits around her. First, I hire her to be Anna's nanny. Then I offer her a midnight meal portioned for two, followed by threatening her.

I chuckle to myself at the thought. As if that strike was meant for her and not me.

"Listen, we all have our days. It's just that, um, you always seem to be the one telling us to get our heads out of our asses. But now that you're being all"—he waves his hand in my general direction, as if it explains everything perfectly— "well, you know, I guess I have to be the one to tell you to cut the shit. Besides, I thought I'd save your ass before Coach Weston tries to wring your neck. We all know he's one bad play away from being featured on *Snapped*. Ain't no way someone can be that calm and stick to themselves that much." He smiles, bearing his annoyingly white teeth at me like the little brother I most certainly didn't ask for.

I shake my head slightly. He's right. I've never given Coach a reason to ride my ass, and I'm sure as hell not starting now.

I never bring my personal troubles onto the field. Not when I found out the woman I was having a casual relationship with was pregnant. Not when Anna was born and I realized what it meant to not only be a single parent, but the sole parent of a newborn.

So why the hell is this rattling me so much?

"My bad. Rough morning. It's Anna's—"

I don't get to finish my sentence. Torres may be one of the biggest jokesters on the team, but he's a devoted father of three. And he does not mess around when it comes to his wife and kids.

He grabs my shoulder and uses his glove to cover his mouth. Something we do when we don't want cameras reading our lips. Even though we're just at practice, we're expected to always believe a camera is pinned on us, no matter where we are. "Anna okay? What happened? I can get Denise to pick her up."

His wife, Denise, would absolutely load her SUV with her kids and drive anywhere for Anna, that I don't doubt. Another reason I should feel lucky to have people like them in my life. But this isn't something Denise can help me with, unfortunately.

"Anna's fine. It's her first day of school. And…" I hesitate, knowing that Torres may have a good heart, but he also has the biggest mouth on the team, and probably the East Coast. "Her new nanny started today, and I guess I'm stressing about—"

"A new nanny, huh?" His shit poker face needs work, because it barely hides his amusement.

"What? Spit it out, Torres."

He shrugs nonchalantly. "Nada. Just find it funny that Denise ran into your mother yesterday, and that's how we found out that our sweet little Isabella was your new nanny."

I'm taken aback for a moment, because, to my knowledge, Isabella has no connection to Torres. Unless…

Before Denise, Torres had his fair share of fun in the dating department, if you even want to call it that. And while he is obnoxiously obsessed with his wife and would never stray, I wonder if he ever crossed paths with Isabella during his single days.

He must sense my demeanor change, because his hands come up as he says, "Wow. Really, my man? It's like that, huh?" He shakes his head while not attempting to hide his smug smile. "Isabella and Denise were in the same class in high school and have been friends ever since. She's my daughter's godmother." He starts jogging backward, as if he doesn't trust me to not aim a fast one at his head as he retreats, chuckling to himself. "Oh, this is going to be fun to watch, Martinez."

By the time I get home, I'm exhausted.

After practice, I stayed behind and had an early dinner with the team. It's something we try to do once a week since this is the New York Monarchs' first season as an MLB team.

Then I avoided Torres like jury duty, since he's been really working overtime trying to get me to open up and talk about Isabella. Even though I now know nothing ever happened between the two of them, I'm still finding myself irrationally annoyed that someone else on my team knows her. And probably knows her even better than I do.

By the time I step into my foyer, I can hear Anna and Isabella in the living room. I give myself a minute before announcing my presence by the kitchen entrance. Enjoying the sounds of their giggles and gasps at whatever they're looking at on Isabella's phone.

They look like two peas in a pod, huddled together on the couch. Perfectly content and comfortable with one another. That's what I should be focusing on.

Anna.

Anna feels comfortable with Isabella. And even though I doubt Isa will survive here until the end of the week, obviously due to my inability to stop thinking about her inappropriately, I do recognize that Isabella's influence is good for Anna. And that she'll most likely always hold a place in Anna's heart.

So with that thought in mind, I tell my dick to calm the fuck down and be mature about this whole situation.

Less than a week left to mildly obsess over Isa.

Maybe if I keep repeating that to myself, I'll start to believe it.

Chapter Ten

ISABELLA

"Papi," Anna yells as she leaps off the back of the couch and into her father's waiting arms.

The same muscular arms I haven't been able to scrub from my brain since last night.

Basilic veins.

Yes, I googled what those stupid forearm veins were last night after I tossed and turned for what felt like an eternity.

I thought for sure I would be awoken by building security, requesting my immediate evacuation. On the grounds of, I don't know, indecent exposure? Grotesque ogling of Mateo's abs? World's most inappropriate and ratty pj's?

I'm not sure, but I definitely feel guilty of *something*.

This morning was so awkward for me, especially because he acted as if nothing happened. Which made me feel crazy and second-guess whether last night was as bad as I made it out to be in my head.

But the slow glide of his gaze over my body as he holds Anna tells me maybe I'm not.

Since I'm not one to make the same mistake twice, I'm currently wearing a long-sleeve flannel pajama top and matching leggings that are four months too early for Christmas, given their red and black checkered pattern. But there's no chance in hell I'll ever be caught airing out my lady bits again.

Then why am I heating up under his inspection as if I'm wearing nothing at all?

Flannel. It's the fucking flannel, of course.

He sets her down but keeps his eyes set on me. "How was dinner? Sorry I'm late. I had to chat with my coach before I was done for the day."

"Dinner was great. Your chef is really talented. I never knew someone could make cauliflower tasty enough for a five-year-old's palate."

Anna beams proudly up at him, clad in a stylish pair of pajamas that she had to wear as soon as she saw that I'd changed into mine.

"Sounds great. And, uh, did you eat your portion as well? I asked the chef to include your meals in this week's schedule."

I roll my lips as I go over his words. Is he trying to make sure I'm fed so that we don't have a repeat of last night? Or is he trying to remind me that only this week of work is guaranteed for me?

Either way, I straighten and answer honestly. "Yes, I did. Thank you for that. You really don't have to keep feeding me." I shut my mouth tightly, hoping Anna didn't catch on to my slip. "I mean, I work for you, not the other way around. I'm more than capable of taking care of my needs. Really, don't worry. I'm of no concern to you."

He takes a step closer to the couch, but I make no attempt to stand from the spot I'm perched on. It wouldn't make a difference; this man would tower over me anyway. He lowers his voice as he says, "I take care of the people under my roof,

Isabella. So I guess that means, for the time being, that your needs *are* of my concern."

I let out a shaky breath at the same time that Anna shouts about having to get something from her room and promises to be right back, leaving Mateo and me at a standstill.

As much as I can't explain what's come over me lately...

Liar. He's a hot, successful, single dad whose love for his daughter could inspire Hallmark movies, while his mouth and body leave me aching every time we're in the same room together.

I clear my throat, hoping subtitles of my thoughts aren't magically floating over my head.

"Mateo, I'm sorry about last night."

"Isa—"

"Please let me finish," I plead. He nods once. "Look, last night, when your mom invited me to sit for dinner, I thought it was some kind of test or something. That I should know better than to intrude on your family time, since you made it crystal clear that this home is your sanctuary and once my duties as Anna's nanny are complete, I should make myself as scarce as possible."

He sighs. "I didn't mean—"

"Mira, I wasn't finished," I snap in a way that's eerily similar to how my mom did any time I dared to interrupt adults while they spoke. I grimace as I realize I just scolded my boss. But if the slight upturn of his lip is any indication, I might have enough wiggle room to finish pleading my case. "Sorry about that. But as I was saying, I was only trying not to mess up on the very first night. And since there was nothing left to do for Anna, I sequestered myself to my room. Which, I promise, under any other circumstance, would be the dream for me.

Since I love snuggling under the covers with a million pillows propped up as I read my Kindle and... you really didn't need to know all of that." I take a deep breath as I try to steer this conversation somewhere remotely to where it was meant to go.

"All this to say, I promise not to be prowling around at night while trying to score some of your food. And I promise to wear better, um, bedtime garments?"

"Is that a question or a statement?" He smirks.

I try, but probably fail, at giving him a slight glare. "I wasn't sure if I should call these pajamas, so that's what I went with." I wave at my current outfit.

His eyes take another unnecessary voyage down every inch of my body. "Well, you can sure call them something. How about Santa's little helper?"

For a moment, I'm left speechless, until a surprised laugh escapes my mouth. "Did you just... make a joke, *Martinez*?"

His eyebrows shoot up at the use of his last name. "We on the field now or something, *Morales*?"

I smile widely. For the first time ever, Mateo and I are having a real conversation, and it's a very friendly one.

Emphasis on the friend, you little hooch.

I quickly remind myself before I do something stupid to ruin this moment, like ask to see his abs one more time.

"Well, we are a team now, aren't we? And that's what your teammates call you."

He nods pensively. After a few moments, Anna shouts for her father to come to her room since she needs help bringing something downstairs.

Without another word, he turns and makes his way up the stairs.

I settle back into the plush couch and grin to myself. I actually did it. I think Mateo and I can overcome whatever weirdness there was between us all this time.

Just as I hear his heavy footsteps hit the second floor, he yells, "Hey, Morales."

"Yeah?" I turn, knowing there's nothing he can say to wipe the satisfied smirk off my face.

"That first strike still stands."

ISABELLA

Fucking hell.

ISABELLA

I'M JUST ABOUT READY to take Anna to her second day of school.

I give myself one final appraisal before I deem my outfit school-drop-off appropriate. It's a red summer dress with short sleeves that hits me right above the knees and my loyal pair of Converse. Nothing too scandalous. Yet I can't be too careful, knowing that Mateo has firmly given one strike to my name.

How was I supposed to know he would take my stupid three-strike rule suggestion seriously?

He barely takes *me* seriously.

I check the time on my phone and decide to make a quick exit from my room before I earn myself a second strike for being late. I grab a brand-new ChapStick from the vanity before I leave, knowing that there are certain simple pleasures in life that are priceless. Like the feeling of opening a brand-new ChapStick and breaking that rigid, circular, smooth... wait.

Did I just make that sound like I'm about to blow my cheap lip-care instrument? Jesus Christ, I need to make sure I don't fall asleep while reading a super spicy why-choose romance again. Clearly, my libido has been all over the place lately, and I'm guessing a broody, sexy baseball player isn't helping.

I walk into the living room right as Anna jumps into her father's arms for a goodbye hug. Mateo leaves today for an away game, so he'll be gone for two nights. I'm hoping those two Mateo-free days bring me a few steps closer to securing this job after the one-week mark, as well as give him short-term amnesia about my whole three-strike system.

Once I got back to the apartment after dropping Anna off yesterday, I was amazed at how much I could accomplish with a whole day to focus on my cover-design business.

I mean, yes. I did spend a good chunk of the morning replaying my interaction with Mateo. And maybe I read a few too many chapters of the romantic suspense that released hours before, but all in all, I was productive.

Which reminds me of the stakes here if I manage to keep this job. I can network with fellow content creators and even indie authors in the morning and further develop my portfolio by designing preset romance covers during the early afternoon.

And let's not forget about the pay. I'm not exactly sure how much my salary would be since I'm still on this one-week probationary period. But if it's comparable to what he's paying me for this week, then I'll be making more than all the finance bros on Wall Street.

Or at least feel like I am, since my previous jobs barely paid above minimum wage.

Plus, let's be honest, can it really be called a job when I'm hanging with a kid as smart and witty as Anna?

Last night, I found myself calculating how far I could push her bedtime so we could continue to watch concert footage of our favorite artist on TikTok.

Concerning, since I should have probably ended my disappearing act and responded to the unanswered calls and texts from friends my own age, but fun, nonetheless.

"Good morning," I greet cheerfully. "Are we ready to go…"

"Cinderella," Anna supplies.

We've been playing this game since I met her. She likes to pretend she's a different Disney princess each day. I play along and sometimes assign myself a character as well.

"Ah, of course, Cinderella. Your chariot awaits." I bow dramatically while waving to the elevator.

She giggles loudly. I swear someone should figure out a way to bottle up her little laughs. They're the sweetest sounds I've ever heard. They make me feel like, if I live in the same world as Anna's joy, then it can't be all that bad.

"Almost ready. Gimme a second." She turns to her dad. "Don't leave yet. I need to go get it," she says before she takes off like a freight train up the stairs and toward her bedroom.

I know the full layout of the place now, thanks to Mateo calling me last night to check in on Anna and asking her to give me an apartment tour since he was running late. I actually much preferred her showing me around since a five-year-old's commentary can't be beat.

The only downside was that Anna was *very* thorough in her tour. Therefore walking me through every nook and cranny of Mateo's bedroom, something I'm certain he would have left out had he given me the tour himself. Which means I now know that he sleeps on silky navy sheets and under a thick gray comforter. And that his impeccably organized closet is the size of my parents' entire apartment. And his shower was probably built with orgies in mind, because seriously, what is one person supposed to do with that many shower heads?

I quickly try to wipe away the memory as Mateo comes to stand next to me. It's hard enough to look him in the eye on a good day, much less if I start imagining him with bed head.

"She'll be down in a minute. She's getting a... thing for me."

I quickly tell myself it's none of my business if he didn't immediately offer up what "thing" meant, but then I remember who I am and ask him anyway. "Thing?"

His soft smile catches me off guard. "When she was a baby and old enough to crawl, she started putting a toy in my away bag. I remember the first time she did it when I left her with my mom while I was a thousand miles away. The first year of her life, I took her on every trip, but she was sick that time, so I thought it'd be best for her to stay behind with my mother. I was miserable. Hated that she wasn't feeling well, that I was too far away to console her, and that she was too young to understand why I was gone. But then"—his smile widens at the memory— "I opened my away bag, and right on top of my spare jersey was her teething toy. I swear I believed that thing had magical powers, because it took me out of my funk, and I ended up playing one of the best games of my career. So, naturally, like any respectable—and superstitious—baseball player, I started bringing it with me to every away game. We didn't always win, of course, but it made me feel closer to Anna while I was gone."

"That's very sweet."

He looks at me then, and for this brief moment, I know it in my bones that I'm getting the real Mateo. The one the public has no access to. The version of him that isn't seen by many. "Last year, she asked me why I traveled with a teething giraffe toy, and I told her the truth. Now she likes to choose a random toy and hide it in my away bag for me to find while I'm gone. Sometimes it's a doll. Other times a random piece of a toy set I don't even recognize. But I love how much fun she has with it. How it takes her mind off me leaving and instead allows her to focus on me finding whatever she's hidden within my stuff." He nods toward a black duffel bag by the foyer table. "I even had to upgrade my bag to something with more zippers and compartments, since my previous one didn't make it hard enough for me to find her surprise."

"According to Anna, I assume." I bite down on a smile.

"Of course. Anything for my girl." His eyes smile back at me, and for a moment, I forget to breathe.

It suddenly hits me then, as his eyes hold me hostage.

I thought I wanted us to stand on common ground. Thought it would be best if we somehow managed to develop a platonic friendship, to help ease the working relationship.

But I was wrong.

Dead wrong.

Because what I didn't know was the power behind his eyes. Their potential to let me forget about my past. And the simple rule I implemented for myself five years ago. Because I can see it right there, reflected back at me. The way I'm slipping, and I didn't even notice it.

How foolish of me.

I know I can't fall for him.

I vowed never to fall for another professional baseball player.

Because the last time I did, my whole life came crashing down.

And the entire world stood by and watched it burn.

Chapter Thirteen

MATEO

I did it.

I managed to have a normal conversation with Isabella without picturing her naked.

That came after I left. But still, progress.

I don't know what I expected to happen after we talked, but having her give me a wordless wave goodbye wasn't it. I guess I'm a bit jaded toward the women I'm not related to.

At this rate, it's easy to spot a vulture among the crowds or people who only want a piece of me.

Well, not a piece of me, but rather a piece of my brand. Because the media doesn't know who I truly am. Thanks in part to the thick skin my father warned me I'd need if I ever had dreams to make it in the big leagues.

It's been over fifteen years since he passed, and I'm still leaning on his life lessons. Which is a true testament to what a great father he was to me.

Something I need to keep in the forefront of my mind if I aspire to be half the man he was.

"Yo, Martinez. You finally coming out with us tonight?" Marcos Sánchez, my second baseman, asks me.

Torres snickers next to him. "Yeah, right. You know Mateo never goes out unless it's part of those team-building exercises they keep trying to shove down our throats, as if we don't play like a team that's been going at it for years."

We're standing in our hotel lobby in Los Angeles, waiting to be handed our room keys.

He's right, though. I never go out with the team. Not because I don't enjoy their company, surprisingly enough. But rather because the idea of sitting in the VIP section of a bar or club is about as appealing to me as eating gas station sushi.

I spend enough time trying to dodge professional cameras as it is. So being in a room with a bunch of drunken strangers, in another team's town no less, sounds like my own personal nightmare.

All it takes is one perfectly aimed shot to paint whatever picture the media is hungry for that week. Which is why I make their job easy for them and avoid leaving my home or hotel room at all costs.

After a while, the paparazzi got the hint and knew it was probably a safer bet to try and follow my teammates if they wanted to post something about the Monarchs.

"Come on, Golden Boy!" Ace Middlebrooks, my third baseman, taunts. The entire team knows how much I despise the title the media has bestowed upon me, so naturally, they use it to rile me up.

Yes, I know how to behave myself in public, and I smile at children and wave at fans, which nowadays is more than enough to brand me as America's Sweetheart.

Clearly, the bar is set extremely low for athletes.

"Come on. Don't be a dick, Ace. We're trying to actually convince him to leave his hotel room this time around. Haven't you ever heard that you catch more flies with honey than with vinegar?" Julian Delgado, my left fielder, pipes in, his signature grin on full display.

I wave them off. "It's late, and we have a game tomorrow. You guys should be resting, not drinking."

"Late?" David García, my center fielder, chuckles. "Do you not know how time zones work, Papi? It's three p.m. west coast time. Which means if we leave now, we can get you the early bird special and have you back and in your jammies before six." The team starts to gather in a half circle, laughing. They're gonna be assholes tonight. I can already sense that ditching them won't be easy.

Torres leans his forearm on my shoulder, which makes him look ridiculous, since I'm at least half a foot taller than him. "Look, man, they're just looking to blow off a little steam. Even I agreed to go, and you know Denise would have my balls in a vise if I went out and made a fool of myself," he assures. "Mateo, we've got a good crew here. They mean well. And besides, we all agreed to a two-drink maximum. None of us here are rookies, and we know how to get the job done. So what do you say to taking the stick out your ass and having some real fun with us?"

I give him a blank stare.

"Besides," he continues. "It'd probably be best to dispel those rumors about you once and for all." He pointedly looks at me. Ever the jokester, I know he's about to say some stupid shit. But I've been listening to Anthony's stupid shit for years, so why stop now?

"Do I even want to know what these rumors are that you are alluding to?" I ask with a deep sigh.

At that moment, our first baseman, Tommy Henderson, walks past me while chewing on a questionable burrito. "That you stay holed up in your room because you're able to jerk off with both hands, bro," he casually explains. Loudly.

The full team now surrounds me and bursts into uncontrollable laughter.

Fucking children. All of them.

Ace puts his hands up, "Listen, man, if I were ambidextrous, I'd probably be doing double-handed crisscross applesauce, too." More roars of laughter follow.

I wipe an exasperated hand over my face.

This shit again.

Because let's forget that I've been ranked best in the league five years in a row. And let's also ignore the fact that I'm able to perfectly pitch upward of ninety-six miles per hour with either arm. And while we're at it, let's not discuss my strategic ability to swap throwing arms mid inning to best attack a batter's weak spot.

Yeah, all that is pretty bogus to my team, apparently, when all they interpret when they hear the word *ambidextrous* is the fact that I can probably masturbate efficiently with both hands.

I can. But that's beside the point.

"C'mon, man. One drink," Delgado pleads. "If you don't come, could imagine how many bottles of lube these guys will prank you with. An alarming number that I bet will leak to the press, and I'm sure you don't want that kind of media attention—"

"Fine," I relent, and the team goes silent.

"Did he just fucking agree to go out with us?" Sánchez whispers out the side of his mouth.

Torres's smile could not be more blinding if the annoying fucker tried. "You heard the man. The team is going out tonight!" The guys cheer, causing a crowd of bystanders to start gathering around us, blocking the hotel's reception area.

"All right, all right. Let's go upstairs, clean up a bit, and meet back down here in thirty. Sound like a plan?" I don't wait for a response and instead turn on my heel and head toward the elevators.

But I should have known they wouldn't let me get the last word in.

"Yes, Daddy!" they shout in unison.

Oh yeah. I forgot they liked to call me that too.

An hour later, we've pulled up to a popular LA hotspot.

With our level of fame and recognition, it's virtually impossible to simply wander into a normal neighborhood sports bar together. We stick to preapproved places in every city we play in.

It's usually the same song and dance. We enter through a back entrance that the paparazzi absolutely know about. Hell, they're probably tipped off by the club's owner to get good press for their establishment.

Then we head through back hallways that are never meant to be seen by the average patron and quickly slip into a VIP section. There, we're usually greeted by an owner or manager who drones on about getting us whatever we may need, followed by a parade of bottle service girls who act like they've hit the jackpot by being assigned to our section.

And I, being the *Golden Boy* of the league, make sure to look over our private section and wave at party goers, maybe even give a thumbs-up, as if I'm some kind of crummy politician, and sign at least a few jerseys. Usually that's enough to keep my PR team happy and keep potential "Mateo is actually an asshole" chatter at bay.

I sit back on the low-rise couch, picking the spot farthest from prying eyes, and take a deep breath. Torres comes to sit next to me. "C'mon, it's not that bad." He nudges me with my elbow.

He's not wrong. Instead of a club, we ended up in a high-end sport bar with an old-school arcade built for adults. The music isn't too loud, more like restaurant level, and there are screens everywhere, so I can see multiple games playing from where I'm sitting.

Fuck, I'm assessing music levels in public places. Does this mean I'm getting old?

"So how's it going with Isa—I mean the new nanny?"

I pick up my beer, the one and only I'll be drinking tonight. "Don't start."

Torres gives me a droll look. "I'm not being a dick. I actually really want to know how she's doing."

I raise a brow as I take a sip of my drink, my eyes never leaving his.

He chuckles. "Correction, *my wife*, that nice lady I never stop talking about or putting a baby in, you know, that one?" he deadpans as I roll my eyes. "Yeah, well, she is quite fond of Isa. The girl is basically family. Yet Denise can't get her to call or text back. Know what that's about?"

Huh. That's interesting.

"She's my employee. I have no idea what her texting habits are, aside from when I need her to update me on how my daughter is doing." I grab my phone out of my pocket and decide to send Isabella a text. It's seven p.m. in New York, so she should be having dinner with Anna right about now. I could text my mother, since she will be accompanying Isa and staying in my home with her while I'm away, but I decide to text Isa instead because she is my employee. And it is her job to update me on my daughter. Yep. That's it.

"You texting her now? Be chill about it. Don't throw Denise under the bus. She understands that Isa sometimes needs... time. But I don't want to make her feel like—"

"Yes, I'm texting Isabella. As I mentioned a second ago, she works for me. No, I am not asking her about why she hasn't gotten back to Denise. That is out of the scope of our work conversations." I put my phone down on the low table in front of us and turn slightly to give him my full attention. "And what did you mean about Isabella needing time?" I know I shouldn't ask, but it's better I do it now that he's just mentioned it rather than hours from now while I'm still dwelling on the comment.

He sighs. "You know, man. After all that bullshit went down with her and... she was different after. I guess, who wouldn't be?"

My hand tightens around the beer bottle, and I force myself to relax, knowing that if Torres spots my white knuckles, there will be more than playful curiosity toward my instinctual reaction. "Yeah. I remember when that went down. But it's been, what, five years since the news broke?"

He looks off into the crowd as he says, "Yeah, I think so. But it was rough, man. The poor girl's face was plastered everywhere online. There was no escaping it." He shakes his head. "Things got better once she left the state and finished her degree out of sight. But when she got back, I dunno... I think she might have slipped back into herself and doesn't know how to let herself live." He faces me now, any trace of my usual humorous friend gone. "I swear, Mateo, had I ever crossed paths with that sick fucker, I would have put hands on him. Fines, punishment, even reaming from my old coach be damned. When he hurt her, he hurt a lot of us." He takes a sip of his beer. "And to think he got labeled a playboy and went on with his life, his pathetic career, while Isa had to—" He stops abruptly. "Sorry, man. Only a few things get me really fired up nowadays. But knowing that I got two little girls at home makes me want to rid the world of scum like Anderson."

I suppress a low growl at the mention of his last name.

Jeremy Anderson.

A poor excuse for a man and a stain on the league, if you ask me.

Very rarely are athletes penalized for indiscretions they make in their personal lives. Although this one was.

"He was drafted to your old team, wasn't he?" he asks, rubbing his chin. "And then randomly got swapped out to another team only two months into his contract." He leans his forearms on his knees. "You wouldn't know the real details about that deal, would you?" He eyes me skeptically.

This time, I can't hide my reaction. Mostly because I'm proud of my actions and the power my name has in the major leagues.

A slow, mischievous smile unfurls on my lips as I shrug. "Nah, man. No clue at all." I pause, my voice turning conspiratorial. "But I will say, it is a shame that he got downgraded to a team that hadn't made the playoffs in more than a decade and was bound to a contract that would keep him there *four long years*." My devilish eyes meet his. "But like I said, I haven't got the slightest of clues." I finish the rest of my beer in one long pull.

I'm still relishing the memories of how I spoke to the higher-ups and played hardball with them. I was a free agent that year and fresh off a World Series win. They maxed out the amount they could offer me for a one-year extension, and I had every plan of taking it, but once my mom called me in tears, telling me about what happened to her best friend's daughter and who was responsible for it all, it was an easy call.

My agent was confused, but he knew better than to question me since the 15 percent of my earnings he receives is more than some players' full contracts. So I made the team a counteroffer they couldn't refuse.

I'd sign on the dotted line if Anderson was out.

All it took were a few quick glances, as if this deal were a no brainer.

Because it was.

Me or him.

He never stood a chance, especially fresh out of the draft.

He seemed so confused when the news was broken to him. I didn't have the slightest idea how HR spun it, and frankly, I didn't care.

Yet that didn't stop me from giving him a word of advice on his way out.

"Watch how you treat women. If not, there'll be much more hell to pay. It's a promise, rook." I still remember his face as I said it. The puppy dog eyes he usually reserved for me, his "baseball hero," as he proclaimed multiple times while we were at practice. All that awe and admiration melted the moment it all clicked for him.

That I had just given him his walking papers, and the team he'd worked his entire life to be drafted to had turned its back on him.

Because of me.

The satisfaction was all-consuming.

I hadn't even met Isa, or Izzy, at the time. I had heard of her via my mother's many stories about a funny, smart, beautiful young lady whose smile could light up a room.

But I didn't need to meet her.

I didn't even need to know who she was.

Because the second that tabloid started circulating, it awakened the protective side of me that I never shy away from.

Because as long as men like *him* exist, men like me will be here, waiting to pick up the slack. Reminding those fuckers that we'll always be here, and we'll never hesitate to help right their wrongs.

I'm still so lost in the memories that I don't even hear my phone ringing on the table in front of me.

Instead, what I hear is a "No fucking way, Martinez."

My head snaps to Torres, and I internally curse myself. I'm such a such a fucking idiot.

He's holding my ringing phone up by his head, with his jaw dropped open. Pointing at the device, as if there would be any confusion for his shocked reaction.

Because there, lighting up my screen, is Isabella's contact picture. A photo she took with Anna while we were in the Dominican Republic.

In it, they're both smiling and in their bathing suits.

Anthony's mouth closes just enough to stretch into his signature smile.

"Okay, so I'm only gonna ask this once, Martinez."

"Don't," I warn.

"Respectfully..."

"Torres, I swear to God."

"Are you *fucking* the nanny?"

Chapter Fourteen

ISABELLA

"He didn't pick up," Anna pouts as she hands me back my phone.

"I'm sure he'll call as soon as he sees the notification, munchkin."

She wrinkles her nose. "Munchkin? Of all the cool nickname options I've given you, you decide to go off script and call me munchkin?" She sighs dramatically. "This is why I have to provide the adults with princess names. They're hopeless without me." She throws her hands up in the air as I pull her in for a side hug and suppress my laughter.

"I fear my Mateo has his hands full with this little one," his mother says as she walks with us toward the awaiting SUV. "Serves him right. He was an absolute terror growing up. His toddler years were enough for his father and me to call it and decide that we couldn't handle two Mateos running around, causing havoc. So if you've ever wondered why he's an only child, now you know." She chuckles, and so does the tall, muscular man in a suit next to her.

Not only do we have Hank, Mateo's driver, moving us around town, we also have Charlie, Mateo's head of security. He has short, black, perfectly combed hair and deep green eyes that assess every square inch around us as we walk.

His main job is supposed to be guarding Mateo at all times, but according to Bethzaida, Mateo asked for the best of the best to be put on security detail for Anna.

Doesn't surprise me. The more I get to know Mateo, the more apparent it is that this man will go to any lengths for his daughter.

Charlie opens the back door for us to get in. Beth helps Anna settle into her middle booster seat as I round the car to the driver's side, where Hank is waiting with a warm smile as he opens my door.

Once the five of us are settled, we pull into traffic and finally start our journey home.

We've finished having dinner at a local pizza joint that Bethzaida mentioned they love to eat at when they're done with Anna's ballet class. Before that, we stayed an extra hour in her classroom for after-school homework prep... homework prep for five-year-olds.

Yesterday, I saw her in action during her gymnastics class, and let's just say that she has more than enough energy to burn off during these extracurricular activities.

Even if I still think her schedule is a bit overkill for a kindergartener.

Hell, it's a bit much for me, a woman in her mid-twenties in a never-ending existential crisis, and I'm not even participating.

My phone starts ringing in my hand, and I see that it's a video call from Mateo.

He has never video called me, but I guess since Anna previously tried him on FaceTime, he must have hit on the missed call without thinking.

I swipe to accept the call, and a moment later, his face comes up on the screen.

I hope the tiny puff of air that escaped my lips was inaudible, because we are all sitting pretty snug back here in the back row, and I'm sure nothing, and I mean nothing, would escape his mother's chisme senses.

It looks like he's standing outside somewhere, his face molded in concern. His eyes don't stray from an exact spot on the screen. It's unnerving to think that he's looking at me that intensely, so I don't. Maybe he has a poor signal and his video hasn't turned on yet. Or maybe he's not—

"Isabella, everything okay?"

Shit.

"Hi," I croak, then quickly clear my throat. "Hey, Anna was trying to call you earlier." Then I quickly shove my phone into Anna's hands, where they rest on her lap.

Real fucking smooth, Isa.

"¡Papi!" she squeals, and his face melts into a look of pure adoration. "I had a super fun day at school today. During recess, a few girls invited me to sit with them, and we made friendship bracelets. Look." She brings her opposite wrist up into camera view and shows off the three colorful bracelets. "But they take a while to make, so we were thinking of maybe having a playdate soon so we can make them at home and then bring them to school. That way we can make enough for the whole class, and then everyone can feel like they have a friend." She smiles as she looks down at her new jewelry.

My heart surges at her kindness.

Anna is many things. She can put you in your place in a funny, endearing way one moment, and the next, she's thinking about how to make sure everyone feels included and cherished.

I know I haven't spent much time with kids her age, but it doesn't take a rocket scientist to know that she's a special one.

Before Mateo has time to respond, because, like me, he clearly has hearts in his eyes, I lean in and give her wrist a light squeeze. "That is so incredibly nice of you, Anna. Your classmates are very lucky to have you."

She moves the camera to include both of us in the frame and asks, "Can you ask Papi if we can do it at our house? That way, you'll be there, and we'll be able to make them together?" Her eyebrows shoot up eagerly.

"Anna, slow down there. First, I need to get into contact with their parents and see what we can work out."

"Okay. And then—"

"And then," he interrupts, "we'll see if Isa is even working that day in order to supervise."

"I don't mind," I chime in. A minute too late, I realize he's probably accounting for me not having this job by this time next week. But hey, if he's gonna get between the sacred experience of girls and their friendship bracelets, then he can shoot me down directly, right in front of his adorable kid. "Even if I'm not scheduled to work, I'd love to help the girls out. I'm sure it'd be super fun." I smile at his cocked brow and ticked jaw.

I probably shouldn't poke him, knowing I already have a strike to my name, but dammit, it feels good to push back a bit, even if it comes back to bite me in the ass later.

"You hear that, Papi? Isa said she would help. And she lives with us, so it's not like Hank has to pick her up or anything."

"And if I did, I wouldn't mind either," Hank hollers from the driver's seat.

I look up in time to see him winking at us through the rearview mirror.

Now they're just making it hard not to be smug.

"How helpful of you, Hank," Mateo deadpans.

I have to bite down on my lip to stop myself from full-on gloating.

His eyes shift, and somehow, I know my bite hasn't gone unnoticed.

He lets out a long breath, but before he can respond, I hear a familiar voice. "Is that the elusive Isabella Morales on your phone screen, Martinez?" Anthony Torres asks melodically. "Nah, it must be my eyes deceiving me, because I don't think Isabella's phone works anymore." Anthony throws his arm over Mateo's shoulders, which Mateo quickly shrugs off. Then he pierces him with a look I can't decipher.

"Hi, Anthony," I say shyly, all vibrato gone. "I know, I know. I deserved that." I nod bashfully.

I really did deserve that.

After shit hit the fan a few years ago, Denise and Anthony stepped up and were there for me at a time when so many cut me off.

I'm beyond honored that I even get to call myself the godmother to their precious second-born daughter, Hannah.

I know I need to get better at responding to the few friends I actually have when they reach out, but it's hard sometimes.

I feel like everyone out there has somehow figured out life while I'm over here, floating my way through it.

Graduations, engagements, marriages, babies, new job opportunities, even moving across the world, you name it. Everyone in my life is crushing it at one or even multiple things.

And I'm happy for them, truly.

It's the dreaded part of the conversation I try to avoid. The part that happens once I congratulate someone on one of their many accomplishments.

"So what's new with you?"

It sounds so innocent. Polite, even.

But the discomfort in people's eyes. The looks I'm sure they have no clue they're giving me when I respond with "oh, you know; same old" is soul crushing.

So I try my best to avoid awkward interactions by avoiding people in general. It's not like it's that hard, since I don't exactly have people banging down my door to hang out with me.

Just the occasional texts from Denise and this girl named Nikki, who I met while I was in the Dominican Republic with Mateo and Anna. Which reminds me, I really should respond to her text about joining her for drinks and dinner.

But it's hard. All of it. Because when my life was torpedoed, all prior plans went up in flames. And unlike many of my peers, I never had a burning passion for any one specific *thing*.

I was surrounded by so many friends, or shall I say acquaintances, who had dreams and aspirations beyond my imagination. I guess I've always found myself a bit lost in that department.

Instead, back then, I poured so much of myself into being the perfect partner, the perfect support system for someone else.

For *him*.

Making sure his dreams were always the priority, because then everything else would surely fall into place. Or so I believed.

Never thinking to put myself first, because what was the point? I never had a reason to doubt us.

To doubt *him*.

Little did I know he would wield the sharpest knife in my back, hurting me in ways I never knew imaginable. Leaving me behind in the wake of his scandal to fend for myself with only the scraps of my dignity trailing behind me.

And in a blink of an eye, it was all... gone.

The life we had planned.

A life where I had love, a home, and a family to call my own.

A life where I experienced a love so big it would seem ripped out of the pages of a romance novel.

But not anymore. Because I'm Isabella Morales. And once my name became permanent ink on the internet, I knew that the dream would forever remain just that. A dream.

I am now destined to be a bystander. Someone who watches others, whether real or fictional, live out lives like the one I once foolishly dreamed of.

If only I had known that my life would be closer to a dark comedy, maybe I would have put more pressure on myself to pick something, anything, so that I didn't spend so many years confused as to what my new future would or should look like.

Maybe then it wouldn't have taken me so long to realize that my passion was quite literally under my nose, on the cover of the hundreds of books that saved my soul at a time I never thought it would be salvageable.

Now that I have a real shot of making my dreams, not someone else's, come true, I know I can't fuck this up with Mateo. No matter how tempting it is to spar with the grump.

"Knock it off." Mateo slightly shoves Anthony, his biting tone bringing me back to the present.

"I was just messing with you, Isa," Anthony says, staring straight at Mateo. What the hell is going on with those two?

"No, Mateo. It's fine," I say, trying to bring down the tension on the call. "Anthony's right. I've been a little MIA recently."

"What's MIA mean?" Anna pipes in.

"It means missing in action. It's sometimes used as a figure of speech when you haven't seen or heard from someone in a while," I explain as best as I can to the inquisitive five-year-old beside me.

"Have you been MIA because you've been hanging out with me?" she asks, worried she may be at fault.

I nudge her with my elbow. "Of course not. Besides, I love hanging out with you. I even get to make friendship bracelets with you and your friends. What's not to love?" I ask, seemingly putting her at ease.

"Hey, that hasn't been confirmed yet," Mateo starts, but I continue as if I didn't hear him.

"And yes, Anthony, I will be texting your lovely wife back. I haven't seen her in a while, and I'm sure she could use help with the kiddos."

Anthony takes the phone out of Mateo's hand. I can't make out whatever Mateo grumbled, but from the sounds of it, I'm pretty sure it wasn't meant for Anna's little ears. "Thanks, Isa, but don't worry about the kids. My wife is literally Superwoman. Although I do think she could do with a little time away from them, actually." He chuckles. "Her mom basically lives with us, and we have a nanny that travels with us when we do, but I'm sure she'd love some alone time with you." He looks over to where I assume Mateo is standing and smiles naughtily. "Actually, if your boss here isn't overworking you too much and lets you out of that ivory tower—"

"Jesus Christ," Mateo mutters.

"I would love to treat you and Denise to a spa day." He spares one more look at Mateo before he continues. "As a matter of fact, take the whole day and get pampered. Go shopping and head out to a girls' dinner. Get white wine wasted while you're at it, if that's what you're feeling up to. We'll plan it on a day when I'm off and her mom and I can tag-team my little gremlins. What do you say?"

I huff out a laugh as Anthony moves the phone a bit to include a very unimpressed-looking Mateo. "Jeez, who knew a girl only had to do ignore her friend for a few weeks to get wined and dined. Just kidding," I say quickly. "You really don't have to do all of that. I don't mind accompanying her to whatever she wants to do. We all know she more than deserves a break. But you absolutely do not have to pay for me. That's going a bit overboard. Besides, your wife is more into chicken fingers and fries than Michelin restaurants, so I don't think I'll be breaking the bank." I smirk.

Anthony being Anthony, opens his mouth, surely ready to insist, when Mateo says something to shock us both.

"I'll be the one paying for Isabella."

The call goes silent for a few moments as I try to figure out whether I heard him correctly.

Anthony clears that confusion right up. "Is that so? Well, looks like Isabella has quite the benefits package at this new gig. Who knew that spas, shopping, and dinners out were included." His eyes shift to me on the screen. "Shit, if this baseball gig goes south for me, I might need to get on that—"

The screen suddenly points toward the ground, and I can tell someone is trying to muffle the microphone. Although a very gruff "that's enough" makes it through the line.

Then Mateo is back on the screen, and I hear a faint "ouch" coming from somewhere behind him.

"We've arrived," Hank announces. Only then do I realize the car is parked in the building's underground garage, and all eyes are on me... including the very assessing eyes of Mateo's mother.

Mateo must hear Hank clearly, because he asks to be taken off FaceTime so he can say good night to Anna privately, since we're going to head upstairs and start her bedtime routine.

I hand my phone off to Anna after I help unbuckle her from her booster seat. Not like she needs it, but I guess I needed something to do with my clammy hands.

I round the vehicle to make sure Beth doesn't need assistance getting out. She might proclaim to feel as good as new after her hip replacement, but I like to be near when she gets out of high stools or cars, just in case.

To my surprise, she's already out of the vehicle and texting with a single digit. For someone who can only type one letter at a time, she surely is going at it.

But hey, better she be distracted by whatever's on her phone than that weird phone call.

A moment later, Anna hops out and hands me my phone.

I'm not sure what to do with the slight disappointment that hits me when I realize that Mateo is no longer on the phone. So I shake it off and tuck that thought under the very lumpy imaginative rug in my mind, never to be sorted through again.

Hank wishes us a good night as Charlie walks us to the awaiting elevator.

Anna, Beth, and I start the ascent up the high-rise. I'm deep in my thoughts when Beth leans over and whispers, "After we put Anna down for the night, I think you and I should have a glass of wine and talk."

The look she gives me makes it clear we're not about to discuss the latest telenovela she and my mother have been binging on Netflix.

I nod and silently hope that when it comes to her bartending skills, she has a heavy pour.

I'm clearly going to need it.

CHAPTER FIFTEEN

ISABELLA

As soon as we make it into the apartment, Beth shoos me away, telling me to feel free to shower and get out of the clothes I've been wearing all day while she supervises Anna's bath and helps her pick out her jammies for the night.

My first instinct is to insist that I do all of Anna's nighttime routine, given that's what I'm being paid for. But the final look she gives me as waves me off with a flick of her wrist brooks no argument.

Truthfully, I think I might need a minute to myself if I'm going to survive the second portion of the evening—a nightcap with Mateo's mother.

It's not like I haven't had countless wine nights with my mom and Beth, talking about the latest neighborhood gossip or recent life updates from extended family in Puerto Rico or the Dominican Republic.

It may sound weird to some, but I truly looked forward to nights where the three of us lounged on my parents' couch with old-school salsa playing softly in the background.

But in reality, those were some of the few social settings where I felt like I could let my guard down.

It's silly for me to be nervous about having this sit-down with Beth, since she has sincerely become like a second mother to me. But just like my mother, she has the influence and power to make me feel like I'm currently guilty of something. Of what exactly, I'm still not sure, but tell that to my anxious thoughts.

I quickly strip in my colossal bathroom and step into the instantly warm water. It feels like my body releases a deep breath when I'm under the massaging spray. The precision is so exact that I don't even need to wear a hair cap to keep my hair from frizzing.

My body feels wound up. I slowly massage the shower gel into my shoulders and will the stress away.

I know I need this job, but I underestimated all the baggage that came along with it. Even though my primary focus is Anna, I can feel myself slowly seeping back into the world that turned its back on me.

The baseball world.

Seeing Anthony's face brought a mix of joy and trepidation.

Although I love him and Denise dearly, life is much easier when I avoid them and the world they orbit in by staying cooped up in my little bubble.

But now that I've stepped into Mateo's world, all that has changed.

And while I know Mateo is the king of the jungle when it comes to professional baseball, it still makes my skin crawl that this world also includes my ex, Jeremy.

Nope.

Not going there tonight. Or ever.

I turn off the shower and dry myself off with the most luxurious towel known to man.

Mateo's not home for the night, so I forgo a bra and throw on a cozy, oversized sweater along with basic black leggings and fuzzy socks.

I make my way out to the kitchen to prepare a late-night snack for Anna before she goes to bed, along with water for her bedside table.

It's interesting, because when my mother brought up the idea of being Anna's nanny, I couldn't turn down the opportunity fast enough. Not because she isn't the world's greatest kid—I'm sure I saw a trophy naming her that on her bedroom bookshelf—but because I couldn't envision myself taking care of another living, breathing human being when there have been days in my past that I could barely take care of myself.

But now, as I cut an apple and scoop up a spoonful of peanut butter onto a plate, I can't help but smile.

I'm not Betty Crocker by any means, and you won't hear me waxing about how putting others first makes me the happiest woman alive. I made that mistake once, and I've clearly learned my lesson.

And seriously, if you've never sat on the couch watching *Vanderpump Rules* with a glass of sauvignon blanc and Thai takeout food in front of you, have you truly even lived?

But I can't deny that there's something to be said about a child's unfiltered joy entering your life. I would happily push back watching any of my Bravo shows for one of Anna's YouTube tutorials on whatever subject is scratching her brain that day. And swap that glass of wine for homemade slushies she loves to make in the fancy blender. Although the wine here isn't the two-buck chuck kind, so I might swipe a glass for after her bedtime. But still, the sentiment is the same.

Like I'm quickly growing accustomed to, I hear her before I see her.

Anna flies down the stairs and starts making her way to me. By the time she swings around the counter, I'm holding her snack plate and glass of water out to her.

"Peanut butter before bed? Yes! You're the best, Isa." Anna empties my hands quickly and heads over to the plush couch.

Beth makes her way to me in a much slower fashion than Anna did and simply says "red or white."

I smile as I look into the wine fridge built into the island and scour my options. "There's an opened pinot noir if you're up for it."

She nods. "Yes, that's perfect. I asked Mateo to open it for me before he left. No matter how fancy the electronic wine opener, I can never seem to figure them out and always end up ruining the cork. And besides, what good is a son if he can't leave a bottle of wine perfectly decanted for his mother?" she jokes.

This is good.

She's asking for wine while Anna's still awake, and she's cracking jokes. So, clearly, whatever she wanted to talk about can't be all that serious. It shouldn't set off my internal panic alarms.

I serve us two glasses of wine with dignified portions. As I put the bottle down, she gives me a bored look, and I chuckle.

At home, I sometimes overdo it and have our guests sipping off the rim of the glass on the table before they can safely lift it.

"Okay, okay. Just remember to tip your server," I jest, as I pour more wine into each of our glasses.

"That's more like it. Now, come sit next to me while Anna finishes her apples and watches that show I'm pretty sure her father doesn't let her watch."

I look up to see her watching a show with preteens that looks pretty innocent, but it's on a streaming service, so I have no clue whether it's inappropriate.

Beth must see my look of concern, because she shakes her head. "Anna lives in New York City. Her father is undeniably the world's most famous baseball player, and she has me as a grandmother." She points at herself as she lifts her glass. "Trust me when I say that she'll be exposed to worse in due time."

We laugh as we clink our glasses. I take a healthy sip of wine and almost moan. "God, that's the good stuff." I stare lovingly into what must be a very expensive glass of wine.

"So." Beth takes a sip of her wine, and I quickly follow for another taste. She then lowers her voice as she says, "I guess my son is into you. What I wanna know is if you're going to be my future daughter-in-law, or if your mother and I still have more work to do."

I try, for the love of God I know I do, but I can't save the decadent wine from being violently spit out of my mouth. Thankfully, it lands in the island sink to my right.

I lose all sense of my bodily functions as I cough roughly and attempt to wipe the mixture of booze and drool from my lips and chin.

Beth, looking completely unperturbed by the whole scene, just rolls her eyes as she says, "Ay, por favor," and hands me a paper towel.

A real empath, that one.

Once I'm sure I can take a full breath, I wipe at the tears that formed during my coughing fit and make sure I've cleared all the evidence of the crime off my face. Then I turn to Beth and plant my hands on the island. "Bethzaida…"

"Save it. Your mother was right. I approached the subject too soon," she says nonchalantly.

"My mother?"

She looks down at her nails, as if her cuticles have all of a sudden become incredibly fascinating. "I may have told her what I witnessed on the car ride over here and filled her in on my suspicions."

I slowly nod my head. "Uh-huh, suspicions. And would you, and I guess my mother, like to elaborate?"

She sighs. "Oh, come on, Isabella. I know you don't know my son as well as I do, but that phone call was a show of barely restrained passion." She fists her hand in front of her face.

"Passion," I say, dumbfounded, "for me?" I point at myself.

Then, slowly, I feel my shoulders shake as an ungraceful snort and laugh combo escapes my body. "Passion." I gasp between laughter. "For me!" I start slapping the counter, garnering Anna's attention.

"Abuela, is Isabella getting the nighttime sillies like I do?" she asks, earnestly concerned for my wellbeing as another bout of laughter forces me to bend over with my hands on my knees.

"No, mija." She sighs as she takes another sip of her wine. "She's just a woman in denial. Nothing to see here."

CHAPTER SIXTEEN

MATEO

IT'S THE TOP OF the final inning, and the game is tied, but I'm not concerned.

This is where I thrive. Where all the outside noise of my life goes completely silent. Where I let the young boy who will forever live inside me play out his dreams.

This view, my view from the pitcher's mound, is a privilege. And it's one I don't take for granted.

I swing both of my arms, shaking out the tension that has built up during the game.

We're on their home turf, and the Los Angeles fans are hungry for a win.

Unfortunately for them, I ain't gonna let 'em have it.

I see who's up to bat and internally smile.

There are a lot of good men in this league, many of whom I have had the pleasure of meeting. And some of those men are still in those early stages of their careers, like Velázquez, who's settling into his batting position as he tries to seem unperturbed by stepping into my line of fire. I've had many conversations with Velázquez, mostly about how he looked up to me when he was in little league.

Which first of all... ouch.

At thirty-three, I've been playing at a professional level for well over a decade. But my ego could really go without everyone pointing out the age differences between me and the fresh blood coming up the ranks.

Yeah, those are conversations I could go without.

Especially when my mind betrays me and continuously keeps calculating the math between my age and Isabella's. Eight years.

Fuck off it, man.

I shake my head and settle back into the present as I berate myself for even slipping for a second. If I let Isa infiltrate my head while I'm on the field, then I'm well and truly fucked.

I focus on the man currently set to bat. And on one of our previous chats.

Because I remember very vividly Velázquez speaking of my left-handed fast ball and how it's a death sentence to players on my turf.

So, with exaggerated movements, I pick up my right glove and drop my left. When I straighten and look at Velázquez, his poker face has shattered into a mixture of annoyance and amusement accompanied by a good natured "este *cabrón.*"

With only one out left for his team, I allow myself to chuckle and wink at him, confirming that we both know exactly what I'm doing. Well, he may think he knows, because I'll definitely be throwing a curveball first, just in case he thinks he can throw up a few Hail Marys and pray for a home run.

I get in position, and after two head shakes, Torres knows exactly what the play is. Our kind of connection during a game is what baseball dreams are made of, since you're only as good as the team you rely on, and Torres is truly the best catcher in the league.

I close my eyes for a fraction of a moment and take a deep breath.

With my eyes open and pinned on Torres's glove, I smirk slightly, then rear back and let the ball fly.

"Come on, Martinez, we won! You've gotta come out with us again. It could be the start of a team winning streak," Ace argues. The tattoos adorning his dark skin are on full display as he walks toward me in a designer tank top and probably a couple million dollars of jewelry adorning his neck, ears, and hands. He's definitely the flashiest on our team, but it somehow suits him. If I ever saw him with anything less than three diamond chains, I would assume he'd been robbed.

"We've won the last three games. Not exactly the start of anything, my man." I walk past him to make my way to the hotel elevators. The guys will probably hit the town tonight since we fly out late in the morning.

We had a small celebration in the locker room, because it always feels nice to win in someone else's stadium. But after we hit the showers and loaded onto the bus, the adrenaline wore off, and exhaustion seeped in.

Most guys like to party and fuck away the tension radiating off their bodies after a game. But most guys on this team aren't single dads. Not only do I have a responsibility to my daughter to not get caught up in a scandal, but I also, guiltily, enjoy the quiet. The time when I don't need to worry about anyone's needs besides my own. And my needs right now are about twelve hours of sleep. But I know I won't be able to pass out until I hit the gym or go swimming in the hotel pool.

Pitching does a number on my arms and shoulders, and after big games, I usually have our strength and conditioning trainers work me out.

But some days, like today, I don't really feel like being around people and would much rather cool down my muscles myself.

"I'm hitting the hotel pool. If you guys want to swim some laps, you know where to find me."

"Ugh, this guy is a machine. Way to make the rest of us look like chumps." Delgado groans.

"Suit yourself." I hit the elevator button.

"Mira, Martinez. Some players, like you, have to be a machine. And then other players, like me"—Molina rubs his rounded belly— "just have to go *bam* with that bat, and then there you go, Papi. A home run for the team. I don't need a pool. I have plátano power," he says gleefully in his thick Dominican accent.

And he's not wrong.

Pedro Molina may look like one of the most unathletic players in the league, but all his power is in his arm strength and hand-eye coordination.

The man doesn't need to run and steal bases when, more often than not, the ball flies out of the stadium once his bat comes into contact with it.

"You're right, *Papi*." We laugh. "But I'm actually wiped. I'm going to get a few laps in, then call my daughter before it's time for her to go to bed."

Most of the guys nod in agreement. When it comes to my time with Anna, they know not to push.

I head up to my room and quickly text the hotel manager, whose contact information I was given at check-in, that I will be using their Olympic-size pool. They respond immediately that the facility has been cleared out and confirm that there will be hotel security on guard to make sure I'm not disturbed.

A part of me grumbles. It's a bit overkill. Yet the other part knows that it's the only way I'll get this workout in without bumping into fans, or worse, people looking for salacious things to post about me. Unfortunately, some aren't above trying to take pics of me having a wardrobe malfunction while I'm in the pool.

So I don't dwell on it and quickly change into my swim trunks and a hotel robe.

I make it down to the pool, and as I was told, it's empty except for one security guard standing at the entrance and another standing inside the pool area, saying he'll be nearby in case I should need something.

I walk over to a pool lounger and disrobe, then place my phone by the edge of the pool.

As a parent, even when I'm at away games, I never allow myself to be far from my phone in case my little girl needs me. Even during the games, I usually have someone on staff hold my phone so they can inform me of anything I should be immediately made aware of.

We're not supposed to have our phones in the dugout, since we're supposed to be focused on the game. But there are a lot of supposed-tos in life that I don't follow, or, I guess, don't apply to me, given that I've dedicated my life to the game, and now Anna.

Even Coach Luke Weston was ready to rip me a new one when he saw what I was up to. Although a full scolding from Coach is usually an assortment of grunts and disapproving stares. To get that man to talk is an impossible feat.

He's the youngest coach in the league, which naturally brings him extra media attention. But like me, he avoids it at all costs. No one even knows where the guy lives. There's always locker room chatter that he must live somewhere in the mountains, since his looks went from Hollywood A-lister to reclusive mountain man during the years he escaped from the spotlight. But given what he went through after he gave up professional baseball at the top of his career, right after a World Series win too, I guess I wouldn't have much to say to the world, either.

But just because he doesn't talk, that doesn't mean he isn't perceptive as fuck. Which is how he must have known I would only be texting someone in regard to Anna during a game and only gave me a slight nod and turned back to the field.

Again, people know not to push when it comes to her. Even Coach.

I release a deep sigh as I wade through the water. Then I waste no time in getting to work. On my third lap, I hear my phone ringing and quickly make my way to it.

And staring back at me is Isabella, wearing an alluring smile.

I told myself after last night that I should remove her contact picture, but I just haven't had the time to do it.

Liar.

Whatever. I'll get to it when I get to it.

I have to try a few times to swipe and answer the call since my fingers are wet, but I finally manage it, and when I do, my precious little girl's face fills the screen, and my heart swells.

"Hola, mija." I greet her.

"Hi, Papi." She squints as she takes in my surroundings. "Are you at the pool? No fair. I thought you were at work," she pouts.

I smile at her. "Yes, I am at work, sweetheart. I'm swimming for my workout after my game. Trust me, the pool isn't as fun without you here."

"Okay," she mumbles, probably still upset that she's not here with me. Because my daughter loves nothing more than being in the water.

So I try to move on to safer conversations to get her mind off what she thinks she may be missing out on. "What did you do today after school?" I'm sure she had soccer scheduled for today, or was it French class? I always get those two mixed up.

Anna looks off screen to someone as she says, "*Um.*"

"Anna, honey." My dad voice fully activates at her suspicious avoidance.

"Well, I-I mean we—" She stutters over her words.

I hear a delicate sigh, and I instantly know who it must belong to. "It's okay, Anna. You can tell your father."

"She can tell me what?" I ask as I make my way out of the pool and in search of my towel. I may not be close enough to get to her immediately, but my body knows it needs to move.

I hold the phone farther away from my body in a futile attempt to keep it from getting any more wet than it did when I abruptly leaped out of the pool.

"Hey," Isabella—now taking up most of the space on the screen—says as she greets me while still giving my daughter a soft look. When she faces the camera and catches sight of me, I don't miss her reaction.

I may have been concerned about what they need to tell me, but I'd be lying if my chest didn't puff up a little by the shocked look on Isabella's face.

And just like the night I caught her in my kitchen, it seems like she's not keen on looking away from me any time soon.

Anna must whisper something I can't hear, because Isabella shakes herself out of her daze and focuses on where I assume my eyes are on the screen.

Definitely not where she was looking before.

"So, yeah. Hi. Um, I already said that, didn't I? Anyway..." She takes a deep breath, and I can't deny that I find her incredibly cute when she fumbles her words. Makes me want to do it more often.

Stop it, you idiot.

"Spit it out, Isabella," I say harshly, even though my tone was meant more for myself than her.

She visibly straightens as her eyes narrow slightly.

There she is.

I can't deny that I love seeing her all fired up. I've only had a few glimpses of that backbone she possesses, and if it isn't the sexiest thing about her...

"It's really not a big deal," she starts.

"Not a very promising way to start a sentence, Isa."

The little minx rolls her eyes at me, and I fight the urge to smile. Can't let her know what her insolence does to me. Fuck if I know what to do with it myself.

The fire in her eyes only burns deeper. "Look, I made an executive decision today as Anna's nanny, that's all."

"And this executive decision consisted of what, exactly?"

"For the record, your mother was with us, and she signed off on the plan. And obviously, as you can see with your own eyes, Anna is perfectly fine. No need to worry. I've got it all under control."

I take a calming breath. This woman is saying everything and nothing at the same time. And as much as I want her to get to the point, it's also nice to have her on the phone. So with the same patience I reserve for Anna, I lower my voice and slowly ask, "Isabella, what aren't you saying?"

She bites down on her thumbnail until she finally makes the decision to fess up. "We ditched her after-school activities today."

"You what?" Those activities are some of the best in the city. Hell, probably the country. And I'm sure I'm probably paying an exorbitant amount for them. But I'd hand over every nickel for Anna.

"Cálmate, papa bear, and hear me out first," she sasses. "Your daughter had an exhausting day at school because they played basketball during physical education, and apparently the whole class was having such a great time, they allowed them to keep playing throughout recess. Do you know how much cardio that is? You probably don't remember, since you stand on that pitcher's mound and beat everyone to a pulp with your fastballs."

I'm no longer able to hide the amusement on my face. "Is that so? Is that what you think I do for a living?" I smirk. "You watch me play often, Isabella?" I mercilessly taunt.

"No," she responds way too quickly.

"But we just watched his game," Anna chimes in helpfully. I respond with a look that clearly shows I know she got caught bullshitting me.

Her cheeks turn a pretty shade of pink.

I don't think twice and turn up the brightness on my phone to get a better look.

"Oh, yeah. Well, that." She tries to discreetly wipe both cheeks, as if she can rub her natural blush away. "As I was saying before, we ditched—I mean, I made an executive decision to take a break from her prior engagement *because* your lovely daughter said she was too tired and would much rather get home in time to watch her father play against Los Angeles." She nods in a triumphant manner, having gained back that confidence as she spoke.

I'm so entranced by her that I almost forget to give her a hard time.

Almost.

"So what's the answer, Isabella? Do you or do you not watch me play?"

I must be certifiably insane.

Because there is no reason under the goddamn sun for me to be messing with Isabella this way. It seems like the physical distance from her has made me bolder, and much, much stupider. The clear boundary I've kept between us is slowly blurring, and while I can clearly see it happening, I can't deny that having her full attention on me feels nice. Like I could talk to her for hours, just to see the many hidden facets of Ms. Isabella Morales.

She huffs, and I swear if I had a full body shot of her, I would put money on the possibility that she may have even stomped at my line of questioning. "Yes, I watched the game *today* because that's what Anna wanted to do. She's your daughter and she misses you, so of course I joined her on the couch as you pulverized that Velázquez guy." She takes a frustrated breath. "But no, Mateo, I don't watch you play, aside from today. Because I don't watch baseball... at least not anymore."

Well, shit.

Now I feel like a dick. All that teasing to get her to admit to watching me, as if my sick ego needed some kind of validation that I'm not the only one secretly losing my mind over here when it comes to our tense relationship, just to inadvertently step in it. Massively.

Of course she doesn't watch baseball. Why would she after what my world has put her through?

I obviously took it too far, and we are much better suited to continue standing behind the very clear boundary line I initially had carved in stone for us. The apology is on the tip of my tongue, but it seems like she's not finished talking.

She looks off camera, and I'm glad she is. It makes it easier to stare at her beauty while simultaneously hiding my guilt over teasing her. "Although I will say that it was nice to watch a game for the first time in years. It used to be such a big part of my life." She turns back to the phone. "I grew up on baseball. I'm Dominican, for God's sake." She chuckles slightly, warming me from the inside out. "I let that part of me go a while ago. And I guess it was nice to finally get a tiny piece of that back. For one game. Even if you were sloppy during the third and fourth innings. Though I guess you still put on a decent show, right, Anna?"

Her blinding smile is back, and while it's not aimed at me, it is directed at the piece of my heart that lives outside my body, which only hits me harder.

Hell, this woman will be the death of me.

Just when I think I have her figured out, she surprises me. I'm not a fan of surprises, but I am becoming a big fan of hers.

I watch the girls as they continue to laugh at my expense.

The fact that I'm still dripping wet and standing by myself at a hotel pool doesn't even faze me, because I'm too lost in them.

As much as I enjoyed riling Isabella up, I decide then and there that I would much rather see her smile, just like this.

And although I know it's a bad idea to keep her on longer than her one-week trial, I convince myself that there would be no harm in helping her fall in love with baseball again. And I'm going to do it by getting her to come to one of my games.

It's the least I can do with the way she dotes on and advocates for my daughter. And sure, deep down I know I can't keep her on as the nanny for good—God knows my willpower wouldn't survive it—but Anna deserves to have Isabella in her life. Their growing bond is clear as day, and I would never do anything to jeopardize it.

They deserve to have each other, even if I can't be a part of that equation.

With my mind focused on a new direction, one in which I'm not fantasizing about my daughter's nanny, I break up their cackling and set my plan in motion.

I make a note to text my pilot after I hang up and let him know that I need him to fuel the jet, because I want to fly out on a red eye instead of flying back with the team tomorrow morning.

I sleep better on my own plane anyway.

"Hey, Isa, I've made an executive decision of my own."

CHAPTER SEVENTEEN

ISABELLA

MATEO LEAVES US ON a cliffhanger.

He won't tell me what he has planned, and the mischievous glint in his eye has me slightly concerned.

It seems like every day, I'm getting to see different pieces of the man who used to be as personable as a brick wall. I hate to admit that it gives me a little thrill each time, knowing that I get to see a part of him that the public has no access to.

The Mateo on TV is mysterious and quiet. He smiles for the cameras and poses with kids.

I didn't think it was possible to have such a squeaky-clean reputation in this day and age. Unless you're a psychopath or a serial killer. Which I'll try not to think about while I'm living under his roof.

Although it might not be a bad idea to ask if he liked lighting fires as a kid or tortured small animals...

Beth lets me do Anna's bedtime routine on my own tonight, which took us an extra half hour because we couldn't stop yapping it up.

Anna is so expressive and has such a creative imagination. I'm constantly in awe of where her mind takes her, and with the way she can whip up a make-believe story out of thin air, she is definitely destined for a life in the arts.

I think I'll type up one of her stories and turn it into a small children's book. I'll make the cover and have it printed for her little library. I think she would love it.

I say goodnight to her, but not before she makes me promise to wake her up a little early so we can make breakfast together, since her dad won't be back until tomorrow evening.

I make my way down the stairs and watch as Beth brings two piping-hot mugs of tea into the living room.

"I'm surprised she didn't convince you to sleep in her room tonight. After I got my new hip, I told her I felt good as new, and she almost had me sleeping on her shag rug." She smiles lovingly up at the second floor.

"I did get pulled into breakfast duty, so hopefully I don't make too much of a mess. Wouldn't want Mateo walking into a disaster zone."

I make a mental note to clean as I go tomorrow.

I recall one of Mateo's previous nannies being fired for wearing inappropriate nighttime wear, and... ahem, I think I already got them beat on that one. Which, unfortunately, landed me my first strike.

The last thing I need is to get my second by making a mess of the kitchen like the other nanny who got fired.

Beth waves my worries away as she hands a tea over. "Mateo is all bark and no bite. Make the mess, enjoy breakfast, and worry about the clean-up later. It's not like he doesn't have a small army cleaning every nook and cranny a couple of times a week." She rolls her eyes. "I don't know how they're able to clean without music or at least something on the TV. I could never."

I smile and think about all my weekend morning wake-up calls from my mother, blasting music while cleaning our modest apartment. There is a sense of home that comes with the little things, like listening to heartbreak merengue and belting the lyrics alongside your mother at the age of eight, only to realize many years later that you had no idea what you were actually singing about.

Which makes a thought pop into my mind.

I lean closer to Beth. "Please tell me Mateo used to sing to Aventura, or something more old-school like Hector Lavoe."

She grins. "Oh, he's been known to belt out a few good ones around the house. But you'd never guess by who."

I take a quick sip of my tea, then promptly place it on the coffee table. I can't be trusted with hot liquids at a time of juicy chisme like this. "Who?" I plead.

She looks around us conspiratorially, as if someone is going to pop up behind the couch. Then gives me the most devious smile ever sent my way. "Olga Tañón."

I give my best telenovela gasp, hands over chest and mouth at once. "No. I can't... *Olga*?" I burst into laughter, knowing it's gonna be the kind that makes you feel like you did a hundred crunches.

I start wiping away the tears that had no chance of being repressed as I say, "I fucking love Olga Tañón. She's an icon. But Mateo... I'm sorry, New York Monarchs' starting pitcher, Mateo Martinez, belting out those notes as a kid? I will never emotionally recover from that visual. Thank you for this gift, Bethzaida."

She sips her tea casually as she murmurs, "Who said it was when he was a kid?"

My momentary shock quickly succumbs to my second round of laughter.

Smacking the couch mercilessly, causing Beth to quickly drop her tea on the coffee table in an attempt to keep it from spilling, I internally vow to mock him relentlessly about this little tidbit.

That is, if I don't get fired first. Priorities and all.

"And here I was, making tea, thinking it was a safer option than you spitting up red wine. But clearly, consuming any liquids around you is a hazard," she teases.

"I need to hear him sing in Spanish. I haven't heard him speak much of it while I'm around. I wonder how I can catch him in the act."

Beth's face falters for a moment, and I wonder if I've said something wrong.

Once she realizes it's safe to do so, she picks her tea back up and stands. "I'm going to add a little whiskey to this." She half smiles as she walks toward the kitchen, and unease settles in my gut.

"Beth, is everything okay? Did I put my foot in my mouth or something? You know me well enough to know that I do it very often, so it's extremely probable," I say as I aim to bring the mood back up.

She empties a bit of the tea into the sink, then fills it back up with a swig of whiskey. "No mija, cosa mía. I get this way when I think about Mateo and his Spanish."

Confused, I ask, "What about it?"

She makes her way back to the couch and lowers herself onto an oversized cushion as she says, "He doesn't speak it."

Huh?

I'm pretty sure I've heard him say words here and there to Anna. And there must have been a time or two where he's been interviewed in Spanish, no?

Then there's the way he pronounces my first name in Spanish, as if it's his favorite melody.

Isabella.

Beth must see me running my mental calculations. And continues. "He understands it perfectly. But he can't read much of it, and he certainly doesn't speak more than a handful of words. I know he can say much more, but I guess he refrains due to his accent." Her short, manicured nails tap nervously against the ceramic mug. "And it's my fault, really." She stares down into the brown liquid.

"Beth—"

"No, really, it is." She sighs as she looks off into the New York City skyline beside us. "When I left Puerto Rico, I was sixteen. I barely knew English, besides the lingo I learned from some of my favorite TV shows. That is a delicate time in a girl's life, so you can imagine, it was hard for me to assimilate into a different culture while trying to learn the native language of my new home." She tilts her head as she offers me a sad smile. "I was bullied relentlessly. No matter how many tutors or after-school programs I attended, there was no way humanly possible for me to erase my accent. Trust me, I tried.

"And back then? In the early eighties? Forget about it. I was called every disgusting name under the sun. My older brothers got into fist fights almost every day that first year. It was horrible." Her voice hitches, and I scoot closer to hold her hand. "I practiced for hours on end. My voice would turn hoarse until there was no more accent to correct.

Every intonation and pronunciation perfected. I went from Bethzaida to Beth. And once I felt as though I could pass as a native speaker, I made a promise to myself. That if I ever had children, they would speak perfect English. That they would not be subjected to the kind of cruelty I had experienced."

My heart hurts for teenage Bethzaida, hearing how much pain she endured as a teenage girl in a scary new city.

I try to reassure the woman who has, on more occasions than I can count, come to my rescue. "Beth, you took your pain and did what you thought best to ensure that your child never faced the same struggles as you did. It sounds to me like you were being a protective mama bear and nothing else." I squeeze her hand.

She makes a noncommittal noise before saying, "Yes, I was protective. But I fear that in my quest to shield him from my past demons, I also kept a part of his identity hostage from him." She squeezes my hand in return. "Now, I would give anything for Mateo to speak freely in his native tongue, or at the very least have the option to if he so wished. And I know he does. I can tell by how he prioritizes Anna's Spanish and French lessons as much as her other after-school activities. And how his terms of endearments for her, like mija, are in Spanish. I sense, in his own way, he's claiming that piece of his culture I never gave him and is doing his best to instill it in his daughter. And I couldn't be prouder of him for it."

Language is such an important part of one's identity, and I couldn't imagine not speaking Spanish, even if, most times, it's Nuyorican slang at best.

I guess I'm one of the lucky ones. Not only did I learn Spanish in my home, but my mother is a high school Spanish teacher, so there was no escaping it. Although I'm sure her students would be tickled by the colorful Dominican Spanish she reserves for outside the classroom.

Without a second thought, an idea is firmly planted in my head. "I can help him. You know, teach him some Spanish? I'm sure he's too busy for any type of formal tutoring, but maybe I can speak more Spanish in the home? Or give him homework... potentially?" The more I speak, the sillier it sounds.

Yet Beth's growing smile offers some encouragement. "If you could get my hardheaded son to do *homework*, then you, my dear, are truly a saint. I could barely manage to get him to do it when he was in high school. Instead, he was focused on all the scouts attending his games." She raises her hand and cups my cheek. "Thank you, Isabella. That is very kind of you. Even if it's a few sentences, I'm sure Mateo would appreciate it. And so would I." She pats my cheek gently before lowering her hand.

"Now, what kind of breakfast extravaganza are you and my granddaughter going to create? My only suggestion is that you steer clear of Anna's extensive collection of sprinkles. Those fuckers light up like the fourth of July in the oven for some odd reason. I'd bet it's all that dye."

And for the third time tonight, I find myself bent over laughing while Beth mercilessly teases me.

CHAPTER EIGHTEEN

ISABELLA

"I THINK WE MIGHT have taken it a tad overboard." I wince as I look at the disarray on the kitchen island.

Pancakes.

All we were supposed to make were simple pancakes on this ordinary Thursday morning. And it started out easy enough.

While I pulled out the flour and sugar, Anna snuck out the chocolate chips, which I absolutely approved of.

When Beth came down and made us espressos on the stovetop, I got distracted while we chatted away, talking about how coffee always tastes better from the stove than from a fancy machine.

Meanwhile, Anna continued to raid the pantry like she was a mini bank robber.

Before we knew it, she had everything under the sun out. She proclaimed it to be a "ladies breakfast," and therefore, there should be more color on our plates.

And by color, she meant sprinkles.

More sprinkles than I could even fathom.

Unicorn sprinkles, glittery sprinkles, alphabet sprinkles, more, more, more, just kept appearing out of thin air until Beth and I decided to go with it. Because who is really going to hold a hard limit against sprinkles when you'd have to do the walk of shame at least a dozen times to get them all put away again?

To be fair, having Beth there felt like I had adult supervision. Even though I was technically supposed to be the adult supervision.

But there's something about having an older adult in the room that allows me to hand in my grown-up card and defer all emergency contingencies to.

If Beth seemed okay with it, then why shouldn't I?

While they made the batter, I finally figured out how to connect my phone to the cool built-in speakers that surrounded the home. I scrolled through my mom's Saturday cleaning playlist, because yes, she did upgrade to streaming her music after she realized she no longer had to smack our old CD player to life every day, and picked a song I knew Beth would get a kick out of.

An Olga Tañón classic, of course.

Within minutes, we were dancing merengue by the stove, whipping up enough batches to feed the whole building. Every time I tried to reel Anna in, Beth waved me off, saying there were enough staff in the lobby that would probably appreciate the free sugary goodness.

So, in my mind, we were providing a service for the building employees. And with that good deed to justify this madness, we carried on.

Anna ate between batches, since I wanted to make sure that she still made it to school on time, even though it seemed like she'd woken up with the need to compete on a Food Network competition show.

By the time she was done, we were working on our final batch.

She was already dressed and ready in her uniform, so I took over powdered sugar duty.

Funny how this was all Anna's idea, yet I was the one constantly wiping sweat off my face. But I couldn't deny how entertaining this was. How nice it felt to cook for fun and not have to stress about appropriate measuring tools when it came to pouring chocolate chips and sprinkles.

There was freedom in indulging Anna's whims, almost like I got to be a five-year-old again myself.

Hell, my twenty-five-year-old self will now forever find boozy brunches a bit underwhelming if they don't include blasting salsa and merengue music and include enough sweetness to put me in a sugar coma.

Yet all good things must come to an end. So with my eye on the clock, I grab the last pack of unopened sprinkles to wrap up this pancake party. I'm so enamored by the sight of Beth twirling Anna to the beat that I don't bother reading the label.

I'm also distracted when Olga hits that note that makes you feel that grown woman's pain that I don't hear the distinct *ding* of the elevator doors opening.

I think this is the point at which the wheels fall off our runaway train.

Because what happens next could only be described as my worst nightmare.

Just as I'm about to twist off the lid of the sprinkle container, Anna's eyes widen comically. I think she might be saying "no" with the way her mouth opened in a perfect, shocked O, but I'm too stunned to react.

Since I'm staring straight into Mateo's confused eyes. As if he must have walked into the wrong apartment.

My knuckles strain as they continue to twist, when the sprinkles in my hand explode... everywhere.

I'm talking multiple feet in the air and covering every square inch of the kitchen all the way up to where Mateo stands tall.

As far as my eyes can see, those little colorful traitors scatter like thieves in the night.

Mateo's expression instantly goes from confused to furious.

"Isa, those were the cannon sprinkles! They're supposed to be for rainbow explosion cakes!" Anna tries to run up toward me, but Mateo holds her shoulder to keep her from stepping in the mess I've made.

"Daddy, you're home!" She leaps into his father's arms. His eyes close and his body sags slightly. For a second, just a tiny one, I think that he may forget about this whole debacle if I quietly slip off to my room. That is, of course, until he opens his eyes to pin me in place. As if he knows I've got the urge to bolt and wants to make sure I stay put for my punishment.

A shiver runs down my spine at the very naughty thoughts of what punishment from Mateo might look like.

Beth's quiet chuckle almost breaks the tension in the room. "You're home, mi hijo. And right on time. We were about to get into Olga's greatest hits."

His cheeks turn slightly pink as he directs that same glare at his mother, although, by the way she's patting his arm, it clearly has no effect on her. "Anna, let's go upstairs and finish your hair before Isa drops you off at school."

Mateo leans down and lets Anna hop out of his hold. I can sense his wrath coming my way, but before he makes a move, Beth speaks again.

"Oh, and Matí, hijo? Can you thank Isa for slaving in the kitchen all morning to make your daughter happy by making her dream breakfast? And for making all this food for your building staff? We couldn't have done it without her." She smiles smugly, knowing she gave him a public motherly warning to go easy on me. I squeal on the inside.

She makes her way to the stairs as she says, "And don't forget to leave an extra tip for your cleaning crew. Something tells me we're going to be pulling sprinkles out of nooks and crannies for a few weeks."

Damnit, Beth. You could have left that part out.

Once they're out of sight, Mateo starts to make his way toward me, his sneakers loudly crunching over the rainbow runway.

Naturally, I open with the dumbest statement possible. "You're home. Um, yay?" I smile awkwardly as he stands close to me. "I, uh, thought that you were coming in later, and, uh, I'd have this whole mess cleaned up by then." I gulp audibly as I take in the disaster zone that was formerly a kitchen. "Well, maybe not *this* mess we're standing in." I point to the ground below us. "I didn't know sprinkle cannons were a thing, but I promise I'll figure out a way to have it cleaned up. It was my fault, and your cleaning team shouldn't have to—"

"Isabella."

My name on his lips stops my entire body from fidgeting, as if it recognizes the need to follow the simple command from this man only.

"Yeah?"

He leans in even closer. "Thank you."

A startled laugh escapes my lips. I know I shouldn't look a gift horse in the mouth, but I can't help but ask, "For what? Turning your home into a sprinkle bomb testing center?"

The side of his mouth tips up slightly, almost teasing me with a smile I didn't realize I wanted so badly until now.

"My mother told me to say thank you." He pauses as he slowly takes me in. "You think I wasn't raised right?" he taunts, his voice playful while his face remains lethal.

His eyes trail over my face, stopping at my right cheek. The front of his hips almost touches mine. The only reason we're not breathing each other's air is because he's probably got a foot on my height. But then he dips his head, and I almost forget to breathe.

I notice him raise his hand in my periphery, but my eyes are glued to his. The gold in his hazel eyes seems to grow darker with every passing second.

He clears his throat. "You have some flour on your cheek." His hand continues to hover, waiting for permission, it seems. I try to nod but can barely move out of this hypnotic state. I must have dipped my head just enough for him to proceed. Cradling my face in his massive, callused hand, he uses his thumb to lightly brush away the white substance from my face.

"It's powdered sugar," I correct him. "I was adding sugar to the batter before you got here."

"Is it now?" His voice turns low and dangerous.

With his eyes holding mine hostage, he continues to lower his face.

Fucking hell. He's going to kiss me.

We're in the middle of the kitchen, with his mother and daughter upstairs, but in this moment, I couldn't even tell you my birthday.

Mateo is going to fucking kiss me.

And apparently, I'm not going to stop him.

Just as his breath mingles with mine, he sticks out his tongue and licks the sugar off his thumb. A rush of breath leaves my chest as he whispers, "So fucking sweet."

I bite my lip to hold in the moan that's on the verge of escaping. His eyes latch on to the movement, and in my libido induced haze, I ask, "Is there sugar on my lips too?" without realizing what I've done.

He lets out a low growl so deep in his chest I can feel it through where he's holding me.

He moves too quickly for my mind to understand that he's no longer within kissing range. Instead, his lips ghost over my ear as he whispers, "Strike two."

And then he's gone.

CHAPTER NINETEEN

MATEO

"Did you step in a rainbow turd this morning? Was it the food we ate on your plane?"

I grunt as I ignore Torres's concerned voice and continue to push my body to its limits as I lift more than my usual amount. It's reckless of me, and I run the risk of potentially injuring myself, but I need the challenge. Need my brain to turn off and focus on the burn, the pain that comes with overexerting myself.

But it's no fucking use.

I still imagine the sugar on my tongue as if it were the taste of Isabella.

Plus, my annoying best friend, who jumped at the opportunity to see his family sooner, and invited himself onto my plane, is of no use either. Especially since he decided to tag along to my gym session as well after his wife requested he do his training early in the day so they can take their kids to the museum later.

Normal family shit.

Normal family shit that I can't seem to figure out how to do.

I let the dumbbells drop to my sides as I ask, "How do you do it?"

He stops his reps while looking at me through the mirrored wall. "Do what?"

Right. This fucker isn't actually in my head. Only when we're on the field or he's riding my ass about Isabella.

"The normal family stuff. Going to public places like the museum. You're a Monarch. How the hell do you avoid getting mobbed? How can you not worry about your family's safety when you're out?"

He nods slowly as he drops his own weights and makes his way to take a seat on the bench across from mine. "You struggling to do stuff like that with Anna?"

Anthony Torres might be a pain in my ass, but he always means well. He's a family man through and through. It shouldn't surprise me that his tone has shifted to take me seriously, but it does soften me up a bit. Just a fucking bit.

"Yeah. I guess. I don't know. I don't think we've really even tried. I see how hard it is to sometimes do the most basic things by myself, so I don't even bother bringing Anna into that mix." I pause, thinking about earlier in the week when I decided to run a quick errand by myself and ended up on over a dozen gossip websites. I would usually defer simple tasks to my concierge team in my building, but when it came to getting things for Isabella's guest room, I couldn't help but do it myself. Especially when the thought of stocking up on her favorite lip balm came to mind. The same one that tormented me during our days in the Dominican Republic.

I shake the reminder away as I continue. "I'd rather fly Anna out of the city and take a couple of vacations throughout the year, to places that provide peace and privacy." I hesitate, because I'm trying to figure out how to ask what's really on my mind. "But I meant, how do you do family stuff, like with Denise too. How does she manage to be married to someone as famous as you and still, I don't know, live a normal life?"

He studies me, and for a brief second, I swear he's there again, in my head. Like he usually is during a game.

I brace for the barrage of questions, but he seems to take a different approach.

"Simple answer? We don't live a normal life." He shrugs. "We live in a secure building. When we want to do activities like the museum, we don't show up on a whim. My assistant calls ahead of time and arranges for us to have an art curator escort us through the place while having one of my security guys walk with us. Sometimes the museum will provide an extra one for us. We skip lines and have access to back hallways, and our car is usually double-parked out front waiting for us when we're done. So yeah, it's not normal. But for the most part, when people see me with my family, they're respectful. I try to take a few pics in the beginning, then I kindly ask the fans to let us be since I'm with my kids." He sighs. "They're usually pretty understanding, and for the few that aren't, well, that's what I bring security for." He smiles.

"Really? Just like that? People give you space?"

He shakes his head. "No, Mateo. I demand it. For me and my family. Because having those moments with them is worth whatever extra hassle I need to figure out. And once you're out enough times, it starts to demystify the experience of seeing a Monarch out, enjoying the city. It's only when one becomes elusive that the media gets antsy and bloodthirsty for any piece of you."

I point at my sweat-soaked T-shirt. "Oh, so we're talking about me now?"

"Meh, I tried starting out that sentence being a little subtle, but then thought, this kind of stuff might be a bit too high-level for you. Best to give it to you straight." He slaps my arm as he moves to get up. "Besides, if you're going to bring someone like Isabella into our world as a WAG, it's best you have all the tips and tricks up front."

A fucking WAG? The atrocious acronym for wives and girlfriends of professional athletes.

There's a special breed of women who are infamous jersey chasers, in it to become WAGs. Isabella is most definitely not one of them. But then again, neither is Torres's wife.

I swipe my gym towel down my face, then aim it at the back of his head.

I don't miss.

"Don't start again with that bullshit," I warn.

Without missing a beat, Torres turns to me, leans down, and rests his hands on his knees. With the most serious face I'm sure he can muster, he asks, "*¿A mí tú me ves cara de pendejo?*"

I can't help it when I start to laugh. "Yes, your face does tend to keep you in a perpetual state of looking like a real pendejo. Might wanna call a plastic surgeon and see what he can do for you about that."

He reclaims his seat on the bench as he revs himself up. "Exhibit A."

"Here we fucking go," I mutter.

"You try to avoid talking about her, but you can't help yourself."

"You brought her up just now, not me."

He waves me away. "Yeah sure, because tiptoeing around the subject of doing 'normal family stuff,' specifically in regard to my wife, was a good cover. If any other man started asking questions about how my wife could be married to an athlete like me, the conversation would have proceeded much differently, and you know it."

The guy is obsessed with his wife. It's a known fact. So I just grunt in response.

"You were almost on the verge of knocking me out when I told you I knew Isa, and you assumed the worst. I've been riling you up for almost a decade. I've done some of my best work to try and make you snap out of this pretty boy persona. Yet the moment you thought I may have had a past with Isa, I saw it in your eyes."

"Saw what?" I ask, aggravated that he's really not letting me off the hook.

"That." He points to my face. "The look of a man who's willing to risk it all. For the right woman," he declares. "I swear, man, I didn't even entertain the idea of fucking with you when I saw what you were thinking, because I saw it. I knew then and there you would lay me out right on our home field if I pushed the wrong button." He tsks as he gives me an exaggerated once-over. "But then I thought *hey, let's give my guy the benefit of the doubt*, right? Maybe he was being a nice guy, protective of those in his circle. That I could get behind." He pauses.

Long enough for me to sigh and have to push him along. "But?"

"*But*." His voice surges with energy, as if he's delivering the best closing statement in a defense case. "But then you went ahead and slipped up."

I roll my eyes. I want out of this conversation, yet I can't make myself move away from it. A morbid part of me needs to know what I'm putting out there that isn't keeping the lid as tight on my Isabella infatuation as I thought.

"And I slipped when, exactly?" I ask, feigning disinterest in the matter.

"When I laid the simplest of traps for you, my friend." He grins mischievously, and now I feel like he's just full of shit.

"All right, that's my cue to get the hell out of here. You are in peak form today." I go to move from my bench, but his words keep me seated.

"You offered to pay."

"What?" I ask, confused.

"Come on, Mateo. Keep up, will you?" He runs a hand through his hair. "When I offered Isa a spa day with my wife? Dinner and drinks too? I didn't exactly do it out of the kindness of my heart." He pauses. "Any other time, I would, but not this specific time," he clarifies before he continues. "Because the second I saw how your whole demeanor changed when she was on video chat, I knew I had to test my theory."

"My demeanor? What, are you saying I was making heart eyes at the woman?" I huff.

"No." He shakes his head. "You were acting like you wanted all her attention on you and you wanted me gone so you could have it." He waits a beat before saying, "You offered to pay. Now, I'm not saying you're a cheap son of a bitch. Hell, we all know you've got enough cash to set you up for a few thousand lifetimes. But when it comes to women, or anyone outside of your mother and daughter? Respectfully, you could give two shits. And I get it. There are gold-digger websites dedicated to how to land a date with you. It's wild out here in these streets. But when I offered to pay for Isabella to go out? Yeah, no fucking chance was Mateo Martinez about to let that fly." He chuckles darkly. "When we won our last World Series and I bought Anna a balloon at Disney World? You went ahead and bought the entire batch from the attendant. When your mother was recovering from hip surgery and Denise brought her lilies, her favorite flower—"

I groan. "I get it. I tend to go a bit overboard—"

"You had lilies planted outside of every window in her apartment and her balcony. She lives on the twenty-seventh floor in Midtown. Those flowers wouldn't survive more than a few weeks at most up there. But the price tag and absurd effort were worth it because her reaction to seeing fresh flowers outside her windows when we live in a concrete jungle was all you cared about."

"Okay, fine. It may have been a bit much. But what's that really prove? That I like to spoil my mother and daughter? And that I was being nice when I, uh, offered to pay for Isabella that day."

"False. You see, I've lived with a woman for many years now, and you know what I've learned during all that time?" he asks seriously.

"How to be a fucking chismoso," I mutter under my breath.

"Yes. The best chisme sessions will always be with your wife. Remember that. But also, I've learned about love languages. And Denise and I both agree that yours is gift giving. So with that little nugget in mind, I deliberately offered Isa a day full of spoiling. An extravagant gift, right in your face."

Crap. Not Denise too.

"And if you cared for her, the way I suspected you did, I knew you would offer."

I stare at him, dumbfounded. "And I offered," I mumble as I run a hand over my beard, resigned to Sherlock Holmes here.

He smacks my knee. "And you fucking offered, bro. Actually, no. You almost demanded you pay. Just like I would have if another man offered the same deal to my wife."

I don't know if it's the brutal workout I just endured or if Torres's masterclass in mindfuckery has done me in, but I sense my resolve starting to slip.

"She's my nanny," I offer weakly.

He grins. "Technically, Anna's nanny. But at least now we can be open and honest about you wanting her to be yours as well." He smirks. "And she's been your nanny for what? Less than a week? I'm sure you can part ways so you can date, if that's what works for you guys."

"No," I say far too quickly. "Anna loves her. And Isabella actually needs the job." I stop myself before I share too much.

His brows furrow. "She got some money issues?" he asks, and now that my mind is caught up on their relationship, it's clear to see that his affection for Isabella is much more that of an older brother than of a former flame.

"No. No money issues. She could just really use the work while she explores other projects. But I'll leave it at that, since it's up to her to decide whether she wants to discuss with you or Denise."

He sighs. "Man, you really care for her, don't you? And before you try to deny it, look over my shoulder and stare at yourself. It's written all over your face."

I look at the mirrored wall behind Torres, but all I can see is a man who has no clue what he's doing.

Like licking the sugar off my thumb while being a hairsbreadth away from her sinful lips.

I don't even think it's a conscious decision between my mind and my mouth when I say, "I don't know what she's doing to me, man. I feel like having her in my orbit is driving me insane. But when I'm away from her, it only gets worse."

He blows out a deep breath. "Fuck, man. I knew you had a crush, but damn. It seems I've underestimated the gravity of this situation. You, my man, are heading toward falling in love. Fast."

I laugh humorlessly.

Love.

The emotion that has evaded every relationship I've ever been in. Even with Anna's mother.

And if I couldn't fall in love with the woman who gave me the world's greatest gift, how could I possibly fall in love with anyone else? Hell, half the battle is getting to know someone long enough to even trust them to not sell stories about me to the press. The likelihood of opening up my heart and soul and trusting that it won't be crushed in the process is statistically improbable.

I can't dwell on the idea of falling in love. Can't bring myself to give Isabella those broken parts of me. She deserves much more than someone like me can offer her.

So instead of taking a deep dive into all the reasons why we probably wouldn't work out in the first place, I say the one thing that I know will get Torres off my back for a bit and most definitely cancel the rest of our workout.

"We also have this three-strikes thing going on that I want to tell you about."

Chapter Twenty

ISABELLA

I DON'T THINK I'LL ever emotionally recover from the sugar lick heard around the world.

Okay, maybe not around the world, but most definitely felt between my legs. Because holy fuck, that was hot.

And no, it is no longer all in my head. I'm sure as a single father, Mateo knows his way around a wet wipe, paper towel, or good old-fashioned hand washing. There is no reason for that whole scenario to have gone down if there wasn't something more behind it.

I'm just not certain exactly what. Because my lovely brain keeps circling the same notion—that there is no chance in hell Mateo would be not only attracted to me but also bold enough to put all that sex appeal on display with no strings attached.

And before my other thoughts join the chat and try to call me an idiot, I remind them that the last man I let in promised me the world with a ring on my finger, and it *still* wasn't real.

So forgive me for my trust issues, but that is something that my friend Kelly and I work on weekly. I call her my friend, but she calls me her client. Even though I secretly know she wishes she could be friends with me. But I get it, professional ethics and all. Which is why I give her a good ten minutes of my best material and personality during the beginning of our therapy sessions before she reels me in and has me reaching for the tissues.

So Mateo must be working on some kind of sexual mental warfare to scare me off before my one-week probationary period is up. I mean, he did give me another strike for the disaster zone in his kitchen. If I keep it up, I'll most likely earn that third strike on my own before the week is up.

Which sucks, because I designed my favorite cover of all time yesterday.

After Mateo disappeared like Houdini yesterday, I dropped Anna off at school, then parked myself at a table in an indie bookstore café. With my wired headphones that only sometimes give me electric shocks, I used that morning's breakfast fiasco for inspiration and created a cover bursting with color. It was a remake of one of my favorite indie romances that centers around a bakery owner and her grumpy next-door neighbor. I made a graphic of an exploding rainbow cake that flowed into the book title. Then I drew some freehand designs along the edges to look like the swirls of a vintage cake. It's something I would never have come up with myself, but with the visual of the morning's burst of color and Mateo's intoxicating proximity, I was able to create a design I think I will show the author.

Not only do I now have the time to lose myself in my art for hours at a time, but I'm also more inspired than ever.

Plus, living with a five-year-old will have you looking at colors you haven't seen in years, since the trending aesthetics usually lean toward the muted and monotone colors of nude.

I've yet to bust out the hot pink, but for some reason, I feel like I could probably make it work for a funky cover.

I sigh as I make my way out of my room. I didn't see Mateo again yesterday after my sprinkle fiasco, and I thank the universe for small mercies.

But I can hear him now, and it's almost time to head out and pick up Anna from school and take her to ballet.

Strike two.

I need to get it together and fast. I don't want to lose this momentum I have going with my small business. Even if that means I have to hide from him for the next seventy-two hours to pass the one-week deadline.

And hide my growing attraction to the hottest man on the planet.

I straighten up as I make my way to the kitchen, where I spot Mateo sitting on a kitchen stool.

The second I'm out of the hallway, his eyes find mine. I stagger for a moment before I secure my footing and continue my way toward him. The last thing I need is for things between us to be awkward, so I make my way to the counter separating us and clear my throat, ready to dive into another well thought-out "I'm sorry for almost ruining your kitchen" speech.

He crosses his arms across his broad chest as he leans back, eyes pinned on mine. "Open that mouth with another apology, and you might as well end it with giving yourself that third strike you're so eager for."

My mouth drops, and I do a very unladylike Scooby-Doo impersonation. Followed by the death stare I have no grounds to give as someone in a precarious situation, but the Dominican in me controls my facial features so I truly have no say in the matter.

His eyes flash with amusement. As if he already knows which buttons of mine to press to get a reaction out of me. If only he knew all the reactions he could so easily incite.

Jesus Christ, girl. Stay on task and worry about your dry spell when you're not directly staring into your boss's hypnotic eyes.

"Well?" he taunts, no longer hiding the small smile playing on his lips.

I place my hands on the counter as I lean forward, hoping this power pose gives me some sort of equal footing. "Me? Apologize profusely for making a mess out of your kitchen, which, in fact, did result in me getting my second strike? Yep, nope. Wouldn't dream of doing such a thing, Mateo. What kind of woman do you take me for?" I cock my head to the side.

He chuckles, causing his upper body to shake mildly, and my eyes to eat up the slight movement. When my eyes reach his again, all the humor has vanished, and in its place lies a tangible tension.

"Speaking of strikes." He shakes his head slightly. "I wanted to talk to you about something."

I straighten. "You're firing me?"

He rolls his eyes. "Dramatic much? No. Well, actually..."

"Actually what?"

"Well, Isabella, it depends on how you handle what I'm about to ask of you."

To get on my knees?

Holy hell. At this rate, I need a sexorcism.

"What, um, will you ask of me?" I ask, much breathier than intended.

He sits up straighter, flexing his right hand as he does but never taking his eyes off me. "I need you to bring Anna to my home game tomorrow afternoon."

And like a bucket of ice dumped over my head, the reality of who I work for finally sinks in.

"As in drop her off?" I ask weakly, already knowing the response.

Mateo stands and starts to round the island. A few moments ago, I would have taken in how his workout shorts hang a little low and offer up a sliver of tanned skin. Or how his black long-sleeve shirt molds to his arms in more places than I even knew possible. But as he comes to stand in front of me, my eyes are unseeing.

All I can think about is the idea of being back in a baseball stadium. Surrounded by thousands of fans I fear may know who I am. Or at least who I used to be.

Only when I feel Mateo's warm knuckles nudging my chin up do I realize he's been talking to me this whole time.

"Isabella. Are you all right?" Concern laces his tone as his eyes bounce over every inch of my face.

I nod. "Yeah, sorry. I think I spaced out there for a second. No biggie." I force a smile.

"Listen, if it's too much of an ask to come to a game—"

Panic starts to rise within me.

I can't let this be the reason I earn my third and final strike. And I won't let reminders of my past keep me from moving on.

So with more confidence than I actually feel, I say, "I can do it. I can go to a game with Anna. It's, of course, a part of my job. So it shouldn't be a problem."

He doesn't seem convinced as he says, "I was going to say that if it's too much for you to come to a game, I would never force you. Wouldn't use it against you as a way to fire you. I promise."

The kindness in his eyes takes me by surprise. I keep a hand on the counter to remind myself to stay upright.

My immediate reaction to his offer is to take the out. Use this strike-free zone to avoid willingly walking back into that world at all costs.

But I don't want to hide anymore. Don't want to feel like I should be banished for actions that were not my own.

Besides, I've survived the worst of it.

The online trolls, the unflattering paparazzi pictures, the whispers behind my back from those I thought were my friends.

And all while I was a naïve twenty-year-old girl figuring out how to be a woman in this confusing and at times cruel world.

I am no longer Izzy, the girl who had treacherous blond highlights to match the hair of the girlfriends of my ex's teammates. I no longer go by a nickname that leans into the whitewashing of my identity, even though when I picked it, I had no idea that was what I was doing.

I am now Isa. Someone who stands in her power. Even if it's in the safety of my bedroom most of the time.

I have learned, through many wine nights with my mother and Bethzaida, along with some professional help from my therapist when their advice seemed a bit on the unconventional side, that I am not the culmination of circumstances that surround me.

Even though I know these things to be true, I also know I've shielded myself from having certain experiences in my attempt to keep my head and heart safe from the level of destruction it once faced.

Relationships, close female friendships, and, silly as it may sound, even baseball.

Something that was so intertwined in my identity as a kid felt like it was taken away from me. All the games I used to attend as a preteen with my dad. Or the games we would watch at home while trying to convince Mami to make us a "stadium hotdog." She refused each time, saying "eso no es comida." *That's not food.* Instead, she would make us a Dominican feast, as if to remind us of what *real food* should taste like. Each time, my father and I would snicker, as if our intention wasn't to get her to cook for us.

I miss watching Anthony play and attending the games with Denise. After everything came crashing down, all those game nights at their home came to an abrupt end as well.

And I, not knowing how to navigate certain relationships while extracting the baseball aspect out of them, took the coward's way out and ran.

I don't know if it's my new living environment, having a renewed vigor for the work I'm accomplishing on my own, or even the positive voice of an always chipper Anna in my head telling me I can do anything I put my mind to, but with a newfound determination, I take a deep breath as I address Mateo again. "I can do this. Actually, no. I *want* to do this. It's been too long, and I think it's time I get back to my baseball roots." I smile. This time, it's a genuine one.

He slowly nods as he takes a step back, taking with him the warmth I didn't realize was enveloping me. "All right. I'll have my assistant text you all the information you need. Hank will drive you guys there and will have all the passes you'll need to access the family area. Anna's been to more than a couple of games, so I'm sure you'll need no better tour guide." He smiles softly.

I swear, if you want to see the sweetest smile known to man, just mention his daughter to this guy. Doesn't matter where or when. If Anna is near or mentioned, you are one of the lucky ones to get to experience the gentlest expressions that Mateo Martinez reserves for his daughter.

And with her in mind, I check the time and see that it's time for me to head out and pick her up for the day. I grab my purse from the counter and make my way to the foyer. "I'm off to get Anna. We'll be going to her ballet class after, and then we'll probably grab some food before we head home," I say as I slip on my Converses.

"Hmm. Is she actually going to ballet, or will you be making another one of your, how did you put it? Oh right, 'executive decisions'?" He looks at me pointedly as he leans back on the kitchen island, as if he's in some kind of at-home photoshoot, while I hop around like a madwoman who doesn't know how to sit while putting on her shoes.

"Hardy har har. That was one time, *Martinez*."

"Getting real comfortable with my last name there, *Morales*."

"Cause we're a team, and don't you forget it," I singsong as he shakes his head.

I'm about to call for the elevator when he shouts, "Hey, Isa?"

"Yeah?" I spin to face him.

"Have dinner with me tonight."

My eyes widen as his sparkle with amusement.

"Tonight? As in tonight, tonight?" I ask, as if any form of clarification would help his request make sense.

He scratches the back of his head, dare I say, nervously. "We're a team, right?"

"*Right.*"

"So yeah. I have dinner with my teammates all the time. Especially the Monarchs, since we're new. Helps us be more… comfortable around one another, and therefore, helps us play better."

"You wanna play with me?" I ask, confused.

When he doesn't immediately respond, I hear the mental playback of what I just said and how it could have sounded. "Uh, I didn't—" I scramble.

He chuckles. "Dinner, Morales. After Anna goes to sleep, we can order pizza or something. Promise not to make you eat the carbless prepackaged meals I have in the fridge." He nods toward his refrigerator.

"Dinner. Yeah. Sure. Why not? Ha." Real fucking smooth, girl. "I'll, uh, yeah. Be here and so will you, and we shall eat. Later. Tonight." I curtsy.

I fucking curtsied.

Then I spin and jam my finger into the elevator button more times than necessary. Why can't I magically disappear as easily as Mateo does when he's done mindfucking me? I swear he has the elevator timed in his head, so he knows exactly when to retreat. Yeah, that's it.

"Isabella."

Fucking hell.

"Yep?" I squeak.

"Do you have something against pizza? Should we order Thai instead?"

I can hear the humor in his voice but turn my head anyway and spot the smirk overtaking his handsome face.

My eyes narrow a bit, and right on cue, his smirk widens into a blinding smile.

The elevator doors finally open, and I launch myself inside.

"Pizza is great. Can't wait. Wouldn't miss it for the world." I salute him.

I know he's far too pleased watching me squirm, but I just curtsied, so I have no choice but to flee at a time like this.

The doors close to the sound of Mateo's soft laughter, and I can't help but join him.

I don't think this is a normal crush.

My body shouldn't be short-circuiting every time he's near.

Especially if we're entering a new phase of our relationship where we have dinners together. Alone. Without Anna.

I grab my phone and lightly smack it against my forehead a few times.

What am I going to do? I'm clearly not equipped to handle this alone.

I need backup. Hell, I need an arsenal of tools at my disposal if I have any hope of surviving.

Shit. I need girlfriends.

Without overthinking it, I shoot off two text messages before I hit the ground floor. I don't know if either will reply, since I have a terrible track record when it comes to keeping up with friends lately.

But by the time Hank is driving out of the underground garage, I've gotten two responses, and a group chat is created for the three of us before I even reach Anna's school.

I sigh in relief as both Denise and Nikki quickly go through introductions and start offering up ideas for a girls' night out.

By the time I'm seated at Anna's ballet class, another member is added to the chat. Nikki's best friend, Amelia.

I don't know how I went from curtsying in front of my boss to feeling like I've joined a girl gang. But I do know that I feel safe, cared for, and thoroughly entertained.

God bless women.

CHAPTER TWENTY-ONE

MATEO

FOR A MINUTE THERE, I thought I shat the bed when I called her my "teammate."

Don't know what I was thinking, calling her that.

Actually, I wasn't thinking at all. Because the plan to ask her to have dinner with me must have materialized the moment the words left my lips.

But that seems to be how it goes when it comes to me with Isabella. An unmistakable force leading me right to her, no matter how hard I try to keep things professional.

Well... except that one time I caged her between the kitchen island and my bare chest after I caught her rummaging in my fridge at midnight, wearing next to nothing. Or that other time, when I licked the sugar off my thumb and leaned in so close, I could have easily licked her lips.

Aside from that, I'm a total professional.

I sigh as I look up to the second floor where Isa is putting Anna to bed. Of course, I offered since I always do it when I'm home, but she insisted. A part of me feels like she needed those extra moments with my daughter before she heads down and has dinner with me. Her boss.

My stomach revolts at the title.

I've never been one to want to be a boss. I thrive better being part of a team, working in collaboration. Not being the sole person responsible for someone's paycheck.

And I'm not blind. I can see the power imbalance between us from a mile away.

Even though I know she's stronger than she seems at times, I'm still a rich man who controls her current livelihood and living arrangements. One she believes is one strike away from firing her and sending her packing.

If only she knew what my strikes really meant.

No matter what develops between us, I want to make sure she knows that she is not at my mercy. Which is why I think this dinner might actually turn out to be a good idea.

And if I ever try and pursue something with her, it would be nice to at least say we've sat down together as friends first.

Footsteps on the stairs bring my attention to Isabella, who cautiously makes her way down.

I think it's incredibly adorable that she and Anna change into their pajamas at the same time of night. I know it makes Anna feel like Isa will be going to sleep when she is, and therefore, she won't be missing out on any fun downstairs.

Isabella's night wear has been very conservative since the night I caught her in my kitchen. Usually lounge pants and some sort of long-sleeve top. I want to tell her that she doesn't need to cover up completely for my sake, but then again, it might be a small reprieve for my sanity, so I say nothing.

Tonight, she sports black leggings that mold her thick thighs and perfect ass, as well as a loose navy top that hangs off one bare shoulder. By the twitch in my pants, you'd think she walked down in lingerie.

Her hair, curly and in a loose bun on the top of her head, bounces as she makes her way over to me with a small smile playing on her lips.

"We hit a new record tonight."

"Let me guess, you read two books for her, and she made up... three," I predict.

She grins. "I read one, and she made up five. Although I think I egged her on by asking so many follow-up questions. Each one sprouted a new idea in her mind for a completely new story, so, of course, she had to start from scratch."

My heart melts. No matter what goes on in my life, I know I'll forever be the luckiest man alive to be able to call myself Anna's dad. I don't know how I won the kid lottery, but I really did.

I know most parents are biased, but Anna is such a creative and loving soul. How she went from asking for one more bedtime story to creating her own is beyond me.

What I do know is that I'm grateful to Isabella for helping foster that imagination and not trying to dim it to make her job easier.

"Thank you, by the way. I'm not sure I've thanked you all week for how you've cared for Anna. I hope you know it doesn't go unrecognized. Although I am kicking myself now for not making that clearer to you."

Her cheeks pinken slightly as she nods.

"You're welcome. And trust me, it's hardly a burden. Anna is a very cool and kind kid, and I'm sure that's all thanks to you. So thanks for making my job easy."

I absentmindedly take a step closer her, then force myself to stop.

I have no idea why my body keeps doing that. Gravitating toward her.

I'm an athlete who has trained and conditioned my body to do things that most people could never fathom. Yet I cease to hold any control over my legs when I'm in the same room as her. They inevitably lead me straight to her, and more often than not, I stand much closer than a boss should be standing by their employee.

"Pizza," I blurt out, refocusing on the present. "I left it warming in the oven for us. Never know how long Anna's bedtime stories will take, and I didn't want to order too late either." I head toward the section of my kitchen with four ovens. A bit overkill, if you ask me, but with a kitchen this size, the extra appliances seem to fit in well.

I put on an oven mitt, then open the oven door, pulling out the three racks with a flourish. "So, we've got a basic margarita pizza, a half-pepperoni half-veggie, and the best Sicilian pizza in the city, half-cheese and half–meat lovers."

She comes to stand on the other side of the oven door, her eyes wide, taking in the extra-large slices of pizza.

"Yeah, so quick question. How many people exactly are coming over to help us eat all of this?"

"Haven't you ever heard of leftovers, Isa? Come on, are you even a real New Yorker?" I taunt.

"Says the guy who probably hasn't had a carb since the nineties."

"Ouch." I put my mitten-covered hand over my heart. "Coming for my age already? At least let a man lick his wounds with some pizza before you go for the jugular."

"I wasn't coming for your age. I was mocking your strict athlete diet." She rolls her eyes as she points at a pepperoni slice and a Sicilian slice. "Besides, I don't think you're old."

"Thanks, because the eye roll really sold it for me." I plate her selections, then put them on the place setting I arranged on the kitchen island. "You do that quite a bit." I plate my own slices, not playing much attention to what I choose, since I know I'll be back for seconds.

"Who? Me? Roll my eyes to my gracious boss who's offering me a gratuitous pizza night? I would never." She smirks as she opens the fridge and grabs one of my usual electrolyte waters.

"Careful, Isabella. Don't want me treating you like you're a brat now, do you?" She freezes momentarily at the change in my tone. "And you can put that water back. If I'm having pizza tonight, I'm also having wine."

Her eyebrows almost hit her hairline. "Pizza and wine on a weeknight?" She tsks. "*Careful, Martinez.* I don't want to be blamed for being a bad influence on you," she shoots back.

I close the oven doors and pull down two wineglasses as I say, "Morales, don't go assuming who could be the bad influence in this situation." I pause to see if she has another rebuttal ready.

"Duly noted," she says into the wine fridge, doing a terrible job of hiding the rosiness in her cheeks. "Red or white?"

"We'll do your red."

She pokes her head out. "My red?"

Shit.

"Well, you liked that brand of pinot noir you had with my mother when I was out of town, right?"

She squints a bit. "This sounds like a trick question. Do I or do I not confirm having wine with your mother—while Anna was asleep, of course? Hypothetically speaking," she adds quickly.

I chuckle. "My mom told me you enjoyed it. You're more than allowed to have a drink while you're not working. So I went ahead and ordered more of it. Guess I now refer to it as your wine." I shrug.

She pulls out the wine as she looks at me, eyes assessing. "Huh. I, uh, guess that was really nice of you. Thanks." She looks back into the wine fridge, then smiles. "But that's a lot of wine bottles in there. So either you think I'm some kind of closeted alcoholic who can put a dent in all of those bottles, which you obviously don't, because you would never allow someone like that around Anna, or..."

"Or?" I join in on her conspiracy.

"You plan on keeping me around for much longer than a week, which means I'm safe from a third strike, at least for tonight?" She smiles cautiously.

I sigh. "Isabella, come here."

It takes her a moment, but eventually she obliges. When she comes to stand before me, I take the wine bottle from her hands and uncork it easily. I pour us each a glass. "Tonight, we forget about the strikes, okay? Tonight is about thanking you for what you do for Anna and, therefore, me." I put the bottle down and pull out her chair. She tentatively takes a seat, and I slowly glide her closer to the counter. "And if I'm being completely honest, it seems like everyone around me knows you a bit better than I do, and let's just say, I think it's time we change that." I force my hands to unclench from Isa's seat and take my own next to hers.

She grabs the stem of her glass and swirls her wine as she asks, "So tonight we get to know each other better? As in, I get to ask you questions, and you'll answer them? And not answer them like you do in magazines or postgame interviews, but like a real straight-shot answer?"

I smile. Something I seem to be doing a lot more of in her presence. "Tread lightly, Isabella. You've watched one of my games, and now I know you're keeping tabs on me. Might give a guy a complex or something." I lift my glass to hers.

I go to clink her glass, but she pulls hers away. "Hold up, let me just get the terms and conditions straight before I step in it. So you're telling me I can ask you anything? Anything at all? Nothing off-limits?"

I laugh, because fuck, she's cute. "Hmm, I suppose, but..."

"But?" she asks, her eyes wide with anticipation.

"It'd have to go both ways. Anything off-limits on your end?"

She mulls it over for a moment and then surprises me when she casually shrugs her shoulders and brings her glass closer to mine. "Deal."

Fuck. The things I want to know about her are not exactly things I should be asking over pizza.

What makes you wet? Would you spread your legs if slipped my hand under your tight leggings? How do you sound when you come undone?

I try to adjust myself subtly as I scold myself. She's probably only curious about my astrological sign or some shit like that.

Not about becoming acquainted with my dick. "So what are we toasting to?" I clear my throat.

She taps her chin playfully until she finally settles on "let's toast to you potentially regretting this." She clinks her glass mischievously against my unmoving one.

Well, shit. What have I just done?

"Seriously? You've never looked at each other's penises while you're in the shower together?"

Fucking hell. Isabella has been relentless tonight. Although I can't say I haven't been thoroughly entertained. She most definitely surprised me with her line of questioning. Gone is the woman who couldn't run away from me fast enough this morning. She's been replaced with someone who couldn't derive more pleasure from watching me squirm.

I knew Isabella had a backbone. Hell, I try to rile her up at least once in every one of our conversations. But little did I know how brutal she could be once she got comfortable with me. I fear she may never go back to being docile.

That's a lie.

I actually like her much better this way. Even if I've become her comical punching bag.

We're lying on our sides, facing each other, on different ends of my U-shaped couch. It feels intimate to lie this way with her, but the ten feet between us seems to give us a false sense of safety.

"You can't tell me a guy like Ace Middlebrooks walks out of the shower with a third leg, and you're not looking."

Okay, fun time is over.

"You like Ace?" I love the guy, but at the moment, I'd love to take a fastball to his sac.

She rolls her eyes again, and for a split second, I think of the ways I want to punish her for being insolent. She makes an unpleasant face. "No, but he walks around like he has big dick energy, so I assume he's packing. And my question was if you look, not if I like." She points her almost empty wineglass at me.

I groan. "No, Isabella. I don't look. Eventually, they all blur into my periphery, I guess. Happy?"

She bobs her head from side to side. "Good enough, I guess. But at least I now know you don't like Ace. That's some prime chisme. Because sheesh. The way you looked at me when I mentioned his name? Got the message loud and clear. Bummed to know that he might not be a good guy after all, though."

Oh, Isabella. If you only knew. Hell, if I only knew why I react the way I do around you. "Sorry, too much dick talk. Didn't mean to give a look. Ace is actually a nice guy. Likes to lean into the whole playboy persona, but it's a front. He's actually one of my favorites on the team. But I'll never tell him that. His head is big enough as it is." I chuckle as I remember the picture he sent in the team group chat earlier today, asking us which bracelet he should buy his mom for her birthday. One was covered in pink diamonds and the other in yellow canaries.

And they say I go overboard with gifts.

I look over at Isa when I realize she's been quiet for the longest stretch of time tonight. Which happens to be ten seconds. "Everything all right in that head of yours, Isa?"

She shakes her head subtly, staring into her empty glass. "Yeah, sorry. Nice to hear that he's actually a nice guy, even though he plays into the whole, you know, 'I'm an athlete and I'm a womanizer' bit."

This is usually where I would bolt. I would give Isa the out and not try to pry into her past. But tonight, I've learned so much about her.

She even brought out her work backpack after I asked to see one of her book cover designs. I couldn't get Torres out of my head once I saw her cracked screens and headphones with exposed wiring. The fucker is right. Took everything in me not to get up right then and there and take her to an electronics store.

Guess gift-giving is my fucking love language.

But now, seeing her reaction to the subject I know caused her the most pain, I can't help but feel like I want to peek behind those curtains too, if she'll let me.

"Are we still operating under nothing's off-limits agreement?"

She smirks as she places the glass on the low coffee table between us. "Is this my karma for asking too many dick-related questions?" A soft sigh escapes her as I keep quiet. "You already know what happened, Mateo. If your mother didn't tell you, ESPN sure did."

"I know what was reported, but I want to hear it from you. What did he do to you?" I half pray that she refuses to answer, because if I didn't like the guy before, I sure as hell won't be able to hold myself back when I'll eventually have to play against him.

She nods solemnly. "I'll try to give you the short version. But I'm Dominican, and I've had wine, so listen at your own risk." She sits up from her lying position, and so do I. She brings her socked feet onto the couch and hugs a pillow. She hasn't spoken a single word, and already, I can see how she is crawling back into herself at the thought of retelling her story. And it fucking guts me.

This time, when my body pulls toward her, I don't stop it. Not until I've taken the seat cushion next to her and pulled her hands into mine. "Please, Isabella. You don't have to tell me. I'm sorry I asked."

She stares at our joined hands, then into my eyes. I thought I would see tears, sadness, or a sense of helplessness. Instead, what I find is pure determination. "It's fine, really. I'm just warning you that it's a bit of a mood killer, and I've had such a great time tonight... mostly at your expense." She smiles brightly as she gives my hands a gentle squeeze. "Besides, I'm going to my first baseball game in over five years tomorrow, so it only seems fitting I get this story out of my system." She leans back on the couch. She doesn't move to untangle our hands, and neither do I.

"We met during my freshman year in college. I thought I wouldn't really be getting the college experience since I decided to stay in the city, but boy, was I wrong. Living in the dorms, attending parties, classes with guest speakers who I've only ever seen on TV... it was incredible. And then, I met him. I think I was enamored immediately by his confidence and charisma. He was a senior, and somehow, he was interested in someone like me." I don't realize I've squeezed her hand until she squeezes mine back. "Oh, don't worry. I'm not trying to sell myself short here. But he always seemed larger than life, with goals of making the major leagues, and I was happy to be along for the ride, to bask in someone else's glow."

I start to rub soft circles on her wrist, which pauses her momentarily.

"Anyway, we dated for two years, and near the end, he had made it to the minor leagues. He said he probably would have been drafted to the major leagues from college, but he had a shoulder injury that he was still rehabbing." She rolls her eyes, and this time, it carries none of the sass I've grown to appreciate. "We never talked about marriage. I'm sure I assumed it was something that would have come up at some point down the line, but I was only twenty years old." She looks up briefly, and I ache to comfort twenty-year-old Isabella. "When the day came for the draft, as he got the call that he was being drafted to his dream team, with cameras he paid for to have there that day, he got down on one knee and proposed to me. And do you want to hear what's funny? When it happened, all the blog sites gushed about how I was so stunned by the ring that I was left speechless. When in reality, in my mind, I was freaking out about what my mom was going to say."

She laughs, and the sound alone makes my shoulder release some tension I was apparently holding in tight.

"Like, I'm technically a grown-ass woman, being recorded on live TV as my boyfriend proposes to me, and all I could think about was how my mom would not approve. And wonder how I managed to be with someone for so long and not explicitly talk about our plans for the future, like engagement timeline, family planning... all of that. I think for the longest time it was all assumed, probably by the both of us. Because I obviously wanted those things, and he was the person I was sharing my life with, so maybe we subconsciously put two and two together. But I truly had no clue. And this man was publicly professing his love for me, yet he didn't even know that I loathe the idea of a public proposal. And the ring was too large and generic for someone like me, who loves jewelry that's more sentimental and artsy rather than showy. If he really knew me, he would have known that I was not in a place in my life to think about marriage. I was still knee-deep in figuring myself out."

Removing only one hand from her hold, I lift my glass of wine and offer it to her. She smiles as she takes a sip, then hands it back to me. I drink from the exact spot her lips touched before I set it back down and reclaim her other hand.

"But even with my racing thoughts, I couldn't bring myself to say anything but yes. I got swept up in the moment and decided we could talk about the engagement at a later time, like when there weren't cameras pointed at us. But that time never came. Because immediately after the cameras went down, he kissed me goodbye and said he was going off with his old teammates to celebrate. And truthfully, I needed a moment to recover from the whirlwind that I had been thrust into. By the time I got home, his proposal had gone viral everywhere. People on campus knew my name, acquaintances were coming out of the woodwork, and every wife and girlfriend of every MLB player infiltrated my social media, asking if I wanted to collaborate on brand deals. And yes, I did find it weird that a man proposes to me and immediately goes MIA, but everything about my life had just been turned upside down, so nothing felt normal. Three days later, the infamous 'seventy-two-hour engagement' came to a crashing halt when photos of him partying in Vegas were plastered everywhere online. Pictures of him with a woman's head between his legs while he made out with another topless woman."

She removes her hands from mine, and it takes everything in me not to ask for them back.

"The betrayal? The pain? It was brutal. But what he did, or claims to have accidentally done after I dumped him? *That* was earth-shattering. Because gone were the photos of me with a ring on my finger on the internet, and in their place, sexy photos I had sent him in private were now available for the entire world to see." She looks at me with a pained expression.

"I swear to you, Isabella. I never saw them."

"I wouldn't blame you if you had. They were everywhere."

I shake my head. "Even though I didn't know you personally back then, I would never have done that to you, or anyone else who had private images shared without their consent."

She points to my glass on the table. "I'm gonna need a little more of that now."

I grab the bottle and top off her glass before I hand it to her. "I didn't even show any nipple," she mumbles into the wineglass, and I'm hit with a coughing fit. "No, seriously. He always asked for nudes, and I always told him I wasn't comfortable with that. But he kept pushing and pushing. Eventually, I sent him something that I hoped would knock his socks off, even though I strategically covered my face and body in ways that wouldn't show it was me. But when the guy you're engaged to 'accidentally' posts those photos on social media after getting caught in a cheating scandal... yep, it didn't take much of a leap for people to know who the mystery woman was." She takes a large gulp of wine before handing it back to me. Her tongue peeks out to wipe a rogue droplet away. "And then I dropped out of school, ran to Puerto Rico where my cousins were attending college, registered there for a semester, and ended up staying the whole two years it took to wrap up my bachelors. I finally came back to New York with my tail between my legs once I felt the coast was clear. And ta-da, sob story complete. Okay, you next. Go."

"Isa..."

"Mateo, I said nothing is off-limits, but I didn't say pity party included." She looks at me sternly. "Will I ever recover from that kind of public humiliation? To be determined. But I've slowly clawed my way back into society, and I'll be damned if I spend another moment sitting here, watching you feel sorry for me, when I could be asking you really inappropriate dick questions."

"You're deflecting with humor."

"Ding, ding, ding. Yes, my therapist thinks I'm very funny too, thank you very much. And maybe I just need to get laid so I stop thinking about dicks, but regardless of where I was going with that, I would like to take my baggage back now and put it in a nicely contained compartment, away from the world to see, and specifically, your sad eyes," she pleads.

"What do you mean you need to get laid? Are you, uh, seeing someone?" Try as I might, I didn't hear a word of what she said after she mentioned getting laid.

She bursts into laughter, barely saving the couch from being splashed in red wine. It's cute that she thinks I would give a damn. I'm still waiting for my answer.

"This might be hard for you to believe, but this hot mess is still single. Haven't been in a serious relationship since I was engaged for a millisecond. Of course, after a while, there were some guys in Puerto Rico who were fun to—"

"Got it. Message received loud and clear," I bite out, much rougher than intended.

She sits up on her knees, eyes wild with accusation. "Oh, I'm sorry. I wasn't aware Anna was made by immaculate conception," she throws my way.

Touché.

"No, you're right. She wasn't. She was made by me and a woman who couldn't run farther away from the idea of being a parent."

Her face drops as she sucks in a breath. "Shit. I'm sorry. I shouldn't have said that."

"Can I get some of that back?" I nod at the wine she's cradling in her hands. "Or will you hold it hostage while you throw *me* a pity party?"

She bites down on a smile as she hands me the glass. Don't know when we decided to go from using two glasses to one, but I much prefer it this way. "No pity parties here. Only pizza parties," she declares.

I look at the time on the microwave. It's only ten p.m. "If we're digging into my sob story, do you think we could at least order some dessert? I'm thinking we keep it on brand with our Italian night and order gelato from Luciano's."

She gasps. "Mateo Martinez. Pizza, wine, *and* sweets? Hand it over." She starts looking behind me. "Give me your athlete card. You clearly aren't allowed on the field for your game tomorrow." She stops, eyes widening. "Shit, if you guys lose, will it be my fault for getting you boozed up the night before?"

I feign indecision. "I don't know. You were a pretty bad influence there for a minute. Offering to get me a third serving of pizza."

She lightly shoves my shoulder. "Your head was on a swivel, turning to look at the ovens every couple of seconds. The moment you realized half the Sicilian was left, you couldn't focus and got slow on your answers about what your favorite Olga Tañón song was."

I groan. "Is my mother too young to be put in a home? I'm never forgiving her for that."

"As if you would ever put her in a home. You worship the ground she walks on, as you should."

I tap my phone a few times, opening up the food delivery app to Luciano's. "To answer your question, you are guilt free. Because tomorrow, we're not losing. Now hurry up and order. I'm going to need some dulce de leche if I'm going to talk about Anna's birth mother."

She takes the phone cautiously as she asks, "And how are you so sure you're going to win?" She starts adding flavors to the cart at an impressive speed.

I take the final sip of wine, earning her attention. "I've got someone I want to impress coming to the game, so I won't lose."

Chapter Twenty-Two

ISABELLA

Things I learned last night:

Good wine doesn't give you hangovers.

Mateo is an ice cream hog.

And everything about Anna's birth mom.

Maria, a woman from Europe, who works in the art world.

Seems fitting that Anna has some creative blood in her, even if they've never met or spoken to each other.

I learned about how he met her at a charity afterparty and dated her casually for over a year. They'd see each other when she popped into town. How she found out she was pregnant and, after seeing Mateo's instant paternal reaction kick in, offered to have the baby, with the understanding that she would not be a part of the child's life, since she never planned on having children of her own.

Mateo went into detail about how he tried to convince her to co-parent, for Anna's sake, once she was born. How he even proposed the idea of dating again to see if there was a chance of them being a real family.

But in the end, Maria wanted a clean slate and walked away. And Mateo vowed to respect her wishes—with more grace than I could muster if I were in his shoes. She signed away her parental rights once she was out of the hospital, and a boatload of legal documents to ensure that later down the line, she can't pop in and threaten to take Anna away from him. Something he felt like she would never do, since he swore up and down that she truly was a kind person. But having a daughter changed him, and he made sure there was no box left unchecked when it came to ensuring he could keep his daughter safe in his arms.

She did leave behind a letter for Anna, for when she's old enough to understand the circumstances around her origin story. Letting her know that although she couldn't hold the role of Anna's mother, she would leave an open door for her in the future, if she ever were to have questions or simply want to have a conversation.

By the end of the night, it seemed like Mateo needed to tell the story for his sake, more than mine.

And the way he was going to town on that dulce de leche gelato was quite the sight.

But as promised, no pity parties were allowed.

Any time I seemed to be on the brink of tears, he'd threaten to eat the rest of my pint of cookies and cream. When my lip quivered and I asked if I could give him a hug, he said he would reconsider the no strike peace treaty. But he gave me one anyway.

I'm pretty sure the hug lasted longer than appropriate, and I clung to him harder than a needy koala, but the way his face nuzzled into my neck makes me think he didn't mind.

And when he walked me to my room, he tried to slip back into our previous roles by warning me not to be late to the game tomorrow and to make sure Anna and I wore matching jerseys.

Yet when I rolled my eyes at his request, his whispered "don't test me" unexpectedly sent shivers down my spine.

So naturally, today, I must test him.

I know I'm not officially in the clear, but after last night, I really don't think Mateo would fire me.

I mean, we freaking trauma bonded.

I smile as Anna hops into the car before me, wearing a very bedazzled jersey with her father's name and number. She's in jean shorts, a navy tank top, and converse. Dressed exactly like me, minus the bedazzling. We are even sporting matching Monarchs baseball hats—my idea, given that a bit of my bravado has faded from last night, and I feel like I could use the extra layer of armor against potentially curious stares.

The closer we get to the brand-new stadium, the antsier I get.

"Isa, you're almost shaking the car with your leg. Do you have to go pee? I know where all the bathrooms are at the stadium," Anna offers sweetly.

I push my hands down on my knees, forcing them to stop their incessant bouncing, and try to act as if I don't feel Hank's concerned gaze from the rearview mirror.

"Yeah, sorry. Forgot to go before we left. But it's all good. We're almost there, right, Hank?" I add a fake level of chipper to my voice.

"Just pulling in now, actually," Charlie answers from the front seat.

It still feels weird to go everywhere with a security detail, but I've been able to crack a smile or two out of Charlie since we've met, so I consider that a win.

We pull up to a security gate, and Hank hands over a family pass lanyard. After a few guards circle the car and scan the bottom with extendable mirrors and other CIA-type gadgets, we're cleared to pull in.

Hank parks by a large open area that resembles more of a loading zone than stadium entrance.

"It's going to be a great game. I can feel it, Isabella. You make sure to enjoy yourself today, all right?" Hank says as he opens the door for me.

For a second, I wonder if he knows why I'm nervous.

Which leads to the other devastating side effect of my public humiliation.

The guessing game.

I never truly know who knows and who doesn't. Who acts coy or dumb to simply spare my feelings.

Knowing that someone is actively trying to go out of their way to make sure I don't feel bad actually makes me feel guilty. It's a never-ending cycle that sometimes puts me in a funk for days on end.

But for now, I take in Hank's kind eyes and words at face value. He's right. This is going to be a great game, because we have two New York teams going head-to-head.

I take Anna's small hand in mind and ask her to lead the way, even though it's obvious that Charlie is leading and directing our every move now that we are out of the car.

Every so often, Charlie brandishes a badge, and doors are magically opened for us. The impressive experience of being able to walk through the behind-the-scenes areas of Monarch Stadium pushes my nerves to the back seat.

That is until we make it to the family suite that overlooks the field.

A stunning young woman meets us by the door. Her golden-brown skin glows in a way that tells me she's been in the Caribbean sun recently. She's dressed in what I recognize as a two-piece Chanel pantsuit and nude Louboutin heels. I discreetly look down at my scuffed Converses and wonder if matching a five-year-old's outfit was really the right call.

"Hi, I'm Daisy." The woman extends her hand to me while sporting a kind smile.

"Hi, I'm Isabella. Uh, Anna's nanny," I say nervously.

"Oh, I know who you are," she says, giggling.

I freeze. It's already begun. Fuck, this was a bad idea.

I clear my throat as I take my clammy hand back and subtly start rubbing it against my jean shorts.

"Anna here hasn't stopped talking about you since she took that trip to the Dominican Republic. Isn't that right, Anna?" she says smoothly, not noticing my current freakout.

Wait, what?

"Yes, and when Papi told me you'd be my nanny, I told him to tell Daisy immediately, since she's one of my favorite people here."

I release a deep breath. The tightness around my chest loosens once I realize Daisy didn't mean she knew who I was *because* of my past, and I almost chuckle to myself.

Almost, because the next questions banging down the front door of my brain are whether Daisy and Mateo are close and why it is that she is Anna's favorite person here.

As I struggle to form the psychotic question in my mind, her gigantic engagement ring catches my attention. She sees me looking, and her smile dims a fraction. "Yeah, my fiancé went a bit overboard, didn't he?"

"It's beautiful. Breathtaking. Massive—"

"You could see this shit from space, Isabella." She starts laughing in a manner that doesn't quite match the wardrobe she's currently donning.

I'm taken aback by a woman who suddenly looks like she's wearing a costume. Her phone lights up in her hand, and it quickly quiets her laughter.

"Sorry about that. If your dad asks, I've never cursed around you. Got it, kiddo?" She nods at Anna, and Anna nods right back.

"Got it. Besides, you always get me the best snacks. Why would I snitch on you?" I tug on Anna's ponytail and laugh at her humor.

"It's not usually my job to greet the family members, but I knew you were coming with Anna, and I just had to stop by before all the action started. Hope you don't mind." Slight vulnerability slips through her tone, and I wonder how a woman in a power suit somehow seems intimidated by meeting me.

And then I recognize something in her eyes. Something I've seen mirrored in my own reflection for years now.

She looks like she could use a friend.

I could be wrong, but I decide there's no harm in taking the leap anyway.

"Thank you so much for stopping by. This is my first time here, so I'm a newbie." I hesitate for a moment, hoping I'm reading the room correctly. "Listen, totally feel free to say no—I know we literally just met—but if you'd like, maybe we could exchange numbers and—"

"Yes. Absolutely!" She coughs slightly. "I mean, yeah, totally. Sorry, got a bit ahead of myself there for a second." She laughs awkwardly. "I'm still kind of new to the city and don't have many friends my age, so it'd be nice to hang out." A slight panic flashes over her eyes. "Unless you only wanted to exchange numbers for game-related purposes, which is totally fine as well."

I shake my head as I smile. I really shouldn't derive an ounce of pleasure from seeing this sweet woman so flustered. But a teeny tiny part of me—okay maybe not *that* tiny—finds a form of comfort in knowing there are other women out there that are maybe just as lost as I am in the world and don't have their entire lives perfectly put together.

Makes me feel like I'm not so alone in this journey I seem to be taking.

"Oh, I meant full-on hanging out. I don't have many girlfriends either... actually, that's changed recently. There's even a group chat created and working on planning a girls' night that should be happening soon. I don't know if you'd be interested in that, but you're more than welcome to join us if you'd like."

I swear her eyes almost glass over before she composes herself and nods enthusiastically. "Yeah, that sounds incredible, actually. Here." She thrusts her phone into my hand, and I dial my number into it, then call myself. Once my screen lights up, I lift it and say, "Okay, got it." I end the call and hand her back her phone as I start saving her contact information. "I'm

Isabella Morales, by the way. Unless you want to save me as Isabella Nanny or whatever works best for you."

"Isabella Morales," she murmurs as she types. "Got it."

"And you're Daisy..."

She cringes a bit before whispering something I can't make out.

"I'm sorry, I didn't catch your last name. What was it again?"

I can see the wheels turning in her head until a look of resignation takes over her face and she says, "Stonehaven. My name is Daisy Stonehaven."

Ho-ly shit.

For a second, I contemplate playing it off like I don't know the Stonehaven name, but then I realize I'd be doing what I hate being done to me. So I keep it honest.

"I'm not going to lie. For a split second I was going to play dumb and act as if I've never heard that name before, but I know a thing or two about name notoriety, so I'll spare you the bullshit and let you know that I'm aware of who you must be."

She chuckles as her shoulders drop a fraction. "Thanks for your honesty. It's refreshing in a place like this." She waves around the state-of-the-art entryway leading up to what I can only assume are just as impressive suites.

I type in her very famous last name, then slip my phone into my back pocket. I'm aware of an increasingly antsy Anna at my side. She's probably trying to hurry up and get into the family suite so she can put a dent in the snack selection. But in true nosy-Isa form, I have to ask.

"So does that mean that your..." I start.

She smiles. "My older brother, Nick. He's the new owner of the Monarchs, as per our grandfather's living will." She smirks at some kind of inside joke I'm not privy to.

Must be a joke rich people make, because who the hell inherits a whole baseball team?

Billionaires, that's who.

Because even though Nicholas Stonehaven comes from money, word on the street is that he cut all ties with his father, and at thirty-four, he's turned himself into the youngest self-made billionaire in the world. He's also the world's hottest Black billionaire according to every magazine publication. And that's a title I can easily agree with. Because hot damn.

Yet Nick Stonehaven is a mystery to the world. We know he has a very white and very British father who's a big player in the business world. But we know nothing of his mother, the woman who clearly gave him all his good looks, given that his father's face is permanently stuck in a manner that suggests that he's just sucked on a lemon.

And given he's grown up in various boarding schools across the world, there's no pinning exactly where his roots come from.

Listen, I'm not proud of knowing all this background information, but while doom scrolling, searching for my name on the internet, his name popped up more than a few times, so sue me.

"Well, I'll be inheriting an overactive kindergartener if I don't let her loose in that suite any second now." I laugh as Anna rolls her eyes.

Oh, her father is going to *love* that.

"So... are we still on? For, like, texting and girls' night?" Daisy asks shyly.

"Listen girl, the only thing your last name changes is me not feeling bad if you offer to pay for my slice of pizza." I wiggle my eyebrows playfully.

A relieved look comes over her face as she nods. "First slice on me, promise."

"But please don't feel like your wallet is what brings value to me and my girlfriends. I promise it doesn't. As long as you have a sense of humor and don't mind having friends who love having inappropriate conversations, then you're golden," I add quickly. "And spoiler alert," I whisper. "I'm the one who starts all the inappropriate conversations." I wink.

She smiles widely. "Sounds like I've met my perfect crew." She goes to wave us in, but stops abruptly. "Oh, I almost forgot." She pulls two tickets out of her immaculate pantsuit and hands them to me. "In case you want to get close to the action, these seats are right up front, off to the side of the Monarchs' dugout. We always set them aside in case Anna wants to go down and say hi to her dad before or after the game."

Seats out in the open, right by the dugout? Absolutely not.

But I smile politely anyway. "Thanks, but I'm pretty sure we'll stay up here and stick by the free food." I nod toward the long table lined with food that I've already let Anna make a beeline for.

Daisy nods. "Sure thing, but um... maybe keep them close in case you change your mind." She squeezes my wrist with a secret smile, then turns on her heels back toward the elevators that must lead to the executive suites.

I shake off the foreboding feeling Daisy left behind and enter the suite to find Anna stacking her plate sky high. Mini stadium dogs, nachos, fries, and other fried foods I can't make out from the pile she's created.

"Think you got enough there, kiddo?"

"For now." She shrugs.

We walk over to a high-top table, and I help her scoot up so she can eat comfortably. I've been so focused on Anna and her truly impressive food choices that I've neglected to take in my surroundings.

And by the time I do, I fear I'm a bit too late.

Apparently, I've entered WAG headquarters, and I didn't even know it.

Everyone seems to be wearing some version of tight patent-leather pants, racy tops, sky-high boots with matching designer bags, and professionally done hair and makeup.

And all their eyes are on me.

I smile in their general direction and try to play it cool by focusing on Anna. But it's hard to start up a conversation with a kid who's currently inhaling food.

Finally, someone I assume must be the queen bee makes her way over.

"You're new. Are you the girlfriend or the nanny... or both?" Her tone, fake as her hair, drips in condescension.

And here I thought these types of women were extinct. The kind that somehow still derive pleasure from another woman's discomfort instead of opting to play on the same team.

Unluckily for her, she caught me at a moment when I'm with Anna. Any other time, and I may have cowered and just moved it along, but I'll be damned if I let Anna see that. She deserves to see better role modeling.

Which is also why I am trying to desperately filter through all the bad words I shouldn't be using in front of a five-year-old.

"Excuse me. I think the words you were looking for sound a little bit like 'hi, my name is blank. What is yours?' Maybe even add in a 'nice to meet you and welcome' if you're feeling truly wild." I give her my scary Dominican mom smile, the one that taunts "just wait until we get home."

I can sense Anna paying very close attention to us, even though she hasn't abandoned her quest for food.

Shock flashes across the newcomer's slightly paralyzed face, but she recovers quickly. "My apologies. Where are my manners? I'm Lexi. My fiancé is number fifteen on the opposing team." A jersey number, not a name. Dear God, put me down right about now. "I know this is the Monarch pitcher's daughter, and we've never seen anyone besides her grandmother bring her to a game. It's why we're all so curious."

I look around and see that most of the other women are waiting with bated breath for my response. I swear one of them is ready to live report this interaction to gossip blog sites as I speak. Which reminds me of where I am and why I should be keeping a low profile instead of bringing this Stepford wife wannabe down a peg.

"Of course. Well, Lexi, nice to meet you. I'm Isa and this is Anna. And if curious minds must know, I'm her nanny." I barely grit out that last part, since they are entitled to none of it.

"And my bestie," Anna chirps in between bites.

"So nice to meet you, Liza."

"Isa."

"Right. That must be nice, being a nanny for a Monarch. How did you manage to get such a gig? My sister would love to get an opportunity to work for one of the top guys on the team. Where did you apply? And you must come to more games and tell us all about working for Mateo. You must have so many juicy stories to tell."

I swear the woman has fangs. Or poorly made veneers.

Either way, I've seen and heard more than enough.

"Thanks for the warm welcome, truly. But Anna and I just stopped by quickly to fuel up before we head down to our seats."

She plasters on a disgusted face. "As in down there? With all the fans?"

"Yep, we are definitely one with the people around here." I nudge Anna out of her seat. Luckily, she's been glued to our interaction and isn't giving me any pushback.

"But there's no open bar down there," a woman behind me shrieks.

"And you might get hit by a foul ball," another exclaims.

"One could only hope," I mutter under my breath. "Sorry, ladies. We'll have to catch up another time. I gotta get this little gal down to her father. Until next time!" I lift Anna's hand and force her to wave as I shamefully use her little body as a human shield and back us out of the suite.

Once we're out and safe from the firing line, I hear Charlie chuckle by the door.

"Lasted longer than I thought you would."

I point a threatening finger in his direction. "You knew."

He shrugs, keeping his hands behind his back as he scans our surroundings. "It's my job to know where all the threats are, Isabella. But I figured you could handle the piranhas on your own." I can see he's trying to suppress a smirk.

I lower my voice as I lean in close. "Next pancake party, no pancakes for you, sir." I take out the tickets that Daisy left for us and remind myself to send her a lightly threatening text later for not giving me a better warning either. What better way to start a friendship, right? "Now please lead us out of the lion's den." I give him the tickets, and he smiles slightly as he takes them.

I was so determined to get as far away from those women that I momentarily forgot where I was running to.

As we step deeper into the stadium seats, the infectious energy starts to rub off on me. From the crowd-pleasing music to the smell of stadium food and beer. I take a moment to look out into the stands and spot couples, families, and buddies in an array of New York Monarchs gear, all gathered together to enjoy this incredible sport of baseball.

I spot so many father-daughter dates, and my mind can't help but flash back to the countless games I attended with my dad and how those games are some of my most cherished memories.

I thought walking back into a space like this would send me into a tailspin, thinking of every terrible word this world spoke of me. Instead, I find myself getting nostalgic about all the things I missed.

And when you're standing in a stadium full of thousands of people, you start to feel silly, thinking that everyone would somehow have their eyes on you. The internet has a cruel way of making it seem like the world is against you. But right here, right now, in this stadium, I feel like I'm a part of the crowd. For the first time since arriving, I allow myself to take a deep breath and release all the pregame jitters.

Until we make it to our seats.

Daisy wasn't lying when she said we would be up front.

We are sitting in the first row off to the side of the dugout, and there is literally a small gate in front of us that would provide access to the impressive field. Guarded by stadium security and, now, Charlie.

I do notice some low murmurs around us. People wondering who we are and why we arrived with our own security. But those whispers quickly turn to shouts when the Monarchs start making their way toward the dugout, being done with their warm-ups.

"There he is. There's Papi." Anna jumps as she points to the reason we're here today.

Number thirty-five, looking every bit a titan in his freshly pressed baseball uniform, slowly making his way to the dugout while chatting with Coach Weston.

He hasn't spotted us yet, probably since he assumes we'll be watching the game from the family suite. So I do what everyone else in this stadium is doing and openly check him out.

I mean, *come on*, baseball pants on a Puerto Rican man?

I can't be judged for how my eyes eat up every inch of him. I'm only human, after all.

Even though I felt like we truly reached a new level of friendship and understanding last night, it doesn't mean I suddenly became blind overnight.

Fans yell his name, shout anything they can to get his attention, but he doesn't break stride as he continues his conversation.

It's a bit mind-boggling, being here and seeing firsthand how the world reacts to the man who had pizza and ice cream with me last night. Who held my hand and listened so intently as I recalled a piece of my past, a piece that's starting to ache less the more I revisit it.

I wonder if he knew how much it meant for me to have someone just listen. To sit in the moment with me without trying to chime in with a positive spin.

It was a shitty situation, and it's okay to let it be that. There's no need to rebrand my story. I just have to continue working on growing from the experience.

I hope I'm able to tell him one day how much I appreciated the fact that he felt compelled to share a piece of his story as well, even though he didn't have to. Although there was a slight downside to him opening up.

I fear my little crush has grown into a full-blown attraction.

Before, I could feign innocence, blame my reaction to him purely on his looks or the power he exudes on the field.

But now? I've seen a vulnerable side to him. A side that didn't hesitate to share his raw feelings, not holding back in an attempt to appear macho or spew toxic masculinity.

I was able to see how much integrity he has. How much loyalty he gives to the ones he loves and protects. And how much depth he hides behind the mask of fame and fortune.

I used to think he purposely played up the mysterious baseball player card when in interviews. I now guess it's more about him feeling comfortable around the person he's talking to in order to open up. To think that I could now be one of those people makes me a bit giddy and a bit protective of him. Which is hilarious, given our size difference.

And apparently, he unlocked a new kink for me.

Grown-ass men eating gelato on the couch. Who knew?

But seeing him here? In his domain? Yep. I'm definitely in trouble.

I've been trying so hard to make sure I keep this job, but now I'm starting to wonder if my growing feelings for Mateo and I will ever survive it.

Just as he's about to step down into the dugout, Anna gives an impressive shout for his attention.

I can only imagine some parental sixth sense alerted him, because the roaring of the crowd around us must have made it impossible for him to hear her.

Yet within a few quick sweeps, his eyes find Anna and then land on me.

And I swear the ground begins to shake.

No, really, it does.

Since the fans behind us go wild when they realize Mateo is making his way straight to us.

Hats, jerseys, and baseballs enter my periphery as they try to reach closer to see if they can get anything signed. I wrap my arms around Anna to make sure she doesn't get knocked over. The gate guard notices and waves for us to stand as he opens the gate slightly.

Now would be a great time for me to stand and unclench my ass cheeks, but Mateo's penetrating gaze leaves my knees feeling a little weak.

Eventually, Charlie moves in and gives me a hand, probably assuming I missed the other security guard's prompt rather than realizing I'm trying to calm down my nervous lady bits.

We make it to the gate, and once Charlie and the other guard cover our backs, it's fully opened for us.

For a second, I forget about it all.

Mateo, the curious stares, the maddening, intrusive thoughts in my head.

All of it.

Once my scuffed-up shoes touch the field, all I see is the impressive stadium in all its glory.

For all the games I've watched in person or on TV, I've never had the vantage point from down on the field.

Seeing the crowd from this angle, the dugout and the thousands of bright lights that are primed, ready, and pointed our way for when the sun set is simply a magical experience.

One I'll never forget.

I'm pulled from my thoughts when Mateo steps up to me, Anna already in his arms. He searches my face intently, something I'm starting to notice he does when he's concerned. He brings up a gloved hand and speaks into it. "You doing okay?"

I smile awkwardly and nod. "Yep. Just another day at the office, right?" His eyes continue their perusal for signs of distress. He's about to say something else when I interrupt him. "I'm fine. I promise. Things will probably feel a little more normal when the mob behind me calms down after you walk away, *Martinez*." I aim for levity.

He looks behind me, and as if it's only now registered that there's an entire section of fans there, he takes a sizable step back.

"I'm sorry. I didn't mean to bring attention to you. I'll be more conscious next time." He puts Anna down softly. "You want to go back up to the family suite? I can have Daisy called down here to get you."

I'm about to tell him it's fine and he's overreacting, when all of a sudden, my feet leave the ground, and the air is sucked out of my chest.

The noise level behind me reaches another level of insanity, and I firmly believe that I should have invested in earplugs.

"*Isabella*!"

My initial panic and confusion morph into muffled laughter when I realize who has fully bulldozed into me. "Put me down, you goofball."

"Torres, really, man?" Mateo yells as he stands next to us, hands on his hips.

"What? It's been forever since I've seen her. You've been hogging her too much. Give the girl a day off or something so she can hang out with cool people like my wife and me." He sets me down softly, throwing a wink Mateo's way.

It feels like they're having a whole conversation with their eyes, and if I didn't sense some simmering tension, I might have found it super impressive.

Anna gets all of our attention by spinning and showing off her bejeweled jersey. "Papi, look. Isabella helped me add all the Monarch colors. I have navy, white, and maroon."

"Dang, girl. You're looking fly. Give Tío Torres a spin. Let me see it again."

Without pause, Anna twirls until she gets dizzy, causing the slight scowl to leave Mateo's face.

"I love it, mija. It's my new favorite jersey of yours." He smiles as his daughter preens under the compliment. Then his eyes find mine, and he nods my way. "Go on, your turn."

My brows furrow. "For what?"

His lips twitch as he tries to maintain an unreadable face. "C'mon, Anna showed off her jersey, so it's your turn now. Go ahead and give us a little twirl."

My eyes widen as Torres belly laughs.

Two seconds ago, Mateo was ready to send me back up to the family suite, away from prying eyes. But after Torres shows up, he wants me to, what, twirl for him in one of the nation's most famous stadiums?

"That's a hard pass." I cross my arms over my chest.

Mateo matches my stance and shrugs. "All right, I'll wait." He looks up and around me. "Not like I have seventy thousand people waiting for me to go and do my job or anything." His smug smirk makes me want to march closer and slap it off his face.

And by slap, I mean kiss really, *really* hard.

I know my eyes are conveying every Spanish insult known to man, because it just kicks up his smile.

So without further ado, I open my arms, letting my unbuttoned jersey hang loosely off my body, then slowly turn in place.

"Happy now?" I say as I finally end my rotation, only to find Mateo's mouth agape and Torres howling with laughter as he runs circles around us.

"Really, Isa? Really?" Mateo asks, seeming genuinely affronted by my jersey.

"She looks like a million bucks, man!" Torres comes and lands a wet smooch on my cheek. "Love you, Isa. Thanks for always repping the Torres household. Anna, quick. Take a picture of us so I can send it to Denise before they take my phone away."

Anthony and I quickly pose, my back to the camera as he points to his last name on my jersey. Anna happily snaps more than enough photos.

I want to laugh at Mateo's reaction, I really do, but the man seems honest-to-God bothered by the fact that I'm wearing my friend's jersey.

The same jersey I went out and bought the second I heard the news that he was signing with the Monarchs. Because even though I was an absentee friend, I still wanted to find a way to support the people I love, even when I needed a little extra time to work on myself.

Coach Weston, who—holy hell—looks like a sexy, unkept lumberjack, yells for Martinez and Torres to "get their asses in the dugout."

I grab Anna's hand to walk us back to our seats, but not before I feel Mateo's presence behind me. He whispers roughly, "This ain't over."

Chapter Twenty-Three

MATEO

I'M AN ANIMAL UNLEASHED.

After the first three innings, I still can't get the sight of Torres's jersey on Isabella's body out of my head.

And anyone stepping up to the plate tonight against me is paying for it.

That asshole Torres, too.

Who makes a show of shaking out his hand every time I throw a fastball into his glove. The permanent grin on his face lets me know he can handle much more. And I plan on giving it to him.

After striking out the last player, I make my way to the dugout. I tune out the sound of the fans and keep my head down to make sure I don't seek her out in the crowd.

I take my usual seat and close my eyes as I chug water while my guys get themselves ready to bat.

I don't need to open them to know that Coach Weston is hovering next to me.

"You wanna tell me what's crawled up your ass lately?" He places his foot on the bench next to me and leans his crossed arms on his knees.

"Got any complaints, Coach?" I open my eyes and toss my water bottle into the nearest trash bin.

He raises a brow at my tone. I have a reputation for being respectful at all times, even in the heat of the moment when our whole season is at stake. So I'm sure my attitude has come out of left field for Coach. "You're playing a hell of a game, but at this rate, you might end up injuring yourself before we have a chance to make it to the postseason. So yeah, I'd say cool it a bit before it's too late." He steps back to leave but pauses. "So, uh, I suggest you sort out whatever's on your mind before we're having a different type of conversation. For the team's sake." He nods his head to where I know Anna and Isabella are sitting.

I bristle, angry at myself for not being able to reel in my emotions while also annoyed that my coach is a fucking intuitive mastermind.

He walks away, and for a moment, I believe I'm about to get a reprieve, at least while my guys are up to bat. That is, until I see *her* coming my way.

A legend in her own right. And someone I'm lucky my daughter will have as a role model.

Luisa Álvarez, the first and only female general manager in major league baseball.

She's someone whose opinion I value and deeply respect.

Except at a time like this, when I know she's coming over to ream my ass over my aggressiveness on the field.

Her job was to create the Monarch team from scratch. Working with the former team owner before he passed to trade and offer deals to the best in the league. And she managed to get every single player on her list. Unlike most managers, she often heads down to the dugout to observe us from up close. Looking for strengths and weaknesses, and putting everyone on alert that we're all replaceable if we're not playing to the best of our abilities.

That's why, when I see her coming my way with a fierce look on her face, I'm put on notice that she's about to hand my ass to me.

And if I thought Coach's chats were bad, I'm in for a hell of a wake-up call with Luisa. Not only is she smart, formidable, and talented at her job.

But she's also Dominican.

And she's free to let loose any Spanish curse words that I'm sure Isabella has on the tip of her tongue every time I'm dead set on pushing her buttons.

"Yo, Martinez. What the fuck's crawled up your ass today?"

"Why's everyone got something to say about my ass all of a sudden?" I ask defensively.

Her brows raise, as if I'm a toddler who just spoke back to his mother. And somehow, it makes me feel guilty.

"Sorry. I'll reel it in."

"Which part? The over one-hundred-miles-per-hour fastballs or the mean mug on your face? Because personally, I'm liking how you're playing. But the aggression, the loud shouts after you pitch, and the evil eye you're throwing the whole stadium? Yeah, that bit has to go before you scare off all the kids sporting your jersey tonight."

I wince at the mention of a fucking jersey.

It shouldn't be taking up this much space in my head. Especially during a game. I pride myself on being a true professional, so why the hell has this gotten so deeply under my skin?

I should shake it off. Rise above it all. I'm a grown man, a father, and a leader on this team.

Or...

I could...

A slow smile starts to creep over my face as I look up at Luisa.

"Ay dios mío. What the hell are you gonna ask me to do for you, Martinez? It better not be some weird superstitious shit."

I chuckle as I shake my head. "I just need you to make a special delivery for me."

CHAPTER TWENTY-FOUR

ISABELLA

MATEO'S BEEN PLAYING LIKE he's about to rip someone's head off.

For the first inning, I think it's all in my head, but then I hear the crowd around me commenting on it too.

I try to engage Anna in conversation when their voices get a little too rowdy, not wanting her little ears to hear something she shouldn't about her father. But it doesn't take long before she takes notice of his change in demeanor.

"Wow, Papi looks mad. Do you think someone said something mean to him? Or is this a World Series game?"

I warm at her innocence. "No, sweetie. This is a regular season game. And I'm not sure what's gotten into your dad. I'm sure he's just very focused on the game," I say, more to placate myself than her, I think.

"Do you... do you think it's something I did? Did he not actually like the rhinestones on my jersey?" she asks worriedly.

"Oh, sweetheart, of course not. He absolutely loved it, I promise. But there's nothing we can do to change his attitude right now, because he's in the zone. I'm sure he'll lighten up at some point."

She takes a bite of her stadium hot dog. I'm pretty sure it was longer than her arm when she started to tackle it. I ordered one as well, because when in Rome and all.

"I wish there were something I could do to cheer him up. His face looks super grumpy, and he's never like that," she pouts.

You're killing me here, kid.

I've been trying very hard to convince myself that Mateo's pitching mood has nothing to do with me or the fact that I'm wearing his best friend's jersey.

Because that would be beyond silly.

Like seriously, Mateo is an actual grown-up. With his life put together, a child, and a retirement plan of some sort, I assume.

He wouldn't be hung up on something as trivial as a dumb jersey.

The crowd around us starts to cheer in waves. Nothing has happened on the field, so I'm confused by the sudden commotion.

"There she is. She's in the stands!" someone yells behind me.

I crane my neck to see if there's a celebrity making their way to their seat, and for a millisecond, throw up a prayer that it's Beyoncé.

That's when a force of nature turns and starts to make her way down the front row.

No way.

That's Luisa Álvarez.

She's like the reigning queen of sports and is currently on the cover of three magazines for earning the spot of general manager for the New York Monarchs.

It probably doesn't hurt that she's drop-dead gorgeous and could probably double as a lingerie model with her height and curves. Her perfectly clear dark skin could easily snag a brand deal with a skin care line. Hell, she could create her own with how perfectly it glows. If I didn't already know that she was Dominican, her big brown eyes would be a dead giveaway. They always seem to twinkle with determination and mischief. And in the sky-high heels she's usually sporting, she could probably tower over most of the men in the stands.

But right now, she's all business, and somehow, deep in my gut, I know she's heading my way.

My excitement and fears are confirmed when she stops in front of me and nods my way. "You Isabella?"

My eyes widen and my jaw drops when I realize that not only is she talking to me, but she knows my name. "Yes, this is Isa," Anna chirps helpfully while I try to recover my ability to speak.

"Special delivery." She pulls an oversized jersey from under her arm and rips off the tag with her perfectly straight teeth. "Fresh out the gift shop." She tosses the three-sizes-too-big material on my lap.

Confused, I lift it up slightly as I smile. "Um, thank you?"

She crosses her arms and rolls her eyes. "It's not from me, sweetheart. It's from number thirty-five. And I have special instructions to make sure you swap it out with the jersey you're wearing before I go. So..." She waves at the jersey in my hand, seemingly exhausted by the task she's been given.

No fucking way.

He did not—

I look around her, and sure enough, Mateo is standing off the side of the dugout, watching our whole interaction go down, with a satisfied look on his face.

I give my attention back to Luisa as I plaster on a fake smile, trying my best not to give any of the attitude that I will keep locked and loaded for when *Martinez* gets off the field. "Hi, I'm sorry he put you up to this. But as you can see, I'm currently wearing a perfectly good jersey. So you can tell him thanks, but no thanks." I ball up his jersey aggressively, making sure to make eye contact with Mateo, and shove it into my small tote bag.

I can tell he's chuckling by the way his chest moves.

Luisa pinches the bridge of her nose, muttering under her breath. "As if I didn't have enough to deal with working with Mr. Fucking Stonehaven."

When she looks down at me, I give her a curious stare, letting her know I heard that juicy piece of chisme. She puts her hands together in a prayer pose as she gives it to me straight. "Listen, I've got work to do, and playing telephone between you and my star pitcher isn't it. So this is how it's going to go. You put on that jersey, he loses the bad temper, and we all get to go home after the game being happy campers. Capisce?"

Anna tugs on my arm before I'm able to give my defiant rebuttal. "Isa, this is a way we can help dad look less grumpy." She worries her bottom lip. "You'll do it, right?" She puts the full power of her puppy dog eyes on me, and before I know it, I'm folding like a cheap lawn chair.

"Okay, fine. But only because you asked so nicely. All right?" I huff as I pull the crumpled jersey out of my bag and stand.

I place it on Anna's lap as I take off my own jersey. I ignore a random whistle and catcalls, since this little display has garnered some attention from the people seated around us. I hand my jersey to Anna as she gives me the new one. I know what the back must say, but I check, to confirm the lunacy of the situation.

In big bold lettering, the name *Martinez* and the number *35* stare back at me. I fix my stare on Mateo as I roughly slip my arms through the oversized jersey. Then I give a tight, closed-mouth smile and two thumbs-up, hoping he knows I really wish they were my middle fingers.

He must, when he uncrosses his arms and laughs.

But then he lifts a single finger and spins it in a circle.

"You've gotta be fucking kid—"

"Oh yeah, I forgot. The man wants a twirl," Luisa says absentmindedly as she types something ferociously into her phone.

I whip my stare back to Mateo as I shake my head. "Nuh-uh. No way, pal."

He taps at his imaginary watch as he mouths, "Ticktock."

That motherfucker.

The teams are switching positions, the Monarchs heading to the bases and outfield. If I take any longer, the crowd and cameraman are going to wonder why the pitcher hasn't made his way to the mound.

It's as if I'm in some fucked-up game of chicken, except he knows exactly who's going to lose. Me.

I'll get him back for this.

I take a deep breath as I tuck my defiance in my back pocket and give a half-assed twirl. And I end it with a curtsy, just for shits and giggles.

The smile on Mateo's face could light up the stadium brighter than all the lights here combined.

And for a moment, I forget that he's public enemy number one once we get home.

Well, actually *his* home. Where I also happen to live, for the time being.

"Huh. Interesting," Luisa muses beside me.

I break our eye contact and hope Mateo takes that as his cue to get his ass back to work. "What is?"

Luisa looks me over, a look of respect taking over her features. "It's almost as if you just slayed the dragon with your mere presence. That guy had a real attitude problem down in the dugout. But one jersey swap and twirl later, and *poof*. All gone." She smiles warmly for the first time now, her mask of authority taking a breather. "It takes a good woman to deal with a powerful man like Mateo. I'm happy you guys found each other." She lowers her voice for my ears only. "Although, if you guys could keep me out of your foreplay in the future, that would be greatly appreciated." She squeezes my arm tenderly.

"No, we're not—I'm not—" I stammer.

"Sure, sure. This was fun and all, but I have my own dragon to slay upstairs, so I'll leave you guys to it. Hope to see you around more often. Enjoy the game." She goes to move away, but I reach out and softly grab her forearm.

I don't know what it is about her, but Luisa Álvarez is a powerhouse that I instantly admire. She's a woman taking charge in a male-dominated sport, and she does so with bigger cojones than anyone I've ever met.

So without much thought, I blurt out a question. It's as if I'm trying to collect new girlfriends like infinity stones today. "How do you feel about girls' night out and group chats?"

Chapter Twenty-Five

ISABELLA

The Monarchs won, five to zero.

A shutout. Not a single home run was made by the other team due to Mateo's relentless pitching.

As if it were even humanly possible, Mateo played even better after I put on his stupid jersey, except this time, he played with a smug look on his face.

I swear they're going to make a million posters of his facial expressions tonight and plaster them all over the city.

The man even smized throughout an entire inning.

Since tonight was such a standout game for him, he texted us to go home with Hank and Charlie.

Mateo:

Hey, I'll have to stay back and handle media for a while, so you guys go ahead and head home. I might not make it before Anna's bedtime because I need my strength and conditioning team to help work out my arms before I call it a night.

Mateo:

> Please text me before she tells bedtime story number three so I can catch her before she passes out and wish her good night.

Me:

> K.

Mateo:

> Excuse me?

Me:

> Oh I'm sorry. Maybe you are older than I realized, although your behavior tonight says otherwise. But "k" means OKAY.

Mateo:

> I know what K means, Isa.

Mateo:

> I'm only 8 years older than you, in case you were wondering.

Me:

> Cool *thumbs-up emoji*

Mateo:

Brat.

Me:

Takes one to know one.

Mateo:

I think I liked it better when you were afraid of getting a strike. Might not be too late to give you one, now that I think about it…

Me:

Cute. You think you have any threatening power? After that very public stunt you just pulled?

Mateo:

You think I'm cute, Morales? You sure know how to make a man feel special. Especially while wearing my jersey *wink emoji*

Me:

You're insufferable today. Now I know never to feed the gremlin pizza and wine. Or maybe it was the gelato that made you this way. Noted!

Mateo:

Friday night pizza, wine, and gelato. It'll be our thing.

Me:

Our thingggg, is me currently trying not to end up in Rikers for fantasizing about ways to put my hands around your neck.

Mateo:

Mateo:

Jeez, Isa. Take a man out to dinner and movie first. But go on…

What the fuck?

Is he… are we? I stuff my phone into my bag, even though I can hear it vibrating with more messages.

I was pretty sure I was trying to put the fear of God in him with whatever intimidation I may hold as an unhinged single woman with nothing left to lose.

But Mateo? Mateo was fucking flirting with me. Or was he only teasing? The man does have a sense of humor once he's not hell bent on giving me a hard time. But we've never texted like this before. It's usually only about Anna, and we keep it very PG. Or at least we used to.

"Is the vehicle too warm, Isabella? I can make it cooler in here if you like," Hank says from the driver's seat.

"Huh? Um, no, it's fine. Thanks."

"You sure? You coming down with something, then? Because your cheeks are rosy. I can see it all the way from here."

I die a little inside. Not even the evening glow of the stoplights can hide how Mateo affects me.

"Nope. All good. Still flying high from that win," I lie.

Hank nods enthusiastically as he pulls us into the building garage. "It was quite the game, wasn't it? Make sure to tell the boss he looked great out there tonight. Even when it seemed like he wanted to tear into the other team." He chuckles good-naturedly. "I swear, he keeps getting better and better."

"Yeah, he's a real peach," I mutter to myself as I get out of the vehicle and start heading toward the elevator with Anna in tow.

"Thanks for putting on the jersey. Papi looked much happier when you had it on," Anna says to me, followed by a big yawn.

"Yeah, yeah. It's bath time, then bedtime for you, little lady. We've had an exciting and long day, so I think it's time for us to call it a night. What do you say?"

She releases another big yawn, this one triggering one of my own. "Yeah, I think I only have one good story in me tonight, Isa. Sorry to disappoint."

I burst into laughter as we enter the elevator and make our way upstairs. "In that case, I'll go ahead and let your dad know we're calling it an early night so he can call you before you pass out."

I dig my phone out of my bag to see four messages from Mateo waiting for me.

Mateo:

> Sorry. That was a joke.

Mateo:

> Shit. I took it too far, didn't I?

Mateo:

> I'm heading into a postgame interview now. Might take about half an hour or so. Please text me regardless once you see this. I'll keep my phone on me. Again, I'm sorry.

Mateo:

> We should talk when I get home tonight.

The first two messages make me chuckle, knowing that Mateo is squirming in his seat just as badly as I have been this whole day. The third one makes me feel a little guilty, because I can see he's genuinely panicking now.

But the last message? Yeah, that one woke me right the fuck up.

There's no chance in hell I'll be able to go to sleep after he drops a "we should talk" text on me.

Is this it? The dreaded moment I get my third and final strike?

He wouldn't really fire me for not responding to his texts immediately.

Would he?

Because I would've never pegged him as someone who demanded I have a wardrobe change in the middle of his game either, so who knows where his head is at.

All I know is that it looks like I'll be waiting up for Mateo tonight.

CHAPTER TWENTY-SIX

MATEO

I'M LOSING MY GODDAMN mind.

I walked off that field feeling that special high one gets after a big win. But it had nothing to do with the game and everything to do with the woman in the stands. Having her eyes on me while wearing my jersey.

I couldn't tell you the names of the players I pitched for tonight, because they were nothing but obstacles in the way of me wrapping this game up and coming home to Isabella.

When I first saw her sitting in the crowd, my heart started to race. I feared that it was all too much, too soon for her. I was ready to have security escort her away and up to whatever suite she felt most comfortable in, since my mother has told me horror stories about some of the women that frequent the family boxes.

But to my surprise, Isabella seemed more than fine. Especially when Torres showed up and didn't try to treat her with kid gloves. Once I saw the shift in her, I knew it was time for me to do the same.

If she was uncomfortable or needed space, I was going to let her take the lead on that instead of me doing that for her and anticipating the worst.

With each passing day, I see more and more of Isabella's quiet strength and how she doesn't need me to coddle her, even though I sometimes selfishly wish she did.

So tonight I went completely off script. I pushed and pushed and waited to see if she truly needed an out.

Instead, what I found was more of the fire that I so love to play with.

All was well, or so I thought. Until I took it too far.

I let myself get too comfortable, and the thoughts that float in my head about her come a bit too close to the surface.

And now, as I step off the elevator and into my home, I have no idea what I'm walking into when it comes to her state of mind.

I kick off my shoes and drop my bag at the entrance.

I know Anna's been asleep for a few hours, since I called to tell her good night, but I'm not sure if Isa's stayed up after the long day I'm sure she's had as well.

I don't have to wait long to get my answer, since I can see her head popped up over the couch as she watches some reality TV show.

She turns her head slightly, as I reach the kitchen. "You." Her eyes narrow as I stay frozen in place, not sure how to handle the sudden onslaught of animosity.

"Me," I answer stupidly.

She stays firmly perched on the couch, only her head visible from where I currently stand.

She points a finger in my direction. "Don't you start. You've already had enough of your cute moments for today. And by cute, I mean tantrums. Which, by the way..." She pushes off the couch to stand, and my mouth goes dry at the sight of her.

"Is this now considered a mandatory work uniform? Or only when you get your panties in a bunch?"

I have more than enough rebuttals ready at my disposal, but the sight of her in a tank top, sleep shorts, and *my jersey* has me reeling.

That, along with that fierce attitude, has me just about ready to buckle and drop to my knees for her.

She takes my silence as permission to proceed with her tirade. She walks around the couch and starts to make her way toward me. Her breasts bounce against her tight tank top, which puts me on alert that she's not wearing a bra.

Fucking hell.

If she knew how close I was to breaking, she'd be a lot more careful in the way she sways her hips, because the back of my couch is looking like a mighty good spot to bend her over and finally sink into her softness.

Maybe then the madness in my mind would quiet long enough for me to get my head straight.

Though a part of me already knows that if I ever were to get my hands on Isabella, it would be game over for me.

"And another thing. You had Luisa freaking Álvarez hand deliver it to me? As if being back at a real baseball game wasn't sensory overload enough, you go and throw in the queen bee of sports to be a spectator to our little debacle? You're lucky she's actually cool, and we're planning to hang out soon." Her bare feet come to stand before me, her ire giving the impression that her petite frame is much larger.

Her sweet-pea body wash scent infiltrates my senses. I know exactly what it is because I bought it for her. I had no idea what she would like to use, so I picked the closest thing to me that was expensive and pink.

Big mistake, because I now want to be the person who rinses it off her body.

There must be a shift in my demeanor, because she takes a slight step back.

Oh no, that just won't do.

I start to circle her. As she turns, she leans her back against the kitchen island.

Perfect.

I move in and grab the edge of the counter on each side of her in an attempt to make sure I don't touch what doesn't belong to me... yet.

Her breath hitches slightly as I lower my face closer to hers.

"Are you done?"

"Excuse you?" she asks, her chest rising with each labored breath.

"I said are you done? Because if you are, then this is the point where I tell you I'm sorry and beg for your forgiveness."

Her lips purse slightly as she gives me a skeptical once-over. "You don't look very sorry to me."

I smile. "Because I'm not. Not even in the slightest. And if I could, I'd do it again, Isabella." I lift a finger and caress the side of her face under the guise that I'm tucking a loose hair behind her ear. I take deep pleasure in noting how goose bumps form along her neck. "So why don't you go ahead and tell me what I have to do to earn your forgiveness?"

Her head tilts slightly. "Are you fucking with me again? Because I swear to God, Mateo. Half the time, I don't know where your head is at."

I groan slightly. "Welcome to the club."

She gives me another hard look. This one I'm afraid might see too much, but I let her, regardless. She crosses her arms under her chest, bringing her breasts closer to me. I'm just about ready to beg for mercy when she says, "All right, I'll play." She straightens up, leveling her cool glare on me. "Two things. First, hire me. Officially. No more—"

"Done. What's number two?"

"Done? Just like that? No more strikes?" she asks, stunned.

I lower my voice slightly, restraint tight as I say, "Isa, the strikes were never meant for you. They were for me. Let's leave it at that for now."

Her lips move momentarily without any sound coming out. Then she continues as if I don't see the confused yet celebratory look in her eyes. "Okay, yeah. Good. And two, I want the night off next Friday. It's hard to plan a girls' night out when I don't exactly have a schedule. Or even—at least as of five seconds ago—a secure job."

I tsk as I say, "Haven't even signed on the dotted line yet, and you're already asking for time off? Doesn't seem very professional to me."

"Neither is my boss's penchant for caging me in on this very kitchen island, but you don't see me complaining to HR."

"You want me to move?"

"You hear me ask you to?"

The little minx. The stirring in my loose track pants has me biting back a curse.

If I don't move now, I will most definitely be causing an HR violation. And probably break a few laws that only exist in the deep south.

I take a slight step back, bringing my arms across my chest to match Isabella's stance. I don't miss the slight pout on her lips when I do. And I vow to kiss it off her face the second I have a less than half-cocked plan to convince Isabella to consider dating me seriously.

I know it's not just about our attraction to one another. My life comes with baggage and a whole lot of spotlights pointed my way, so I've got to make sure I can make her feel safe before she dares take that leap with me.

"Time off approved. My mother has been asking to sleepover with Anna anyway, since I'll be gone at away games next week."

Slight surprise overtakes her features. I hadn't shared my schedule past this week when I initially hired her, but now she's here to stay.

Hopefully, as more than Anna's nanny.

"I'll email you my schedule. I'll be leaving tomorrow morning and coming back Friday evening. Just in time for your... girls' night."

As much as I hate the fact that I might not see her when I get back, I feel relieved that she's reconnected with friends and seems to be in a much happier place overall since she started working for me.

She nods. "Thank you. Will you be gone by the time Anna and I leave for school drop-off?"

"Trying to get rid of me already?"

She smiles as she shakes her head. "Nah, just wanted to know if Anna will have time to sneak a toy into your away bag or not."

Damn. She remembers.

Only this woman can make me go from horny to sentimental in two seconds flat. At the moment, I'm both.

"Yeah, I'll be here to see you guys off."

"Good. So, uh, I guess I'll be going to bed now. It's been a long day." She starts to shuffle toward her room, facing me as she walks back. As if she knows it's probably not safe to turn her back on me. Smart woman. "See you bright and early. Good night." She gives a slight wave and finally turns as she makes it to the hallway that leads to her room.

I should let her keep walking. Let her off the hook for the night.

But the sight she gives me makes it damn near impossible.

"Hey, Isabella?"

She stops momentarily, turning her head slightly to catch my wandering gaze. "Yeah."

"My last name looks good on you."

And if things go according to plan, I just might make her keep it.

CHAPTER TWENTY-SEVEN

MATEO

I'M DREADING TODAY.

We fly out to Toronto for six days.

I usually hate the longer stretches of away games, since it means time away from Anna, but after last night, the weight feels heavier.

I feel like Isa is within reach now. That if I play my cards right, I might have a chance of making a life with her a reality.

I rush through my morning routine so I can spend as much time with my girls as I can before I have to leave. I don't know when I started referring to Anna and Isa as *my girls*. Maybe when I spotted them making breakfast in my kitchen, or last night when they wore mostly matching outfits. Either way, there's no shifting back now.

I head downstairs, hoping I haven't wasted too much time, only to spot Isabella hunched over my unzipped away bag.

Interesting.

"Stealing on your first official day on the job? Doesn't seem too promising from where I stand, Isa," I taunt. She immediately leaps from my bag with a squeak.

She places a hand on her chest, probably in a futile attempt to relax her racing heart from the scare I just gave her. "Good morning to you too, boss. And for the record, I wasn't *taking* anything. I was *giving* you something."

That grabs my attention. "Gifts on the first day? Now you're just brown-nosing, Isa." I live for the slight blush that rises in her cheeks when I tease her like this. Makes me curious about how else she would respond to me if given the full opportunity to explore.

She's about to roll her eyes, right on cue, but she straightens and speaks instead. "It's not a *gift* gift. Just a little something to help you pass the time while you're alone in your hotel room." I raise a devious brow, and that blush threatens to burn brighter. "Jesus Christ, get your head out of the gutter. Go ahead and look for yourself before you get the wrong idea." She waves at my bag.

I give it two seconds before my curiosity wins. I squat down and immediately spot a bright yellow Post-it. I grab it and stand.

"You left me a to-do list, Isabella? If so, we're going to have to work on your gift-giving skills. Stick by me, and I'll show you the ropes." I wink at her as I wave the sticky note by her face.

"It's... you know what? Forget it." She goes to snatch her gift out of my hand, but I quickly raise my arm above her, putting it way out of her reach. "Real mature, Mateo," she grumbles.

"My sincerest apologies. I should have been much more gracious about your offering. For this—" I look up at the neon Post-it to see one word written on it. "Otoño?" I ask, perplexed.

"It's dumb. You can trash it." She turns to walk away from me, but I gently grab her wrist and spin her back toward me before she gets far.

Now all traces of my teasing are gone, replaced by genuine interest. "Really, I'm sorry, Isa." I wait a second for her to see the sincerity in my eyes. "Could you tell me what this is about?"

She nibbles on her lips slightly, and I now realize she seems a bit nervous. I curse my past self for not taking her seriously from the get-go. "Otoño. It means fall, like the season. Today, you're heading to Toronto, where it's much cooler than here, and I figured it might feel like fall." I nod, still confused as to why she had to write it on a Post-it, when she continues. "Okay, please don't take this the wrong way..."

"You have a knack for knowing how to start sentences, Isabella."

"When your mom stayed over during your last trip, she mentioned, very briefly, may I add, that you, um, don't really know much Spanish." She half winces, half smiles.

Shame threatens to drown me as I take a step back and look down at the word she delicately scribbled for me.

It's no secret that I don't speak Spanish. I can understand it perfectly if it's not spoken too fast, and I can say my fair share of words. But I can't really read it well, and my accent is a bit rough from lack of practice.

It's always been a sore spot for me.

I wear the name Martinez every time I'm on the field, yet I can barely hold a conversation with some of my native Spanish-speaking teammates.

And it makes me feel like a failure sometimes.

Like I'm missing something that my Hispanic peers have possessed since birth. I know why my mom didn't make teaching me a priority when I was younger, and I don't fault her for it.

But it doesn't take away from the fact that sometimes I don't feel like a complete Puerto Rican because I can't speak our own language properly.

Like I'm lacking a piece of my identity, my culture. And instead, I'm only bits and pieces of my Puerto Rican heritage, even though I am 100 percent native by blood.

I can feel myself starting to retract from Isabella. This isn't a side of me I was keen on showing her yet. I'm still in the phase where I'm hoping she doesn't realize how far out of my league she is. I'm not ready to present all of my flaws to her.

But just like I didn't let her retreat far earlier, she does the same for me.

Her soft hands wrap around the wrist holding her note as she waits for our eyes to connect once more before continuing. "I promise, this isn't a pity party invite. We don't allow those here, remember?" She smiles tenderly. "And you don't have to do what I was planning. It was a silly idea in case you were interest—"

"What were you planning?" I ask, eager to hear where her mind was going with this.

"I... well. Okay, so I was thinking this could kind of be like a Spanish version of *word of the day*. I give you a word in Spanish, and it's your job to figure out its meaning, use it in a sentence, and maybe practice pronouncing it throughout the day." She shrugs her shoulders timidly. "I figured on away trips, you have some downtime on the flight or after the game when you're in your hotel room, so you could practice then." She blows out a small breath, then quickly adds, "But only if you want to. I can only imagine you must be completely exhausted after games, and that's probably not the best time to study a language. Actually, now that I think about it, it's dumb. I'm sorry if I overstepped. It's not my place."

She rambles on because I'm currently incapable of responding with any coherent words.

I try to think back to an instance when someone has taken the time and energy to think about doing something as thoughtful as this for me, and I come up blank.

Aside from my mother and Anna, of course, who smother me with enough love and attention to let me know that I'm the luckiest man on the planet.

But apart from anyone who's actually related to me?

Never.

And it's never been a problem before. At least I don't think it has. I thoroughly enjoy spoiling the people in my life.

Yet to be given this kind and sincere gesture from the woman I know I'm falling for? Yeah... If I wasn't before, I'm pretty sure I'm a goner now.

"Mateo, really, I—"

"Your method is flawed," I say as I rub my thumb over her smooth handwriting.

"My, um, what now?"

I meet her puzzled gaze. "You said it was word of the day. I'm gone for six days. I'm owed five more."

A short laugh escapes her lips. "You, you want..." She straightens, eyes wide the moment she seems to realize that the serious determination in my eyes is real. "Wait, you're being serious right now? You want me to come up with five more words? Right now?"

I nod toward the drawer I know holds the note pads. "You signed up for this gig, Teach. Now go ahead and give me my homework so I can be on my way."

CHAPTER TWENTY-EIGHT

ISABELLA

I CAN'T BELIEVE I'M officially Anna's nanny. And now, Mateo's Spanish tutor.

I thought I for sure overstepped once I mentioned that I knew about his limited Spanish. And the gutted look on his face almost made me want to give myself the third and final strike.

That feeling alone shook me to my core.

Because I knew I never wanted to see that look on his face again, and I would stand in the way of anyone who tried to put it there, even if it were me.

By now, I know I'm slipping, and fast.

You'd think that after so many sleepless nights and years of agony, it would be easier to resist a baseball player. I vowed to myself to never put myself in that position again.

The problem is that Mateo being a New York Monarch is probably the least interesting thing about him.

With Jeremy, baseball was his world, and it was at the forefront of our lifestyle. Every decision taken into consideration had to go through the "how does baseball impact this?" funnel. And when he was off the field, baseball was still the third, imaginary being in our relationship. From the way he dressed to where he made reservations for us to eat so we'd be seen, to who we hung out with.

All those fair-weather friends who scattered like roaches when the lights turned on the second our scandal hit the headlines.

And the interviews they gave? Painted a picture that couldn't be further from the truth.

People always said that we finished each other's sentences. In reality, he finished mine as he saw fit. And my naïve brain took it as *he must know best.*

I never realized how much that relationship chipped at my sense of self until I was out of it and left with scraps of myself to piece together.

While he carried on living in blissful notoriety.

But Mateo is the complete opposite of all that.

Maybe it's because he's so established in his career, but the man could give two shits about baseball once he enters his home. All the focus is on his family, and lately, me.

He doesn't seek out the media. In fact, he avoids it at all costs. And the persona he feeds to his fans and post-game interviews is a generic and watered-down version of the man I now know him to be.

He's kind, funny, and sensitive, and I swear to God, if he pins me against that kitchen island one more time, I'm going to go full spread eagle.

My poor libido can only take so much.

But I'm still stuck.

Because I struggle with trusting myself, with trusting my judgment after Jeremy, and I loathe that. Even five years after the fact, his fingerprints are still all over the damage on my heart.

And, of course, I couldn't have made it any easier on myself either. Instead, I went ahead and developed a mad crush on not just a baseball player, but probably the most famous one to ever exist. And he just had to be my boss. And he just had to have the funniest kid in existence, whom I'm also starting to grow very attached to.

I'm a true mess.

Which is why I'm so grateful I'm finally having that long awaited girls' night on Friday.

I kind of dropped a bomb on the initial girls when I added Daisy Stonehaven to the chat, quickly followed by Luisa Álvarez.

Nikki texted me separately a *WTF? How are these your friends?* text. Similar to when I sent her my own version once I realized that Amelia's husband, Evan, was Evan Fucking Cooper, tech billionaire extraordinaire.

It's safe to say that I'm never picking up a bill with this crew.

Funnily enough, once the introductions got out of the way, the group chat was firing off as if we'd known each other for years. All of our senses of humor blending in a way that made me feel like I could really be myself with these women rather than worry about being perceived the wrong way. And from what I can tell, it seems like they feel the same way.

My phone ringing on my bedroom desk brings me out of my thoughts and rushing back to the present.

Shit, is it ten p.m. already?

Mateo had an evening game, so he wished Anna good night when she got out of school. He mentioned that he'd be calling me later to report in on his homework.

For a second, I thought he was teasing.

The man has been traveling and playing a professional sport all day. Clearly, he could do with some relaxation time.

But as I pick up my phone and bring it back to bed where I've been lounging, I can confirm it's him, and I can confirm it's a video call, not a phone call coming through. Shit.

I shimmy a bit under the covers and bring the blanket over my chest a bit.

Now that Mateo is gone at away games, my flimsy pajamas have made it back into the rotation. And I don't think that giving him a screen full of nipple is on the agenda for tonight.

Although with the way he was looking at me last night, I doubt I'd hear any complaints.

I swipe to answer the call, and his gorgeous, smiling face comes into view.

Try as I might, a small sigh escapes me at the sight of him. And at the easy smile that seems to be directed at me more and more.

"Well, don't you look cozy? Must be a sweet teaching job if you get to do it from bed, Isabella."

"Hi to you too, Mateo." I squint slightly and realize the tops of his shoulders are bare. "And it seems to me like you've shown up for class shirtless. Not a very good way to kick off your lessons," I scold playfully.

He looks down at his chest, then back up at me, smiling mischievously. "And here I thought I could get some extra credit." He moves the screen back and props it against something so his full upper chest is on display. He seems to be sitting at a desk with a notepad and paper. If I weren't too busy squeezing my thighs under the blanket, I would find the sight extremely endearing.

"And here I thought this was a nip-free zone, Mateo," I chide as I raise the blanket over my chest a bit more. His eyes snag on the movement.

"Then maybe it's time we stop making assumptions about what we're doing and start calling it how it is."

His eyes flare slightly as I bite my bottom lip. He clears his throat before he shakes his head slightly and continues. "Besides, have you forgotten that we've already vacationed together? I was shirtless 90 percent of the time we were in the DR." His brow quirks. "Or can you not concentrate under these conditions?" He smirks arrogantly.

I tilt my head. "I guess a little nip never hurt nobody."

He groans. "Isabella, can we please start talking Spanish now, because all this talk about nipples is affecting me in a way that makes me glad I'm sitting under a desk."

I burst out laughing, releasing the blanket and letting it fall slightly. "All right, Martinez, let's get to work."

For the next five nights, we repeat our nightly "classes."

It always starts off the same. We joke around and tease each other for our nightly attire, then get into the word of the day.

Surprisingly, Mateo is less shy about the whole thing than I would have imagined. He tries repeatedly to pronounce the words I gave him correctly and presents me with a sentence he'd like me to show him how to say.

We usually go back and forth for about half an hour before he's satisfied with his progress. Seems like his competitive streak doesn't end when he leaves the baseball field. He wants to be the very best when he's trying out new words, especially ones I throw into a sentence he hasn't practiced before.

It's quite impressive, how quickly he's picking it up. But I truly live for the moment when he fumbles a word, because he makes the most adorable face when he's confused or stuck.

By the time we're done, we stay on the call for a couple of minutes, asking each other how our days were.

I usually stick to conversations about Anna, and he usually keeps it about his daily schedule.

But as the days go on, those few minutes have turned into late-night conversations about my cover designs and funny stories about him and the team. He's seen every cover I've made thus far and has even given me the push I needed to reach out to authors and show them my work.

By the time we're ready to hang up, we're both comfortable in bed, feeling as though we've been lying together having pillow talk.

And I can't lie; it's been nice. Having a chance to talk without the impulse to jump his bones has let me concentrate on all the little, funny quirks I might have otherwise missed.

Mateo, on the other hand, has not been shy with flirting on his end. Although I will say that it's more teasing than anything. He makes comments about me no longer wearing my "Amish pajamas," and I give him shit for posing like he's in an underwear campaign during our calls. His salacious smiles let me know he's doing it on purpose, and I die a little inside knowing I get this view to myself every night.

By the way he's cautious about mentioning certain aspects of his baseball world, I can tell he worries about me being back in this environment. But he's no longer treating me like I'm made of glass, and the relief it gives me is insurmountable.

And today, he comes home.

I'm lounging in my sweats as I finish my hair and makeup for the night. I'm excited to go out with the girls and have a night on the town. It's truly been ages since I've done anything like this, and I'm so happy we get to leave the group chat and all meet in person.

Daisy got us a table at a very exclusive lounge downtown, so we're all dressing up for the occasion.

Bethzaida is out in the living room with Anna, since she's covering for me until Mateo gets home. She's also sleeping over tonight, which means we all get to have breakfast tomorrow morning, and I'm pretty sure I can convince her to make some Puerto Rican food for lunch.

I'm shaking out the last piece of hair from my curling iron when I hear Beth call for me.

I walk out into the living room and see the concierge waiting by the foyer.

"Hey, did Mateo get a delivery?" I ask as I see the multiple shopping bags surrounding the concierge.

"No, Ms. Morales, the delivery is for you. I was given instructions to take these to your bedroom once I made sure you were available." He starts to make his way toward me, but I put my hand up, halting his movements.

"Hold up. I didn't order anything. And who said to put it in my room?"

The glass Beth is drinking from does absolutely nothing to hide the massive grin she's sporting. So I direct my confused gaze her way. "You do this?"

She straightens. "No, but I'm sure there's a card somewhere. Right, Frank?"

She nods at the well-dressed man waiting patiently for instructions. "Ah, yes. My apologies." He puts a few slim boxes on the kitchen island and produces two cards.

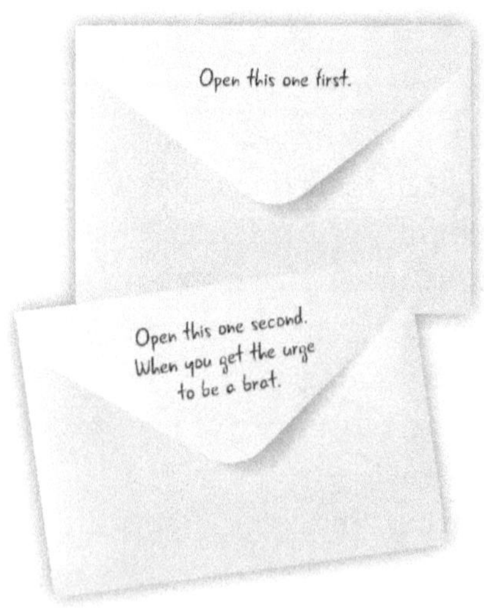

What the fuck?

I open the first one, only because, like a true reader, I hate to spoil an ending.

Isabella,

I don't know how to put into words how much this past week has meant to me, so I'll simply say thank you.

And since I took up so much of your time, I thought it was only fair to buy you a few things to help you and your business grow. I hope everything is to your liking. If not, we can have them replaced.

Yours,

-M

I look up at the stack of boxes and immediately recognize the Apple logo.

No fucking way.

One by one, I move the boxes to reveal a brand-new laptop, a tablet, wireless headphones, and a stylus.

I start looking through the bags and see every graphic design program imaginable at my fingertips, ready to be downloaded onto the new devices.

I'm moving on autopilot. None of this is registering as I tear into bag after bag.

But when I get to the last one, a bright orange item stops me in my tracks.

Frank sees my reaction and chuckles. "That one as well."

"Uh, Frankie? Can I call you Frankie? Actually, no, Frank sounds better." I lower my voice. "That, my friend, is a shopping bag from Louis Vuitton. Do you want to go ahead and make sure you delivered it to the right apartment?"

"Ay no seas tan pendeja." Beth sighs from behind me, picking up the bag and pulling out the massive box inside. "Toma, open it up already. I wanna see what it is."

Undoing the pretty bow feels like a crime, but I do it anyway.

There's a Louis Vuitton soft dust bag concealing the gift. Once I undo the flap and open it up, my hands go flying to my mouth.

It's a stunning black-on-black monogrammed Louis Vuitton messenger bag. Big enough to store all the devices currently on the counter but compact and chic enough to run around town with.

That is, if the rest of my wardrobe weren't highly curated by TJ Maxx.

"Qué bonito, Isa. Try it on so we can adjust the straps."

It feels like I'm having an out-of-body experience.

This is... a lot.

No, too much. Has the man never heard of a gift card?

I can't accept this.

And not because I want to pretend that I would never desire such a thing, but because, hell, that's a graphic designer's wet dream staring back at me.

But I refuse to let Mateo think I'm just another person who takes from him or only needs him for what he can provide.

I take my phone out of my sweats and dial his number. "Hands off the merchandise until I talk to the big guy." I point at Beth, who drops the designer bag innocently.

"Careful, I could get used to being called 'big guy' by you, Isa." Mateo's deep voice startles me. Did the phone even ring? "Let me guess, you got my gifts?" I hear the smile in his tone.

"Oh, yeah, I got 'em, and I'm here to say thank you, but—"

He sighs deeply into the phone, overplaying it a bit if you ask me. "And let me guess—you haven't read the second card yet?"

Shit. I had forgotten about the card after the designer bag wiped my brain clean. I take it off the counter and turn my back to my audience while I read it over.

Isa,

Are you done acting like you won't accept my gifts? I'm sure the effort was cute, but we both know that these items belong to you. And just in case you need a little more convincing, I'll let you in on a little secret.

This past week, you have helped me feel connected to a part of myself that I thought would forever remain dormant. It's not just about learning the words. Being able to carry on a conversation with you in our native language has made me see a piece of myself that I haven't dared look for in a long time.

So I ask you this: was it a burden for you to spend your evenings teaching me? Did you feel like you did it out of obligation?

I'm going to use the knowledge from our time together to answer that question for myself. It wasn't. Because you are a kind and loving soul who doesn't think twice about doing things for others. And while I can recognize that financially, our circumstances are different, please know that I feel the same way when it comes to giving you these gifts.

They are of no burden to me, and I don't feel obligated to give them to you. I do so because I want to return the favor and see you and your business grow in the same way I feel like I've grown in the past few days.

But if you for some reason still feel indebted to me, I sure as hell would appreciate a picture of you wearing that new LV for me ;)

Yours,

—M

I read it again and try my hardest to sniffle quietly.

"You still there, Isa?" Mateo asks tenderly. "Please don't cry, *tesoro*."

I chuckle lightly, quickly wiping a rogue tear before it messes up my makeup. "Tesoro? You picking up some new words without me now?"

"Yeah. Guess you can say I've been practicing. Got a teacher to impress."

"Oh yeah?" I taunt as I step farther away from the kitchen. "Then surely you can tell me what it means."

He pauses momentarily, and I think it's because he's trying to remember. That is, until he speaks, and his words come through like a caress. "Tesoro, it's what you are to me."

I suck in a stunned breath.

Tesoro means *treasure* in Spanish. But it's also a term of endearment. One usually reserved for lovers.

"Mat—"

"We're about to land. I'll be home soon, Isabella. And I'll be seeing you tonight."

"You took my call from the plane? That's currently still flying in the sky?" I ask, shocked.

"Isa, someway, somehow, you will come to learn that there isn't a place on earth where you wouldn't be able to reach me. Sky and sea included. Talk to you soon, tesoro."

CHAPTER TWENTY-NINE

ISABELLA

GIRLS' NIGHT IS TURNING out to be a blast, but I can't keep my thoughts off Mateo.

All I could think about when I decided to switch my outfit to the short sparkling red dress I have on was whether it had the ability to push Mateo far enough over the edge that he'd touch me tonight.

We've been circling each other long enough, and that letter might as well have knocked over the tiny stone left in the flimsy wall I'd erected to keep my feelings for Mateo at bay.

No, it was the moment he called me tesoro.

"What are you daydreaming about, all googly eyed over there?" Daisy hiccups as she puts down her drink. "Sorry, I'm a lightweight." She shrugs innocently as her flushed cheeks confirm her statement.

"Two drinks are all it takes? We've got to get more food in you, then. These tiny finger foods are not going to cut it," Amelia whisper shouts across the table.

"Yeah, Daisy. We've got to take you out for some real Dominican food next time we have a girls' night. It'll soak all that alcohol right up," I add.

Daisy nods as she stares into her half-finished drink. "Yeah, that would be nice. Especially since my mother was

Dominican and died when I was a baby, so I don't have any memories of her."

The table goes quiet, and I feel like we all collectively hold our breaths.

Nicholas Stonehaven is infamously private. And although he and Daisy grew up in the society pages, not a single speck of information has ever hit the tabloids in regard to their birth mother. Something that many have speculated over is that she must have been a woman of color, since both Daisy and Nick have warm, golden skin, and their father is white.

And now, at a crowded lounge full of New York's who's who, Daisy just dropped the equivalent of front-page news on us.

After a moment, Daisy's sluggish brain must catch up to her words, because her head pops up, and she's wearing a terrified look.

"Guys, I didn't—you can't—"

"Sorry, didn't hear a word you said, Daisy," Luisa says as she scans the room, probably looking for anyone who might have been close enough to overhear.

"You sure you said something, Daisy? You did say you were a lightweight, after all," Nikki adds.

"The music is a little loud, and the drinks are a little strong. Did I miss something?" Amelia asks as she takes another sip of her martini.

"No, maybe she said something about wanting another drink," Denise says convincingly.

Poor Daisy looks like she's two seconds away from having a full-blown meltdown, even though all the women are trying their best to put her worries at ease.

I decide now is the best time to take advantage of all these new friendships and divert the attention away from poor Daisy. "So I think I'm falling in love with my boss. As in Mateo. You know, the famous baseball player whose daughter I currently nanny for? And I'm pretty sure he feels something for me too. Anyhow, he wants to talk to me tonight when I get home, and I'm pretty sure it's about us." I pick up the small light-up menu on the table and give it a quick peruse. "Hey, anyone want to order the egg rolls with me?" I raise my hand to get the waiter's attention. Daisy immediately swats it down, her face completely void of her prior concerns.

"Forget about egg rolls. This calls for tequila."

Tequila was a bad idea.

For Daisy, at least, because the woman has probably never had more than a glass of champagne in her life.

I, on the other hand, am nervous about seeing Mateo after reading his thoughtful card, so I've been chugging a whole glass of water between each drink.

Besides, there hasn't been much time to drink when the girls are asking me questions left and right.

The diversion was the right call for Daisy's sake, but I'm afraid I put my ass in the hot seat.

"So you mean to tell me that you guys still haven't had sex yet? Even after all that pent-up tension you guys showed on the field?" Luisa asks, dumbfounded.

"Quit it, Luisa. It's not the about sex. They clearly have a connection. And love and respect for one another. Almost like they're on a team together. And isn't that a nice thought? To find someone to be with that feels like your perfect match," Daisy rambles on as she sighs wistfully.

I give a quick look at her engagement ring, confirming that it's still there and mentally noting to keep Daisy sober next time, because the rate at which she is letting things slip is concerning.

Denise keeps looking at the time on her phone with a worried look on her face. Probably thinking about her kids. "Hey, you okay over there, mama?" I lightly nudged her leg under the table.

She looks up, a guilty look on her face. "Okay, so I kind of fucked up. Please don't be mad."

Chapter Thirty

MATEO

I know I won't make it home in time to see Isabella before she's off for the night.

Doesn't mean I don't haul ass trying.

I made it home in record time.

I expect to find my mother and daughter curled up on the couch watching a movie. Instead, I almost bump into my daughter's bright pink luggage.

"Oh, great. You're home now. Anna, come greet your father so we can be on our way."

"Hold on. What's going on here? And why is Anna's bag packed? I thought you were sleeping over tonight," I say as my daughter gives me a quick squeeze, eyes fixed on the movie she was watching before I got here. "And hello. Can a dad get a better greeting than that? I've been gone for almost a week. What am I, chopped liver?" I tickle her sides and finally get her full attention.

"Sorry, Papi. We were just finishing the movie before we went to Grandma's house to play with puppies!"

I give my mother a stumped look. "Care to explain, Ma?"

She waves me off. "My neighbor fosters dogs, and one of her pups just gave birth. She's up around the clock bottle feeding these little cuties. I remembered when I got here and thought that Anna might want to come to my place instead and help her out."

"*Right.*" I know my mother well, and I know there's something she's not telling me. "Looks like I've got the place to myself tonight, then. Come here and give your old man a hug before you abandon me, mija." I give Anna another big squeeze, then let her run off to the TV.

My mother sidles up beside me as she says, "You know, maybe it's a good thing that we're out of your hair tonight."

"Oh yeah? And why's that?" I ask suspiciously.

"Let's just say that you weren't here when Isabella left for the night. Had you seen her, you'd know exactly why it's best we go." She taps my chest twice and calls Anna over and gets her ready to leave.

I'm slightly disturbed by the insinuation my mother just dropped on me.

But I'm a helluva lot more interested in seeing what Isabella's got on that's sent my mother running with my kid in tow.

I'm about to text her that I'm home when my phone starts to ring in my hand.

"Torres, I saw you on the damn plane. How are you already having separation anxiety?" I make my way up the stairs, on my way to take a quick shower to wash off the travel day.

"Yo, you home yet?" His tone catches me off guard. He sounds abnormally chipper, like he's got something up his sleeve.

"*Yeah*, why?"

"Uh, I was over here thinking that we're due for a night out. You know, grab a drink or something somewhere. Just the two of us. I know a place. Think you can be ready in twenty?"

I shake my head even though he can't see me. No way am I leaving my home, especially knowing that Isabella could walk through that door at any moment. "We spent all week together. I even went out for beers with you and the guys. *Twice*. I'm sorry that you interpreted that as me being open to bar hop in the city." Seems like Isabella's rubbing off on me, since I decided to follow her lead and spend more time out with my team while we were out of town. It was a media circus, as anticipated, but it was nothing we couldn't handle.

"C'mon, man. I really think you should come with me. It's... it's important."

I stop as I get to my bedroom door. "Torres, what's going on? You're putting me on edge. Even more than usual."

I hear him groan on the other line, then curse under his breath before he finally speaks. "Okay, but don't shoot the messenger, all right?"

I'm instantly on alert. "Spit it out."

"Fine, and before you get mad, watch your mouth. It involves my wife." He waits for my confirmation. A grunt is the best I can do at the moment. "So the women are all out at girls' night. You know that, right?"

I sigh. "Yes, I'm aware."

"Well, I just got an SOS text from my wife, basically saying that she messed up. Bad. She apparently invited an old colleague to crash girls' night and to take Isabella on a blind date."

My body temp skyrockets, a blind rage threatening to take over my senses.

"Say that again."

"Listen, man. She was only trying to be helpful, since Isabella's apparently been telling the women that she's open to date now. And that's huge. Denise never thought she'd see the day, and she got a bit ahead of herself. Her heart was in the right place, man," he defends. "But apparently, she knows she's fucked up majorly, because the second Isa got to the table, she started talking about you."

I lean my hand against the wall for balance.

"She what? What did she say?" I take a breath and start to move, making my way to my walk-in closet, tearing down a dress shirt and a pair of slacks.

"I didn't get all the deets, because they're still all there sitting at the table, but she wants you, man. She's down bad."

I almost fold over with some misplaced sense of relief. It isn't real until I hear it from her lips. Hearing it from my friend feels like I'm cheating her out of telling me herself, and I don't want to hear more until I have her safely back home with me.

Knowing that Isabella is out there right now and has somehow proclaimed she wants me, while I'm here at home, has me ready to break every speed limit in the city.

"Look, the guy hasn't even arrived yet. I think if I pick you up in twenty, we can—"

"Where is she? I'll be there in ten. And I'm driving myself."

CHAPTER THIRTY-ONE

ISABELLA

"Oh God, what did you do?"

"Okay, for the record, I came up with this plan while I was breastfeeding, so maybe my baby sucked the brain cells right out of me through my tits. So keep that tidbit in your back pocket when I explain myself, okay?" Denise stammers.

"First of all, don't bring your titties into the conversation at this point in the night. You had your chance to shine when I explained how Mateo found me half-naked in the kitchen. Now talk, so I know if the crime could land you on an episode of *Dateline*," I demand.

"So I might have invited a guy to come by and take you out on a date, like a teeny-tiny one, so you could break the ice on the dating scene in the city."

"You invited a guy to girls' night? That's breaking rule number one," Nikki exclaims.

"What are the other rules?" Daisy inquires.

Nikki shrugs. "I dunno, but that's rule number one. That's for sure."

"Look, I'm sorry. Anthony and I know that Mateo has feelings for you, and I thought a little date might be harmless. You get your toes wet, and if Mateo really wants to be serious about you, he'll step up to the plate."

"Baseball pun. Nicely done," Luisa interjects. I throw her a dirty look, causing her to quickly backpedal. "But totally bad. Bad Denise." She tries and fails to hold in a chuckle. Another victim that will be out for the count tomorrow, thanks to the tequila.

I try to filter out the noise in my head and laser in on one comment Denise made. "What do you mean you *know* Mateo has feelings for me?"

"Well, he may or may not have told Anthony about it... in detail?"

"Oh, Denise is spilling all the tea tonight." Amelia takes a long sip from her straw as her eyes bounce between Denise and me.

"Wait, so you know? For sure? That he—I mean—it's not all in my head?" The last bit of my sentence seems to come out quietly, yet the soft looks on the women's faces let me know they heard me.

"Look, Isa. I've already texted Jeff that there's been a change of plans, but he's texted back saying that he's here and waiting by the bar." She sighs heavily. "This is my mess-up. Let me go find him and tell him it's a no-go. I'll buy him a drink for his troubles and send him on his way. This isn't on you."

I stop myself from nibbling on my bottom lip, not wanting to ruin my lipstick.

I have no interest in going on a date with someone who isn't Mateo, especially now with the information Denise has dropped on my lap.

But my people-pleasing ways rear their ugly head at the thought of standing this guy up, even if it wasn't my fault.

Plus, what harm could come from saying hello and quickly letting him know that this was all a silly misunderstanding?

"Five minutes. I'll go say hi, then tell him you had a lobotomy or something. You know, to explain how you're setting up blind dates so stealthily that even the parties involved don't know about them."

Denise's concerned gaze meets mine. "You sure? He is a really nice guy, Isa. He just got out of a long relationship, and I thought you two could be each other's safe landing. You know, for returning to the dating world."

I wave her away, already focused on getting this over and done with, when Luisa gets our attention. "Coach Weston?" she shouts, baffled.

The man who seems like he would be much better suited for the wilderness than the glitzy lounge we're currently vacating freezes at the mention of his name. His eyes meet Luisa's, and he gives a slight nod, seemingly not intending to get any closer to our table. That is until his eyes land on Daisy.

Maybe it's because I'm the most sober of the crew, but I immediately notice how his body language changes and shifts toward her. It's made much more obvious when he walks out of his way and comes up to stand right next to her.

"Hey, Luke. What are you doing here?" Daisy beams when she realizes he's joined the conversation.

"How much have you had to drink?" he asks gruffly.

"It's girls' night, *so* who knows?" She giggles to herself.

He ignores everyone else at the table when he directs his question to Luisa. "How much?"

She nods at the bottle of tequila. "Let's just say she's going to be feeling that tomorrow. Gonna need some fluids and ibuprofen, for sure."

He nods, as if he's just been given orders and leans down closer toward Daisy. If I hadn't heard it myself, I wouldn't have thought it was possible for his voice to soften so suddenly. "Hey, Daisy girl. What do you say I take you home?"

She pouts dramatically. "But it's girls' night."

He looks around the table, finally paying us some mind, and when those glacial blue eyes land on me, I realize he's looking for backup. I look at Luisa for guidance, since she works with Coach Weston and knows him better than I do.

Our female telepathy kicks in, and she nods. "Oh, um, Daisy, we were all about to call it a night. Isa here was just about to lose this guy and then head home to make sweet, sweet love to Mateo. Isn't that right, Isa?" Luisa smirks my way.

Luke's eyebrows almost hit his hairline. Must be the closest thing the man does to a shout. But he quickly disregards our comments and focuses back on Daisy. "How about we stop for some mac and cheese on the way home? Might even swing for some soft serve while we're at it."

She eyes him suspiciously. "From where?"

"Do you really have to ask? C'mon, I'll take you to see the place you're always stealing my lunch from."

"Dale's Diner?" She hops down from her seat, wobbling in place. But Luke is there, steadying her with a respectful hold on her bicep. "I get to eat their food warm instead of from your Tupperware? Yes! Let's get out here. Bye, girls. I love you so much. You have no idea how much tonight meant to me. I had so much fun," she yammers on as she proceeds to give each of us a loud kiss on the cheek.

"Text us when you get home." I give Luke a stern look. Just because Luisa vouches for him doesn't mean it'll hurt to give him a slightly threatening glare and a reminder that we'll be waiting to hear from her tonight.

I think I see his mouth twitch before he gives me a subtle nod. Then he's off, gently guiding Daisy through the crowd.

"Am I missing something here?" I point to myself.

Luisa shrugs. "From what I can tell, Daisy's a literal wallflower. The complete opposite of her brother, Lucifer."

"I thought his name was Nick?" Nikki chimes in.

"Isn't that what I said? Anyway, any time there's mention of Daisy's dad or fiancé, she shuts down. If I had to put money on it, our girl is struggling to stand up for herself and step out of the shadows of all the alpha men around her."

"And how does the lumberjack hottie fit into all of this?" Amelia slurps the last bit of her frozen margarita.

Luisa sighs. "Luke's a good guy. Tragic past that I won't get into. But he keeps to himself and speaks only when absolutely necessary."

"He was speaking mighty fine with Daisy," I tease.

Luisa taps her nose. "Yes. And there lies the unknown mystery. The man who can barely stand small talk yet can often be found sharing his lunch with our sweet Daisy. We can try to tackle that whole bit at our next girls' night. Preferably doing an activity that doesn't involve alcohol so that we can try and get to the bottom of it."

"Oh, daddy issues. I'm fluent in the subject matter. Can't wait to dig in." Nikki smiles.

I've just about forgotten about my mystery date when a handsome man comes to stand by Denise shyly. "Hi, there. Sorry, I spotted Denise and figured this was the right place." He struggles to make eye contact with each of us, and his cheeks are displaying what I already know.

He's nervous as hell.

I look at the time on my phone and realize it's eleven p.m. If I hurry this "thanks, but no thanks" conversation up, I can be out of here in no time and hopefully catch Mateo before he goes to bed.

With that thought pushing me into action, I say, "Hi, I'm Isabella. I think my nosy friend here arranged for you to meet me."

His eyes meet mine, and his shoulders lower slightly at my humorous tone. "Ah, so we've both been conned. Nice to know we're walking into this on equal footing." He points at a small two-person booth to the right of me. "I actually had that booth reserved for us earlier. Would you want to bring your drink over there so we can chat?"

"Oh, you mean as opposed to you standing there next to Denise while a table full of women dissect your every word?" I shrug playfully. "I guess so."

He laughs, and I feel better knowing that I'm putting the poor guy out of his misery by doing so. We make our way to the booth and take the seats opposite one another. I don't know exactly what I had planned once I got here, but it feels like I have a bird's-eye view of us sitting here, and even though it's innocent on my part, it feels wrong. So I don't waste any time and get down to business.

"Look, Jeff, is it?" He nods, so I continue. "You seem like a really nice guy, but I think our friend got a bit ahead of herself, and—"

"Oh, thank God." He releases a deep breath. "I've been dreading this since the moment I agreed to Denise's plan. That woman can be very convincing. And kinda scary." He laughs. "I just got out of a long-term relationship, and if I'm being completely honest, I don't want things to be over between us. So I'm kind of stuck in the place where I'm respecting her space while still wanting her back desperately."

I develop instant heart eyes for the man in front of me. Platonically, of course. There is nothing my rom-com-loving heart loves more than a man fighting to get his lover back.

And some good groveling. That never hurts either.

It seems like this proposed date has now turned into operation Get Jeff's Girl Back, and I have more than enough romance novels to recommend for this exact task.

"Okay, Jeff. Hear me out. I think I might be able to help. My only question to you is, how fast can you read?"

Chapter Thirty-Two

MATEO

I toss my keys to the starstruck valet and don't break my stride as I make my way toward the heavily secured doors. Eye contact is all it takes for the velvet rope to be lifted and for large men to scramble to open the doors. This is one of those moments where having a recognizable face comes in handy.

I make my way through the hordes of people. Being a head taller than most makes it easy for me to spot Denise and Luisa. I make it to their table in four long strides. I ignore the look of shock on the faces of two women I don't recognize as I scan the table, where there's no sign of Isabella.

I lean into one of the vacant seats, keeping my voice low as I look at Denise. "Where?"

More words aren't necessary. She knows exactly why I'm here and who I'm looking for.

She nods at a booth where a guy wearing a navy dress shirt is sitting and typing desperately on his phone. "She just got up to use the bathroom, but she's sitting over there. Listen, Mateo. I had—"

I stop a passing waiter and hand him my Black Amex. "Cover the tab for this table and that booth over there. Once you're done, leave my card with her." I nod at Denise. "Before you close out, give yourself a 50 percent tip. You got all that?" The waiter nods rapidly and runs off toward the bar.

"Mateo," Luisa starts.

"Torres is on his way. I'm offering up his services to drive you ladies home safely." I make brief eye contact with the women I don't know. "Hope you don't judge me for the man I might become in the next thirty seconds. See you all at a game soon. Have a good night." My media training finished the rest of that sentence for me, because my eyes were already scanning the room for the bathrooms.

My hands itch with the need to touch her, to know that she's safe and that she's within reach.

I find the dimly lit hall to the bathroom right as she's walking out.

She might as well be on a damn runway with the way she's strutting in that red dress. It's cut low enough to give the hint of cleavage before it cuts short by her mid-thigh, molding to her every curve.

Heads turn as she passes, men attempting to get a peek at the figure I know all too well.

She's about to turn off toward the booth when I notice a dark and quiet alcove and pull her by the wrist.

She gasps as she loses her footing slightly, landing between the wall and my chest. I close in around her, making sure that if someone passes by, they can't see her.

When her eyes finally reach mine, her jaw drops slightly, and I can see the questions floating in her gaze. I don't give her a minute to catch her breath.

Why should I? I haven't since the moment I laid eyes on her all those months ago.

"This is how it's going to go, Isabella. So listen *very* carefully."

Her eyes widen at my tone, and she bites her bottom lip.

My large hand cradles her chin as my thumb releases the plump lip.

"Option one: you tell me to get lost and I leave." I lean in close enough for my lips to fan faintly over hers as I speak. "But let me warn you. If you're gonna tell me to fuck off, do it properly and make it convincing." Her eyes flare with heat as I swipe my thumb over her bottom lip, then slowly pop it into my mouth.

Cherry fucking ChapStick.

"Option two: you keep your manners for the time being, walk over to the man I hope has been a gentleman all night, and bid him farewell. I will be waiting with my car outside the private entrance to take you home. If you choose option two and take more than five minutes, I will walk back in here and show you that I have no problem disregarding my manners when it comes to you. I'll haul your ass over my shoulder and out of here. Understood?"

Isabella takes her sweet time looking me up and down. I can see the mischief starting to play out in her eyes.

"And what happens if I want an option three?" she asks breathily.

I give her a dangerous smirk, because I knew she would be a brat and try to push my buttons. So I came prepared.

"Glad you asked. Because there is no option three. But there is a strike three on the table." I don't let the shock on her face fester as I continue. "You remember when I told you those previous strikes were more about me than you?"

She nods slightly in my hold. "Well, you see, the times you earned strikes weren't because you were failing at your job. They were because I was failing at mine. At not wanting you, at not keeping you at arm's length." I lean down her neck, inhaling her sweet scent as my breath tickles under her ear. "That first strike wasn't because you were rummaging through my kitchen in the middle of the night. It was because I wanted to bend you over the counter and take you right then and there at the sight of you wearing pajamas that were begging to be ripped apart by my teeth."

I almost stop talking and get us moving at the sound of her soft moan. But if we're going to do this, I need to get it all out. "The second strike wasn't because you made a mess of my kitchen. It was because you so seamlessly wove yourself into my family, making it hard to imagine a day where I come home and you're not right there, standing next to my daughter."

I lift myself slightly to meet her big, beautiful brown eyes again. "And strike three, tesoro?"

"What happens after strike three?" she whispers, her face inching closer to mine.

I let my hand travel from her chin to the back of her neck, giving her a slight squeeze as I say, "Strike three, and you're mine, Isabella."

I watch my words wash over her face as her eyes flutter closed momentarily. When she opens them fully, she bypasses my awaiting lips and whispers into my ear, setting my world on fire. "I'm calling strikeout."

CHAPTER THIRTY-THREE

ISABELLA

THE CAR IS FILLED with sexual tension as we drive through busy Friday-night traffic.

Mateo maintains a firm grip on my bare upper thigh, as if he's unconvinced that I'm actually here and not going anywhere.

He maneuvers his Mercedes G-Wagon with ease, using only one hand to drive.

I'm tempted to make a joke and break the tension. Ever since he discreetly got us out of that lounge by only using subtle eye contact and chin lifts with the bouncers, he's been quiet.

But a part of me, the part that has some form of self-preservation, knows now is not the time to poke the beast that lies beneath the surface.

I called strikeout.

And now I sit and impatiently wait for what comes next.

We pull into the garage, and he parks in a spot I've never noticed before. "Stay here," he says as he slides out of his seat and closes his door. I take off my seat belt, and in the next moment, he's there, opening my door. I take his offered hand and hop down. He makes no attempts to move when I do, putting us chest to chest.

He gives me one final heated look before he's leading to the elevators. Once inside, I start to break. I don't think I've ever been quiet this long in my entire life. "Mateo—"

He stops me from continuing as he points to the camera at the top corner of the elevator.

Damn.

The man has thought of everything. I wonder if that's what it's like being him. Having to know where all the possible media leaks may be. Not even being able to have open conversations in your own elevator.

The doors open, and he guides me inside with a secure hand on my lower back. The farther we get into the apartment, the farther that hand seems to travel south until it's firmly planted on my ass.

I turn my head with a smirk on my face. Never thought I'd see the day when Mateo gets handsy with me.

As we reach the kitchen, he stops abruptly. Before I know it, his hands are on my waist, and I'm being lifted. I land softly on the kitchen island. Mateo quickly stepping into the space between my legs as I let out a small squeak.

One hand gently digs into the back of my head, intertwining with the loose curls, while the other finds its happy place once again on my upper thigh. "Did he kiss you?" His tone brooks no argument and has me shaking my head.

He hesitates momentarily. "Can I?" His eyes dig deep into my soul. For a moment, the lust dissipates, and in its place is pure devotion.

"Yes," I whisper, desperate for him to finally kiss me and put me out of my misery.

He shifts closer between my legs, forcing them to open more to accommodate his size. The grip in my hair tightens slightly as he maneuvers me toward his lips. I'm mesmerized by the sight of his tongue swiping quickly over his bottom lip. So much so that I'm taken by surprise when he finally says, "Strike three, tesoro."

Then his lips crash onto mine, devouring me.

A kiss filled with desperation and possession.

His tongue demands entry, and I quickly give it to him.

Our hands roam and explore one another.

I take advantage and discover every inch of his broad chest, then lower to where I know lies an impressive six-pack.

His mouth leaves mine in favor of my neck, surely leaving his mark as he goes. My hands dig into his short brown hair, and when my nails scrape lightly, he releases a low moan of pleasure.

He makes his way back up to my lips, kissing and nipping me into oblivion.

"Say it again," he says gruffly.

I'm in no mood to play games, and I know exactly what he wants to hear. "Strikeout."

"And what does that mean?" His nose nudges mine as his eyes drown in desire.

"That I'm yours."

"You sure you want to be mine, Isabella? Think carefully, because there's no coming back from this."

My hands slowly make their way up his arms, noting every muscle from his biceps all the way to his shoulders, until I finally wrap them around his neck. I bring my lips close to his so we're breathing each other in as I whisper, "Yes."

I pull him back into me, no longer interested in anything other than the feel of his lips on mine.

"I can taste the tequila on your tongue, Isa."

"Hmm, want to pour it elsewhere and see how it tastes?" I bait him.

"Fucking hell." He takes a slight step back, leaving me panting and needy. "I can't believe you're real." He stares intently at me, just as out of breath as I am.

Which makes me feel better, since he is a professional athlete and all.

I go to reach for him, but he holds my hand and kisses it tenderly.

Much too tenderly for my liking, because it feels like he's cooling off while I'm burning up.

"Isabella, you've been drinking tonight. Why don't we take it slow and continue this tomorrow, when I know you have a clear head?"

My eyes immediately drift up to the second floor.

Shit. I was so ready to mount this man in the middle of the kitchen that I didn't take into account that his family is currently sleeping upstairs.

"They're not here. If that's what you're wondering. They decided to sleep over at my mother's house instead."

"Oh."

I can see the struggle in Mateo's eyes. The man is good to his core, so much so that not even being splayed open on the counter for him like this would tempt him into taking what he wants if he believes he'd be taking advantage of me.

Which he wouldn't be, because that kiss sobered me up instantly.

For a second, I start to panic that the moment has passed, that maybe this won't actually happen. That I'll be stuck angrily using one of my toys instead of the man standing in front of me, who looks like he can tear my dress off in two seconds.

But then I wait a beat.

Mateo's always been cautious of my boundaries and wanting to make sure I'm comfortable. And as annoying as it is at a time like this, it does remind me that I'm lucky to have a man like him care for me. It also reminds me that I kind of smell like a bar and could probably do with some freshening up.

If this is going to happen tonight, it's going to be because I take the lead and let him know he can have me fully.

So I decide to play along.

"You know what? You're right."

It's a testament to what kind of man he is that not even a flicker of guilt or disappointment is sent my way. Instead, he nods, as if to confirm that he did the right thing.

If only he knew the surprise I have up my sleeve.

"I'm going to shower and head to bed. We can talk about this tomorrow, right?" I ask coyly.

"Of course. This changes nothing, Isabella. We go at your speed. No rush." He dips low and kisses me softly, and for a moment, I forget I have a whole plan I need to execute.

I break the kiss, then hop off the counter. "Good night, Mateo." I quickly make my way toward my room and avoid eye contact, because if he sees my face, he'll know I'm up to something.

"Isa, do me a favor," he says as I get to my room. "Lock your door tonight. For my sake."

I nod my head quickly and dive into my room.

Little does he know...

CHAPTER THIRTY-FOUR

ISABELLA

I TAKE THE WORLD'S quickest shower and send the universe a quick thank-you after I didn't cut myself while shaving.

I used almost half of my fancy body wash while lathering up and brushed my teeth with enough toothpaste to rid myself of any traces of tequila.

I dig into my underwear drawer and pick out a sexy number I got once while online shopping and tipsy. I've never worn it because it's not exactly practical with all the black lace and extra satin strings, but I don't intend on keeping it on for long. The bra opens with a front clasp, which will come in handy, since I plan on wearing one more thing.

His jersey.

If this doesn't work, I'm changing my name and entering the witness protection program.

I silently make it up the stairs on bare feet.

The closer I get to his door, the more nervous I get. I'm not exactly well versed in the art of seduction, so I'm leaning heavily on all those spicy romance books I read, hoping they don't steer me wrong.

I stand in front of his door, ready to knock softly, when it swings open.

Mateo stands in front of me, dripping wet, with only a low-slung towel around his waist.

I lose whatever sexy opening line I had planned and instead ask, "Where are you going?"

It takes him a moment to register me, all of me.

His eyes heat when they stop on my bra, since the lace is see-through, and I know he can see everything.

A rough growl escapes his chest. "I was on my way to break down a fucking door."

In the next instant, he's hauling me up in his arms, and my legs instinctively wrap around his middle. His lips are on mine, and before I know it, we're moving.

I'm pinned against a wall as Mateo kisses me hungrily.

And he wastes no time.

He leans down and traces my nipple with his tongue through my bra. I throw my head against the wall and push my chest farther into his face, needing more of the intoxicating sensation. He moves to give the other breast equal attention, and that's when I decide to intervene.

"I'd prefer if we get this out of the way now." I unclasp my bra and let my breasts bounce out of their confines.

He releases a deep moan and is back on me. This time, his beard creating a delicious fiction against my sensitive nipples.

"My girl likes when I play with her tits."

"Yes." I gasp as he bites down lightly on one of my nipples and pulls slightly.

"Noted."

He keeps this onslaught going to the point where I think I might come from this alone.

But I'm greedy, and I want to feel it all when it comes to Mateo. "More."

"What do you need, baby? You want my mouth, fingers, or my cock?"

I almost want to scream, I'm so deliriously aroused.

"Yes."

"Yes, what tesoro?" he taunts evilly.

"Fuck me, Mateo. I need you to fuck me right now."

The words are barely off my lips when my back lands on his soft mattress with a bounce.

Before I can register the slight pinch, I realize he's ripped my panties right off me, and I think I have a mini orgasm at the sight of my tattered underwear in his hands.

"That's more like it." He tosses my panties aside, not bothering to look where they land. "Now open for me, Isabella. Show me what's mine." He gently nudges both of my knees, and they fall open easily.

His golden hazel eyes darken as his gaze falls to where I've exposed myself. With any other person, I may have felt self-conscious, but with Mateo, knowing I make him this feral makes me feel powerful.

"You know how long I've wondered how good this pussy must taste?" He wipes his mouth as if he's salivating and about to indulge in his favorite meal.

He undoes his towel, letting it drop to the floor, and my eyes almost fall out of my head.

There's no way he could have concealed *that* in those baseball pants he wears at every game. How the hell was I supposed to know that he walked around with a literal bat between his legs?

I don't realize I've started to scramble backward until his hand lands on my ankle and he's pulling me back down the bed. "Promise it doesn't bite. Only I do." He grins down at my shocked expression. "Don't worry, I'll prep you. I'd never hurt you, baby. Not unless you asked for it."

He drops to his knees and pulls me closer to the edge of the bed. "Mateo, you don't have—"

His pointed tongue flicks my clit with one strong lick, and I bow off the bed.

"I'm sorry. You say something up there? I got a mouth full of pussy I need to tend to, so relax tesoro. Trust me, you'll need this."

I don't have time to focus on his words because he's back, eating me out just as passionately as he kisses me. Nipping and sucking, responding to every moan and whimper I make. When he slowly slips a finger inside me, I almost come undone. When he enters another and curves it slightly upward, I do.

I claw at the bedding, thrashing in the tight hold he has on my thighs as the orgasm threatens to take my sanity along with it.

I've never come so hard in my life. My pulse vibrates throughout my oversensitive body as I try to get my breathing under control.

Mateo stands, sucking his fingers as he does. "Fucking delicious."

Even though I've just come, I don't want this moment to end, especially as his cock bobs heavily between his thighs.

Without a second thought, I find the strength to get on my hands and knees and reach for him.

His long, thick cock weighs heavily in my hand as I slowly jerk him up and down. A bead of precum threatens to leak on the bed when I lean forward and lick it up.

He groans above me. "Careful, Isabella. Keep playing with me like that, and I just might let you have it."

I roll my eyes at him.

The look on his face tells me I've made a big mistake.

He grabs his cock at the base and lightly taps the tip on my lips. "Open up for me."

I obey, sticking out my tongue as well. "Good girl." He slides into my mouth, not stopping until he finds resistance. "Now open up that throat for me."

My eyes widen slightly, but I do as he says. His hand grips a handful of my hair, and he slowly sets a pace, thrusting in and out of my mouth. Going deeper than I ever thought possible. My eyes water slightly, and my saliva is everywhere. "*Now* roll your eyes all you want, tesoro. It suits you quite nicely with my cock stuffed down your throat."

I gag, and the action has Mateo bending over me slightly.

"Fuck, I need to get inside you now." He slips out of my mouth, and I gasp for air. He flips me onto my back and prowls over my body.

He's hovering above me, reaching for something in his nightstand—a condom, I assume—when the tip of his cock accidentally nudges my wet pussy. We both hiss at the sensation, meeting each other's heated stares.

"I've been tested, you know. And I'm on the pill," I whisper.

"I've been tested too. All clear on my end as well," he says as he pulls the sealed box of condoms out of the nightstand. He stares at it a moment too long.

"I didn't mention it so that we could, um, forgo that. No pressure. I just thought it was the responsible thing to do. To let you know that I'm safe."

I want to slap myself for being so incredibly unsexy at a time like this. We probably should have had this talk before I presented him with my exposed nipples.

"I've never, you know, without a condom." His pained expression leads me to believe this would be the time he would try to break that streak. But part of my brain realizes that this man must have super sperm if he made a baby with protection. That part wins out and makes the decision for us.

"Let's use it. We can always revisit our stance later on." I raise my arm and grab the box out of his hand and slide a wrapper out.

"You sure?" He looks down at me, studying my face intently. "Because I need you to be the one to make this call. Because at a time like this, filling this pussy up with my cum seems like the perfect idea to me."

He groans as I grab ahold of him and slowly roll the latex onto his hard cock. "You have a breeding kink... noted. Now fuck me like I dare wear another man's jersey," I taunt as I pull on the edges of the jersey I'm wearing.

And fuck, did I push a button.

I'm flipped face-first on the mattress when I feel my ass and hips being lifted by his callused hands. A swift breeze is the only warning I get before his hand comes down on my right ass cheek hard enough to shock me but not hurt.

"You know what? It's about time I teach you a lesson." He fists my hair, pulling me up on all fours.

His dominating voice makes me so wet, I fear I'm dripping down my thigh.

He teases his cock at my entrance, coating himself in my arousal. My breasts sway back and forth as I try to get him inside me.

"Maybe I should edge you a little longer. Make you learn a little patience. What do you think?" I groan desperately as he purposely massages my clit with his hardness from behind. "Because maybe the threat of holding back that orgasm you so desperately need will make you think twice about whose jersey you wear. Maybe after I've fucked you senseless and turned this ass the prettiest shade of pink with my hand, you'll remember the name you should be wearing."

His tip enters me, and we both moan loudly. He slips it out slightly, then thrusts back in, a little deeper, a little harder.

"And maybe, just maybe, after your vocal cords go raw from yelling my name, you'll remember it's me and only me you belong to." He bottoms out inside me, and I scream.

I've never felt so full. He's hitting places that are making my eyes roll to the back of my head. The sounds of our sweat-slicked bodies smacking into one another amplify the feeling.

I feel myself tighten around his length, and I turn my head slightly to get a good look at the man giving me the best sexual experience of my life. His teeth are gritted, eyes on where he's currently pistoning in and out of me.

Seeing him so concentrated on keeping control has me feeling brave and loosening my lips. "What? I wear your jersey, or you'll spank me a few times? Not much of a threat. Think you're branding me or something?" I pant.

His hand abandons my hair and reaches under me to find my needy clit. Keeping pace, he starts to rub firm circles, rendering me speechless.

"No, sweetheart. Once you come on my cock, I'll be branding you by ripping off this condom and coming on your ass. The jersey is so everyone else knows not to touch what's mine." His voice darkens.

And with one tight pinch, I clench around him, and my pussy threatens to milk him dry as I start to come.

With both hands now on my hips, he powers into me harder and faster than before, setting off a second orgasm before I've had the chance to recover from the first. My shouts threaten to prove him right as I scream his name.

When I've just about turned into a rag doll, he gently slides out of me, leaving me momentarily relieved but empty at the same time.

Then he makes good on his promise. I watch him yank off the condom like it offends him and give himself two hard jerks before his warm cum is raining down on my ass and lower back.

I can feel one stream rolling down the hole no man has ever touched before. Once it's close to reaching my pussy, Mateo's thumb stops its trajectory by rolling it back up and massaging it into my puckered hole. "I'm going to make that mine one day too, in case you were wondering. So keep that in mind the next time you want to mouth off while you have my cock buried in your greedy pussy."

I have no energy to respond to his threat. Instead, I'm fighting against my body's exhaustion long enough to ask him for a towel.

Yet it proves to be unnecessary, since he's lifted me in his arms and is walking to his massive shower.

He gently sets me on my feet as he sets the water to the perfect temperature, then pulls me into him.

Noticing the way I try to avoid the overhead spray, he wordlessly grabs the handheld shower head and starts to clean me up. He's lathering me more than necessary, but I'd be lying if I said it didn't feel good having his rough hands glide all over my wet skin.

I'm blissed out, head tilted up with my eyes closed, taking it all in.

Until I feel his tongue on my clit, and I gasp.

"I'm being meticulous. Gotta make sure I clean you up right." His eyes tease as his tongue darts back over my needy center. "Look, I even have reinforcements to make sure I do a good job." He clicks the shower head a few times, changing the rainfall to a more forceful stream of water. Then he's aiming it right at my pussy, the water pulsing against my clit.

"I know I made a mess of you, but look how pretty you look when I clean you up."

My hand lands on his head for support as he lifts one of my thighs over his shoulder and angles the water on and around my clit, teasing me with the loss of pressure.

I never knew it was humanly possible to come this many times in one night, and I fear I'm becoming addicted to the feeling.

"Okay, enough of that." He tosses the shower head aside. "I can get the job done better anyway. Watch." His warm lick has me throwing my head back again.

But the soft bite on the inside of my thigh has me looking down quickly.

"I said watch." He uses his fingers to spread me open farther for him. "Look how nicely I can make you come on my tongue. Now keep your eyes locked on me. I wanna see my handiwork at play."

He sucks my clit into his mouth, and I feel my soul leave my chest on a silent cry. As promised, I keep my eyes locked on him as he works me into a frenzy. There's no direct shower spray hitting him, so I know the wetness on his face is all me. That knowledge, along with the smug, satisfied look on his face, is enough to send me over the edge for a fourth time tonight.

He slowly rises and is careful when he rinses off the evidence of my arousal between my legs, making sure the showerhead is set back to a soft rainfall before the water cascades over my stomach.

"There. Did I kiss it better?" He grins down at me.

"Yes. Much." I laugh as I lean into his chest. "Now get me a towel and put me to bed before you get any more ideas."

"Fine. No more sex for tonight," he fake pouts, then smiles childishly. "But get ready, because I'm going to cuddle the shit out of you."

"Let me guess, you're the little spoon?"

He turns me to walk out of the shower, then swats my ass. "Yeah, you're definitely going to be taught a few more lessons."

"Promises, promises."

Chapter Thirty-Five

MATEO

There are few things in existence I have dedicated my life to.

Baseball, being a father, and now, being the man worthy of waking up with Isabella sleeping peacefully on his chest.

Her eyes flutter when she dreams, and she pouted in her sleep when she rolled over and couldn't feel me.

I spent most of the night awake, watching her. Molding my large body into her soft curves, tracing every inch I could get my hands on.

I'm certain I've memorized every bit of her by now.

When sleep finally came, it was with the surprise of Isabella curled up on my chest, legs intertwined with mine.

I try, desperately, not to recount the events from last night. Simply because my morning wood has turned painful at this point. Having all of her softness rubbing up on my hardness makes it difficult to breathe at times, but I wouldn't have it any other way.

She starts to stretch, eyes closed, as she releases a sound that only sends more of my blood rushing south, and I internally curse my male biology.

When her eyes open, I can see her take in our surroundings and our current cuddling position.

For a moment, I fear that she might freak out and possibly regret the events of last night. But in true Isa fashion, she shocks the hell out of me when she reaches under her pillow and grabs a condom she's sneakily tucked away.

"Well, good morning to you too," I say, amused.

She kicks the blankets off our nude bodies and stares at my raging hard-on. "Looks like everybody's awake. Good." She quickly rolls the condom on and straddles my hips.

She must be sore. I know I wasn't as gentle as I should have been last night. But as she starts to lower herself onto me, I allow her to make that call and take the lead. I put my hands behind my head and fully take in my view.

She hisses slightly as she fully seats herself on me but slowly starts to rock, and that look transforms into raw pleasure.

"You know, people usually say good morning and ask for a cup of coffee or something as soon as they wake up." I try to act affronted, but my moan makes it hard for my delivery to be believable.

"Really?" she asks as she leans forward, rubbing her clit against me. "Huh, interesting. I wonder what most people do when they've been poked and teased with a hard cock that's kept their pussy wet all night." She sighs as her hips change directions and have me buried even deeper inside her.

I tried to play it cool, but that lasted about three seconds. My hands immediately reach for her heavy tits as I teasingly pinch and tug on her nipples. When her pussy tightens around my cock in reaction, I know she's enjoying it. I lean forward, sucking one nipple into my mouth as my hand plays with the other.

"Fuck, I'm so close," she whispers.

So am I. Which means I need to get her there before I do. I keep my mouth and right hand on her breasts as my left hand lowers to meet her clit.

Within seconds, she's coming on my cock, triggering my own orgasm at the same time.

"There, that's better." She smiles as she catches her breath. "Hi. Good morning. Can I get a cup of coffee now?"

We erupt in laughter as I haul us off the bed and into the bathroom for a shower.

That morning coffee is going to have to wait a bit longer.

It takes us another hour before we emerge from my bedroom.

And apparently, I've earned myself my very first sex ban. Minimum twelve hours, according to Isabella. And you can bet your ass I immediately set a timer to make sure I'm not one second late.

It's Saturday morning, and I have a game tonight.

But all I can focus on is how my T-shirt fits Isabella like a dress, and it's the most stunning she's ever looked. Hair slightly curled, sitting in a loose bun at the top of her head, barefoot on my heated floors as she cradles her warm cup of coffee in hand.

"Why are you looking at me all funny?" She eyes me suspiciously above her mug.

I walk over, tugging her close. "You got a problem with how I look at you? Well, tough. Get used to it, because if it was hard keeping my eyes off you before, it'll be well near impossible now." I lean down and kiss her. Just because I want to. Just because I can.

Her smile beams up at me. "Mateo Martinez, you're a big softie, aren't you?"

"I'm pretty sure I proved more than enough times how hard I can be, and that landed me on a sex ban. So look what good that did me," I mutter as I take a sip of my coffee. She swats my chest playfully as she laughs.

"So, game tonight, right?"

I nod. "Yep. You think you girls will be in the same seats as before, or do you want to head up to a suite? I can put you in one by yourselves, without the piranhas." I waggle my eyebrows.

Her jaw drops. "Oh, so you've heard of them too and sent me in there to fend for myself? You know, Charlie lost pancake privileges for such a crime. I should come up with something for you."

I kiss the scowl off her face until she's putty in my hands.

"That's cheating," she says between kisses.

"Really? Feels like winning to me."

My phone chimes on the counter, and Isa breaks the kiss so I can check it.

It's a text message from my mother, letting me know she can bring Anna to my game tonight instead of bringing her home this morning.

I groan at the thought of my mother thinking she's wing-manning for me.

"What is it?" Isabella asks, concerned.

"My mother." I sigh. "She took one look at you last night and made the call to have the sleepover with Anna at her place. Seems like she hoped, or maybe she knew, this"—I wave between us— "would happen. And now she just offered to keep Anna longer."

Panic is clear in her eyes. "So your mom knows about us?" She takes a big gulp of her coffee.

"Suspects. Probably lighting a candle and praying for, if I go by any of her previous subtle suggestions about you."

"And by subtle, you mean…"

"Bull in a china shop."

"Exactly," Isa huffs. "So what happens now?"

Here comes the part I was concerned about. I never worried about what would happen between Isabella and me behind closed doors. But outside these walls, I know that things can be more complicated, especially for her.

I take her hand in mine, opening her palm and planting a light kiss. "Whatever you want happens. We go at your pace, remember."

She nods as she looks out at the New York skyline. "Okay, yeah. But what do you want?" She looks up at me, eyes hopeful.

"I already got what I want, Isa. I got you. And however you want to share that news with the world is completely up to you." I pull her into a hug and kiss the top of her head. "You want to tell your mom and friends? Go for it. Keep it a complete secret? That's fine as well. Want me to call Nick Stonehaven and have his media company plaster it on the cover of every magazine with professional photos of us? That can be arranged as well." She stiffens in my hold. "Okay, maybe not that last one." I chuckle as I lift her chin slightly, placing a kiss on her forehead. "All I need you to know is that this time, it's different."

I pause so she can really take in what I'm about to say. "I'm not him. I would never do anything to hurt you, Isa. And this public world I live in plays by rules. I have power and say in things. I can make deals to make sure you're protected, offer up more personal interviews in return for keeping any type of negative press in regard to you from being printed. It's power I've never cared for before, but I will use it to protect you." I hold her face delicately, letting my thumbs rub her soft cheeks.

"Will I mess up along the way and make some mistakes? Sure. But you can bet your ass I will work harder and do better by you every chance I get. Give me all of your heart in return, and I promise to protect it with all that I have." I bring our foreheads together and release a deep breath.

After a few moments, she responds. "Okay. I can do that." I lift slightly and see the shy look on her face. "I can also try. I don't have these big muscles or any other powerful tool in my possession currently. But I can promise to protect your heart. And Anna's. Which is why I think that before we tell anyone else, we should talk to her. Or maybe you do, and then bring me into the conversation when needed? Either way, you take the lead on that front, however you see fit."

I don't have the proper words to respond with, because every time Isabella puts my daughter first, my heart threatens to burst from my chest. So instead, I kiss her. I pour every single bit of my heart into it too.

The kiss starts to pick up heat and hands start to wander. My voice turns gravelly as I say, "Ever since the moment I knew Anna's heart beat inside her birth mother, I knew she would forever be my number one priority. Never, not once since she was born, have I had the urge to go out and meet someone. I've never felt the need to take a step into the dating world. Not once, Isabella."

"So you're saying you want to take that step now? With me?"

I shake my head and laugh humorlessly. "No. I want to drop to my damn knees. I want to keep you in that special place that you've so delicately carved into my heart. I want to be so pathetic around you and hope that you somehow mistake it for romanticism. Because no, Isabella. I don't want to *date*. I want you, wholly. Forever *mine*. Forever *ours*." I don't waste another moment as my lips threaten to devour her. Letting her body know what my words attempt to convey.

"So, is this the part where you ask me to be your girlfriend or something?" She smirks as she pushes on my chest, her brows raised expectantly.

I smirk. "No, this is the part where I beg."

So much for that sex ban.

CHAPTER THIRTY-SIX

ISABELLA

I'M ON CLOUD NINE.

I don't think I've ever been happier or more sore in my life.

Mateo and I spent the day tangled up in one another until he had to leave for his game.

The cool early September air means that I have to ditch my shorts for jeans tonight. I pair them with a navy bodysuit that does wonders for my boobs and decide to break out my black ankle boots for the first time this season.

I'm about to grab Mateo's jersey, the very same one I had to wash this morning in order to hide the evidence of last night's events, when I pause.

I really shouldn't goad the man. These baseball games are his place of work. And we've been living in such bliss for the last twenty-four hours. Surely I shouldn't rock the boat...

But then I remember what happens when Mateo "punishes" me, and I leave the jersey right where I left it, folded on my bed.

Guess I am a brat after all.

"Isabella!" Anna runs up to my seat and squishes me in a tight hug. I wave at Hank, who brought her down to our front-row seats, and he points up to where the suites are. I mouth, "good luck," and he laughs good-naturedly as he makes his way up the stadium steps.

I direct my focus back to the cuddly kid who's begging for my attention. "Where have you been? I missed you so much." I squeeze her right back and help her climb onto my lap. She's taller than the average five-year-old, and I'm sure that's due to her father's genes.

"I was helping feed tiny little puppies. Their mama was rescued when she was pregnant. Now that the babies are here, they need lots of help to get strong and ready for other families to adopt them so that they can go to their forever homes. I asked Abuela if I could stay over one more night to help, and she said yes. Do you want to come too? Abuela has extra guest rooms. I'm sure she'd be okay with it." She wipes hair out of her face as she comes up for air.

"Slow down there, girl." I laugh. "Maybe I can stop by during the day tomorrow. How does that sound?"

She nods enthusiastically. I'm about to ask her more questions about the pups when the crowd gets loud, and I assume I know the reason why.

Mateo Martinez. Number thirty-five, starting pitcher for the New York Monarchs and the man who's given me more orgasms than I can count while whispering the filthiest words in my ear, is making his way over to us.

Anna hops off my lap, and we make our way to the small gate.

I tap her on the back, and she bolts toward her father. He easily catches her in his arms and kisses her cheek repeatedly. She squirms in his arms until he reluctantly lets her stand and ruffles her hair.

I let them have their moment, admiring how beautiful their relationship is. The crowd *oohs* and *aahs* at their interaction, and it reminds me that there are quite literally eyes everywhere.

The usual panic that starts to rise at the thought doesn't reach its usual fever pitch. I know there will always be eyes on Mateo. And if I want to be a part of his life, then that means me as well.

I never thought I'd be put in a position like this again, but I also never knew a man like Mateo existed.

I would love to say it's a light switch decision, and the fact that cameras are always pointed at him doesn't bother me, but that's not the case.

A part of me will probably always be a little extra sensitive to the limelight. The only difference is that I'm choosing to accept it and slowly learn to live with it if it means I get to be in Mateo's arms at night.

A far cry from when I started a few weeks ago. Back when I was begging for this nannying gig. Crazy how life can change in such a short period of time.

A few of Mateo's teammates walk over and greet Anna.

One in particular has me blushing at the memory of what I did once I arrived at the stadium.

I went to the gift shop and bought a jersey. One without Mateo's name on it.

I was feeling pretty ballsy, but that was before I realized the player whose jersey I'm wearing might actually get close enough to see me wearing it.

As if my guilt were written all over my face, Mateo makes eye contact with me, lifting a questioning brow. I swear it means *what are you up to, Morales?*

I bite my lip and stare at the field as Anthony jogs over and calls my attention.

"Hey, Isa. Come over and meet some of the guys before we start." He nods over to stadium security, and he and Charlie move to make room for me to slip out.

I cautiously make my way toward the half circle of giants. I forgot how tall these men could be. I always assumed only basketball players were tall, but these guys easily dwarf me.

Mateo tracks my movement like a predator, his eyes snagging on my chest for a touch longer than appropriate before he schools his features.

"Yo, guys. This is Denise's friend, Isabella."

"And my nanny and bestie," Anna adds.

Ace Middlebrooks, the Monarchs' third baseman, gives me a quick once-over, then grins at Mateo. "So this is the nanny, Martinez? Looks like you've been holding out on us." He looks back at me and winks. Shit, this might have been a bad idea.

"Hey, Charlie, do me a favor and take Anna up to get some dinner for me, will you?"

Charlie nods. "Right away. Let's go, kiddo."

At the mention of food, Anna darts toward Charlie and starts reciting the concession stand menu from memory.

A part of me wants to turn and go with them, but then I'd have to turn my back on Mateo, which seems like a very dangerous thing to do while he's silently staring down a grinning Ace.

Anthony notices and looks back and forth between Mateo and me. "Isa, tú sí estás bonita. Look at you. It's like you're glowing or something," he teases, and the look I send his way only eggs him on more.

"Let me see, you decide to wear my jersey again? Give us a spin."

My cheeks go bright red, and Mateo notices. "Torres, quit it."

Mateo must be thinking that Anthony is teasing me for wearing his jersey, since we're now a couple. Oh, this is gonna be bad.

"Sheesh, está bien. I just wanted to—" He leans back slightly and catches sight of the name on my jersey. "Oh. Oh, damn." He starts to shake his head as he laughs. "Damn, Isabella. I'm gonna have to tell Denise about this one."

"Torres, don't make me tell you again. Leave her alone." Mateo's teammates start to pay closer attention, their confused gazes latching on to my panicked one.

Anthony raises his hands. "Okay, tranquilo. My bad. Didn't know you were cool with Isa wearing Ace's jersey, though, given how you just about lost your shit when she wore mine, and I've known her forever."

I swear I can no longer hear the sound of the crowd.

When I put on this stupid jersey, I thought Mateo would ask me to spin, and he'd get riled up and take it out on me in bed tonight. I didn't realize we'd have an audience and that the owner of said jersey would be looking at me like he doesn't mind me sporting his name one bit.

"Shit, Mateo. I didn't know your nanny had such good taste." Ace moves to take a step closer to me, but Mateo's gloved hand smacks his chest, stopping him in his tracks.

"Watch your mouth when speaking about my woman."

A choir of *whoa*s and *oh shit*s echoes around the team as they all bow their heads slightly and take a large step back.

Ace's playful face quickly turns serious. "Had no idea, man. Meant no disrespect." He nods my way, his tone much less flirtatious than before. "Nice to meet you, Isabella. Thanks for holding down our guy here. He's a good one. See you around." He taps another player on the chest, and they all head to the dugout, whispering among one another.

Only Mateo, Anthony, and I remain.

They step closer, creating a small circle among us.

Anthony is basically bouncing on his feet. "So... it's true? It happened? You two are finally—"

"Yes. And I fucked it up just now by letting it slip before Isa was ready to tell people." Mateo closes his eyes and shakes his head, seeming upset with himself.

I discreetly poke him in the chest to look my way. "It's fine, I promise. I don't mind them knowing as long as they let us tell Anna before anything gets out."

Anthony shakes his head, losing his smirk in the process. "Nah, don't worry about it, Isa. The team's a vault. Those guys would never talk. They aren't rookies, and we know how to keep our business to ourselves. I trust them." He squeezes my shoulder softly. "I'll let you two lovebirds be and reinforce that notion now so you don't have to worry about it." He nods at Mateo. "See ya out there. Let's get it done tonight."

Mateo nods as Anthony jogs away.

"You know exactly what's going to happen the second I get to that dugout, don't you?" He raises a reproachful brow.

"I'm assuming I'll be receiving a new jersey?" I smile innocently.

"You trying to rack up a collection of my jerseys or something? Say the word, and I'll have your closet filled to the brim by tonight."

"Jerseys, your gray hairs, whichever brings me more joy at the moment." He shakes his head, probably concocting a devious plan for me tonight. "And nice touch with the whole 'my woman' bit." I sigh dramatically. "And here I thought you would test out that new boyfriend title you worked so tirelessly for earlier in the kitchen."

"I look like a boy to you?" he asks, eyes darkening as they quickly rove over my body. He doesn't let me respond as he starts to back away. "Anna's staying another night at my mom's. Be ready for what's coming your way, Morales. Your ass is going to regret this."

ISABELLA

I had no regrets.

ISABELLA

And so began our little routine.

For every away game, I have the appropriate number of Spanish words written on Post-its for him to study while he was gone. Now, I find bright neon notes of my own.

On his pillow when he gets up before Anna wakes up or needs to go to the gym and train. They usually say tesoro, but recently, he's added other Spanish terms of endearment, like mi amor, querida, and mi cielo.

And for home games like tonight, he asks me to reveal my jersey as he stands to the side of the dugout and shakes his head at the name not matching his own on my back.

I could stop, but the postgame sex with a hint of aggression is just too good to pass up. Even though we've had to get creative and keep it quiet for Anna's sake.

Mateo was gone for a long stretch of away games, and we haven't had the time to tell her in person. But I'm hoping we can finally get to it this weekend, since it's a rare weekend that Mateo has off and will be at home with us.

I hear the crowd begin to cheer around me and smile. Luisa or Daisy have been on jersey swap duty for the last couple of games. They don't mind since it gives us a chance to catch up. I never intended to tell my friends before Anna, but after the scene Mateo apparently caused before he found me on the night we got together, I had no choice but to fill them in.

A group video chat later, and all the women were up to date on all things Mateo and me. Well, most things, since I can barely think about our wild nights without burning up at the memories.

The crowd gets louder, and I lean forward to see whether all the noise is for Luisa or Daisy, since they're both loved in this stadium. Luisa, the general manager, for being a girl boss. And Daisy for being the head of community connections, a role she made up entirely. My favorite part of her job is Hot Mic, where random players get mic'd up during the game. She then gathers all the content, along with what the cameras catch, and creates the funniest videos of the shit these guys say when they're not up to bat.

But as I look down my row, it's not Luisa or Daisy heading my way. I suck in a shocked breath as the man who seems more urban legend than real starts to make his way toward me. Tall, dark, and offensively handsome, wearing a tailored black suit and shiny black shoes with an unmistakable number thirty-five jersey in his hand.

Nicholas Stonehaven.

He takes the empty seat next to me, since Anna and Charlie are currently on their second snack run.

"Isabella Morales. Happy to finally make your acquaintance." His hand reaches out to shake mine.

"Nicholas Stonehaven." I shake.

"Please, call me Nick." He smiles.

I nod. "Nick. Nice to meet you as well."

"Yes, I feel like it is a bit overdue. Given that you're good friends with my sister and currently dating my starting pitcher," he says smoothly, running a hand down his immaculate tie. My eyes widen, and he quickly waves my fears away. "Don't worry, my sister didn't spill the beans, if that's what you're concerned about." He turns slightly, facing me. "It's my job to know things about people. And you are quite the interesting one. By the way, congrats on landing a book box deal. I hear those aren't as easy to come by as a newbie graphic designer."

My jaw drops. I only received the email before the game. I hadn't even mentioned to Mateo that I had applied in case I didn't get it. "How did you—"

"Like I said, Miss Morales—"

"Isa."

He smiles. "Isa. It's my job to know things. Which brings me to why I'm here and why I intercepted my sister on the way down to give you your delivery." He hands me the jersey. "Cute, by the way. This thing between you and thirty-five. And I want to make sure it stays that way, so I'm here to let you know that I'm aware of your past with your ex, and I want to make it clear that it won't be a problem here."

I feel my heart drop.

I've been so wrapped up in my own little world that I haven't even given my ex a second thought. How foolish of me to think this kind of high would last forever.

"Isa, are you all right?" Nick touches my shoulder lightly. "Shit, I'm fucking this up, aren't I?" A bit of a British accent slips through as he speaks. He clears his throat, and I meet his concerned eyes. "Listen, all I was trying to say is that you're a part of the Monarch family now, which makes you my family. Whether that's because of your close friendship with Daisy or your relationship with Martinez. You're safe here, and I just wanted you to know that." He pauses. "I'm highly disgusted with how the media handled your ordeal years ago, and I promise that my company will make sure that something of that sort will never happen again. Not under my roof—or, um, stadium." He smiles warmly.

My eyes water, and I try my best to blink back tears. "Oh. Thank you." I reel in my emotions long enough to ask, "But why? You don't even know me." And to be honest, the little I know isn't exactly great since it's usually spewed from Luisa's lips after she's had a glass of wine or two.

He shrugs, looking less like a multibillionaire and more like the guy you'd ask to walk you home. "It's what I would do for my sister," he says simply. "And like I said, you're family now. Daisy told me all about how you asked her to hang out with your friends, and I'll be honest, I was suspicious of your intentions at first. Unfortunately, that's par for the course for us and our family, never being too sure of newcomers. Which led me into having you looked into. My apologies if that sounds too invasive, but when it comes to my sister, there's nothing I wouldn't do to keep her safe and happy."

I chuckle, because this rich guy is talking to me like having me investigated and then suddenly welcoming me into the "family" like the mafia is a normal occurrence for me. "Okay. Thanks again, but that's a lot to take in at once."

I swear his cheeks take on a blush. "Sorry. Again, I don't exactly come from a normal world, and I misstep." He seems uncomfortable and starts to look for the nearest exit. I'm afraid he might just walk out to the field.

"No, it's fine. I just didn't think I'd meet you for the first time under such circumstances, but tell me—what kind of perks do I get as someone who's a part of the Monarchs' fam bam? Are there Sunday lunches? Do I get a monogrammed hat? Matching tattoos?" I whisper shadily.

He laughs, and I see a bit of the tension leave his rigid shoulders when he does. "No, none of that at the moment, but I can now see how you and Daisy have become such fast friends. You're a funny one, Isa."

"Thanks, and you have two fewer horns than I expected—from speaking to Luisa, of course. Wanna tell the fam why she calls you Lucifer?"

He smirks, and suddenly, his face takes on a more devious nature. "Let's just say that our prickly little Luisa and I just... got off on the wrong foot. Shall we?" He stands, straightening his jacket sleeve as he does, looking every bit like someone who owns an entire baseball team. "Although if you see her around tonight, please send her my regards and tell her to start brainstorming on any future pet names for me. I do have a reputation to uphold and whatnot." He winks, and then he's off.

I quickly put on Mateo's jersey in case he looks over during this inning and immediately text Luisa. I would blow up the group chat, but that would probably make things uncomfortable for Daisy, given Nick is her brother and all.

Me:

So why didn't you tell me that the reason you hate Nick Stonehaven is probably because you haven't fucked him yet?

Luisa:

Not you too.

Me:

ME TOO?! Who else has landed on my genius assumption?

Luisa:

Daisy. Which is weird. And for the record, you're both dead wrong. I'd sooner hand in my resignation than touch that egomaniac with a ten-foot pole.

Me:

Sorry, did you say he has a ten-foot pole? Ouch, but intriguing.

Luisa:

You're certifiable.

Me:

Probably, but I know I'm on to something.

Luisa:

Promise you, that's never going to happen.

Me:

Careful. Never say never. Might end up eating those words, friend.

Chapter Thirty-Nine

MATEO

I woke up to Isabella lightly scratching my forearms. After she detangled herself from my limbs, she made her escape downstairs to her room since Anna was sure to wake up at any moment.

Once downstairs, I made coffee while my girls made breakfast. Luckily, Isa was able to reel Anna in this time, and they made a savory breakfast rather than something that would put us all in a diabetic coma.

And now I'm sprawled on the couch, watching the two most beautiful ladies in the world make friendship bracelets for some exchange students who enrolled in Anna's class mid-term.

Seeing them sit on the floor side by side, giggling and smiling while surveying all the colorful strings and beads strewn all over the coffee table makes me have to take a breath and send a silent thank you to the universe. Because I truly never knew that I could know peace and happiness like I do now.

Isabella gives me a weird look, one that screams *why are ya looking at me funny?*

I give her a nod, and she quickly looks between Anna and me, understanding immediately what I'm about to do.

"Okay, kiddo. You keep working on these while I go to the bathroom." Isa moves to stand, and I shake my head and mouth, "stay."

"Hey mija, put that down and come here for a second." I sit up straight and tap on the cushion beside me.

She bounces as she takes her seat next to mine. "Dímelo," she says in perfect Spanish, and I have the urge to laugh and cry at the same time.

"Hey, do you remember a while back, when you kept asking me when I would consider having a girlfriend?"

She nods. "Yeah, and you said that you don't have time for anyone besides me and Abuela, because we're a handful," she says with a straight face.

Kids, man.

I smile and nod. "So if I were to have the time, to have someone join our life as my girlfriend, what would be some of the traits this person should have in order for you to be okay with her?" I venture.

Her face turns serious as she ponders. "She has to be nice. And know how to make sprinkle pancakes. As well as yummy snacks. She obviously needs to like baseball and come to games with me and—" She looks somberly at Isabella, then back at me. "Those are all the things I do with Isa, and she's my bestest friend. So..." She perks up and sighs dramatically. "Can't you just make Isabella your girlfriend so I don't have to find someone else to join us? Because Isabella is here to stay, right, Isabella?" She looks at my woman pointedly, and I can tell Isabella is on the verge of a nervous breakdown.

Isa walks over and takes the other seat next to Anna. "So you wouldn't be upset if your Papi and I are boyfriend and girlfriend?" she asks cautiously.

Anna shrugs. "Not really. What would really change? You already live here."

Isabella bites down on a smile as she continues. "Well, we would hold hands and sometimes, maybe even kiss." She tickles Anna's side when she makes a disgusted face.

"Kissing, gross. I didn't know kissing was part of the package. You would kiss Papi with his prickly beard?" She points to my face, aghast.

"Hey, I thought you loved my besitos," I complain as she giggles.

"Okay, I guess they aren't that bad. What else would change?"

"Isa would be moving into my room. You know, so our stuff can be closer together." I smirk over Anna's head as Isa sends me a silent death glare.

Sorry, but I refuse to continue sneaking around. Any extra moment with Isa in my arms is worth adding to the negotiating table now.

Anna nods. "Okay, that makes sense. That's it?"

Isa and I both look at each other, a bit at a loss as to what else to say. She's clearly taking this much better than expected, and I didn't fear she would struggle with it to begin with.

"Nope, that's all, kiddo. Just means she has a place in my heart, like you and Abuela do."

Anna looks down at her hands as she worries her lip. "Can I ask a question?" she asks warily.

"Of course, mija."

She looks up at Isabella with glassy eyes. "Does that mean I get to have a place in your heart, too?"

That question and her pleading tone almost do me in.

Isabella's eyes instantly well with tears, and I'm right behind her at this rate. She grabs Anna's hands and squeezes them gently. "Oh, Anna, you've had a place in my heart for a very, very long time. And the space you take up just keeps getting bigger and bigger, my love." Anna dives into Isabella's arms, and before we know it, we're all in a tearful cuddle puddle.

"You have a place in my heart too, Isa," Anna hiccups.

Tears fall freely down Isabella's cheeks as her eyes glow with love.

Fucking hell... love.

"Mateo, have the fire department on standby. I'm making an executive decision. Anna and I are making a sprinkle rainbow explosion cake."

CHAPTER FORTY

MATEO

I MAY NEVER KNOW what a sprinkle-free kitchen looks like again, but I do know what a happy home feels like, because I'm living in it.

After having cake for lunch, Anna crashed hard from the sugar high and ended up falling asleep on the couch.

I took the opportunity to suggest we start moving Isabella's things up to my room.

Which is how I ended up staring at Isa's underwear drawer and being completely useless.

"Leave those alone, you perv." She pushes me out of the way with her hip and crosses her arms. "And were you going to include me in this conversation about changing rooms? It's like we're moving in together."

"We already live together," I deadpan.

She wrinkles her nose. "Ugh, you know what I mean."

I move in, pulling her into my chest. "Isabella, will you pretty, pretty please move into my room with me so that I can wake up with you in my arms and give you all the morning besitos for as long as I want?"

"Hmm, tempting. But I've got a sweet setup with my desk in this room. And my clothes are put away so nicely..."

"You're only using up three drawers and a few hangers. We haven't even brought over the rest of your things from your parents' place. And besides..." I turn her in my arms so she faces the floor-to-ceiling windows. "I was thinking we make a few adjustments and turn this into your office. Get a bigger desk and a desktop computer. So when you're in here, you can focus on work, and when you're in our room, you can focus on my co—"

"Don't finish that sentence." She sighs theatrically. "And to think you were doing so well."

I pinch her side, and she erupts into giggles. "Okay, okay, I'll move into your room."

"Our room."

"Our room," she agrees.

"And remember, we're a team now." I lift my wrist, showing off my new friendship bracelet.

Anna made them for the three of us after our conversation earlier. And all three have our initials on them—MIA.

Which is fitting, because mía means mine in Spanish.

Which is what they are.

Isa lifts her bracelet and gazes at it lovingly. "She's the absolute sweetest, isn't she?"

I lean down and kiss her forehead. "Yes, and now she knows. Which also means it's only a matter of time before..."

"Our moms," she shudders. "You know how smug those two are about to be? After months of riding our asses and suggesting I work for you." She shakes her head. "I'm never going to live this down. This'll be the ultimate I-told-you-so moment for them," she grumbles.

"Want me to talk to Anna and see if it's possible for a five-year-old to keep a secret?"

She shakes her head. "No, it's fine. It's actually nice to have my friends know, and now Anna. And I love hearing how much shit the guys on the team give you for dating your nanny." She grins as I roll my eyes. "Plus, I'm sure that after their victory parade, it'll be good to have our family in the know. I don't want it to feel like it's this big secret we have to keep hidden." She wraps her arm around my middle and leans her chin on my chest.

"Except when it comes to the media, right?"

She shakes her head from side to side, contemplating. "I mean, maybe just a bit longer?"

"Whatever you want, tesoro. It's about me and you right now." I kiss her head.

"And Anna. Don't forget our initials, mister." She lifts her bracelet up to my face.

"Would never dream of it."

Later that night, we're both getting ready for bed.

Our bed.

It only took three quick trips up the stairs to get Isabella fully moved into our room. I didn't realize how sad-looking the right side of my empty closet was until I started to organize it with her things.

Which reminds me that I need to take my woman shopping soon. This closet isn't going to fill itself.

Isabella's currently in bed with my biggest competition... her Kindle. I knew my girl loved to read, but I clearly underestimated how deep that love runs. "Just one more chapter," she mumbles without looking up from her screen.

"Yeah, yeah, I've heard that one before," I say as I lift the comforter and settle into bed alongside her. It's not odd for me to catch her reading out on the balcony under a couple of thick blankets or in a nook on the couch when I come home from practice.

We seem to have slipped into this new sense of normalcy, one I never knew I was capable of having.

I think of the moments when I walked in after a long day of work to find Anna and Isabella curled up on the couch together, or in the kitchen making an absolute mess. For the first time in a long time, it feels like I'm walking into a real home. One full of love and warmth. Full of things I never deluded myself into believing I could have with my kind of lifestyle in the public eye.

But Isabella made it easy. She made it easy to come home, because now, along with Anna, she is my home.

My phone dings with a notification.

It's a text from Torres. It's late, and I'd usually wait until the morning to respond, but I don't want to interrupt Isabella as she wraps up her chapter. I'm trying to behave, since I won't be on my best behavior once she puts the Kindle down and I give her fictional book boyfriends a run for their money.

I open the text and see a flyer for a charity baseball game being hosted at our stadium.

Torres:

Yo, man, I know it's late and this is last minute, but this charity event is to help raise funds for hurricane relief in Puerto Rico. I know we always donate and do our part, but I think if you and I show up to this and play a couple light innings, it'll draw a bigger crowd. What do you think?

I look back at the flyer. A bunch of celebrities have signed up to play with some Monarch players. It stings for a moment that I wasn't asked directly from the Monarch organization to join in on the event, given that I'm their starting pitcher and I am Puerto Rican. But I quickly get over it and understand why.

I never go to anything that isn't mandatory. I write a hefty check and ask for regular updates on the charities I'm involved in but never actually show up to kiss ass and shake hands. It's always been the hard line I keep against the relentless media and their attempts to write a personal interest story on me.

Torres:

BTW, I already told Daisy that you'd do it. So don't look like a douche.

Torres:

Plus, I know Isabella will be invited, so that should get your ass in gear.

Me:

I've had just about enough of you referencing my ass.

Me:

And yeah, I'll do it.

Torres:

SHIT, FOR REAL, BRO????

Torres:

Damn, Isabella is a miracle worker. She finally reached close enough to pull that stick out your ass, then?

Me:

What the fuck did I say about my ass? Go to sleep and leave me alone before I change my mind.

"Why is Anthony texting me about being an ass whisperer?" Isabella asks, scrunching her face as she rereads her text.

"Ignore him." I grab both of our phones and set them to charge before turning my attention back to the sexy woman in my bed.

"There's a charity event this weekend. At the stadium, and you're invited. I'll be playing to raise money for hurricane relief in Puerto Rico."

Isabella clicks her Kindle off and sets it on her nightstand, then shimmies under the covers. "That's amazing! We've been lucky to not have any bad ones hit the Caribbean so far this year, but sometimes the infrastructure left reeling in the aftermath can be just as bad, if not worse, than the actual storm. I lived through a couple of bad ones while I was down there, and they were for sure scary, but the worst part was what came next. No electricity or water. People waiting hours in line for gas so they could turn on their generators—if they were lucky enough to even have them. And feeling like the government wasn't doing shit. Like they were just waiting to see how we would dig ourselves out of the devastation." She shakes her head at the memories. "Anything we can do to help, we should. And I know a couple of grassroots organizations on the island that could get the aid directly into the hands of the people who really need it instead of having shipping containers filled with relief sitting on a dock for months on end."

I slip my hand behind Isabella's neck and bring her close enough to kiss her. I don't think I'll ever stop being in awe of this woman, of her heart, or of her fearlessness when it comes to helping others.

"Thank you," I murmur against her lips.

"For what?"

"For helping me see that I wasn't checked in or fully aware of the things happening around me. I've been simply existing for far too long, and I've made peace with sending off money and counting it as my good deed. But now I see that there is more to be done, especially when it comes to my people on the island."

She nods. "It would probably mean a lot more for people to see you outside of your official role, out there making news waves and bringing more attention to the cause because you have such a large platform. But not only that. When people are in the trenches, they don't need fake smiles and rolls of paper towels thrown their way. They need to see you in the trenches with them, shoulder to shoulder. Showing up to things where they can talk to you about their experience and feel the connection happening in front of their faces. There's never a way to fully understand what someone is going through when you've never been through it yourself. But you can listen. You can give people the time of day, make them feel seen and heard. And with a little magic, maybe even make them smile, laugh. Forget about their circumstances for a moment and focus on the joy instead." She traces the slope of my nose with a delicate finger, leading it down to my lips, and I kiss it gently. "If there's one thing I learned about the Puerto Rican people when I lived down there, it's that nothing, and I mean nothing, keeps them down. I thought we Dominicans were the life of the party until I saw how Puerto Ricans got down." She chuckles. "Not only do they rise above adversity time and time again, but they do it with a sense of pride." She smiles softly. "Once, we were in a complete blackout, heating up canned soup over a portable electric stove. All the neighbors were out, and apparently, so were the mosquitos. My cousins were miserable, having lived these same scenarios in the Dominican Republic. I don't remember exactly what one of them said, but it was something silly like 'Why wasn't I born in Bora Bora?' Most of us laughed, but one neighbor shook his head good-naturedly and said, 'Yo soy Boricua aunque naciera en la luna.' And that phrase has always stuck with me. Because I'm a proud Dominican, but I was born here in the states and don't have the same experiences as the majority of my family. But that sentiment, of being who you are, no matter what your birth certificate states, will forever stay with me."

I let out a deep sigh as I let those words sink into me.

My little Spanish lessons, which may have started as a way for me to get closer to Isabella, have now turned into serious business. Whenever I'm not on the field, I'm doing self-appointed homework, since I truly believe my woman is taking it easy on me when giving me small assignments. But I don't want easy, I thrive when pushing myself.

Which is why I know exactly what that sentence meant. "I'm Puerto Rican, even if I had been born on the moon."

Direct translations usually suck, because the Spanish language always has a flair for the romantic while English is pretty straightforward and to the point, but the sentiment isn't lost on me.

The idea that you are a whole version of yourself, of your culture, no matter where you were born or how you were raised, soothes a part of me that's always struggled to figure out exactly where I belong.

Always feeling like I'm part of this or that.

Puerto Rican *but* not from the island. Hispanic, *but* I don't speak Spanish.

Dealing with the ignorant "Oh but you don't look Puerto Rican" comments all my life, because there is apparently only one acceptable version of what a Latino man should look like. Another strike against me not feeling worthy enough to claim my people loudly, proudly.

Yet with each passing day, with the woman by my side—who doesn't even share my same exact lineage—I'm getting closer to my roots.

And for a man who could afford to buy anything, she has no clue that she's given me the greatest gifts of all. Acceptance, education, and love.

There goes that word again, tumbling in my mind in a nonstop loop.

One of these days, once things have settled and I believe she's ready, I'll tell her how deeply and madly in love I am with her.

But for tonight, I'll have to settle with showing her.

Chapter Forty-One

ISABELLA

This is already my favorite game, and it hasn't even begun yet.

The feeling in the stadium is electric. The DJ is blasting salsa, merengue, and bachata through the speakers, keeping everyone in the stands moving and on their feet.

The Monarch players litter the field, greeting their teammates for the day, celebrities and Puerto Rican public figures. They're all in casual jeans and T-shirts, with loose jerseys indicating the teams—one home team Monarchs jersey and the other an away game Monarchs jersey.

The crowd is filled with people who donated to the cause or those who won tickets. Most of the ticket winners were flown in from Puerto Rico. Over a dozen of them on Mateo's private jet. Only I know this because I was there when he was on the phone, asking how we could get more Puerto Rican locals to the Monarchs' stadium. I'm also the only one who knows that he's footing the bill for most of their hotel stays, since he upgraded whatever the stadium was offering and extended their stays—with a stipend.

I look down from the suite I'm seated in, but I can't see him. He must be mingling with the newcomers.

And yes, I'm in the suite. Because not only was I invited, but I was able to bring as many friends as I wanted since Mateo reserved a private suite... for the rest of the season.

Luisa and Daisy are done with their logistics for the day and are indulging in the chilled champagne as Denise wrangles her three kids while also pleading for a glass. She came along with her mom and cousin so they could help her out with the kids, but I swear they're all velcroed to her.

Amelia and Nikki were also able to make it, and they brought their significant others. I remember Tony faintly as the hot guy she was on vacation with when we met, but I truly forgot that the guy was the size of a tank.

Although the biggest shocker was when Amelia's husband, Evan Cooper, walked in and immediately spilled the beans that Amelia was newly pregnant. It took a second for my brain to jump off the fact that Evan Cooper was hanging out in our suite. But the way his smile beamed the moment of his announcement made him seem much more approachable. And a clear simp in regard to his wife.

Daisy's fiancé was supposed to be here as well, but it seems like he's running late. I've been dying to meet the man who's put a ring on Daisy's finger, and not because he has atrocious taste in jewelry. There's a silent sadness in Daisy that sometimes slips through her blinding smiles, and I wish I knew how to set her free from whatever is keeping her down.

Next to Amelia's pregnancy announcement, my favorite moment was when Nick Stonehaven showed up and immediately ruffled Luisa's feathers with his mere presence alone.

"Play nice," I see him mouth to her when he thinks no one is looking. "Play nice," she mouths back mockingly as he chuckles. She rolls her eyes while finishing off her champagne.

And to round off the gang, my parents, Bethzaida, and Anna are here.

Everyone in this suite besides the parents know about Mateo and me. So tonight will be the night I rip off the Band-Aid and let the mothers rejoice in the satisfaction of being right to push us toward one another.

Honestly, now that I think about it, it's a small price to pay for the man I now get to call mine.

Speak of the devil.

He walks in, scanning the room until his eyes meet mine, and his smile threatens to weaken my knees.

Long gone are the days when I couldn't read this man or was greeted with barely constrained scowls. Now, I'm the lucky woman who gets to witness those loving smiles, the ones that are only directed at me.

And the other women in his life that he loves.

Love.

Shit. I'm in deep and I know it.

I'm trying to pace myself, but it's no use. I know my heart has long belonged to that man since before my head ever gave it permission to.

Now I just need to grow some lady balls and tell him how I feel.

Although it wouldn't kill me if he said it first. Yeah, I know I'm probably setting feminism back fifty years with that kind of mentality. But if you only knew the things I let that man do to me in the bedroom, you'd already know that ship has long since sailed.

He moves into the room, greeting people as he gets closer to me, until I hear, "Shit, you're Evan Fucking Cooper, right?"

"Says Mateo Fucking Martinez." Evan laughs as they do that weird bro hand slapping and hug combo.

"Tony, nice to see you again, man." Mateo repeats the same ritualistic handshake.

"You remember me? Uh, I mean, yeah, man. Nice to see you again too. Have a good game out there tonight." He nods repeatedly, clearly still starstruck by Mateo.

Nikki winks at him from across the room and whisper-shouts loud enough for all to hear. "You're doing amazing, sweetie!"

Tony silences her giggles with a stare I recognize all too well. Oh, she's in for it tonight.

Mateo changes trajectories, opting to say hi to my parents before he comes over to me. Smart man.

The wink he throws my way as he hugs my mother lets me know he agrees.

They chat for a few minutes, my mother very loudly singing his praises for giving me a job and a place to stay.

Yep. Looks like it's time to put an end to this dog and pony show.

I simply walk up to Mateo. His gaze tracks my every move, as if to gauge what my intentions are. Yet he doesn't skip a beat when I lean into his body, wrapping my arms around his middle. He slips his hand to my hip and drops a quick kiss to my forehead.

We're barely able to get the words out before my mother and Beth are in hysterics.

We honestly let them be, as Mateo shifts me slightly to shake my dad's hand and whisper something in his ear. Something chivalrous, I'm sure. But my dad has always been a big softie, never one for intimidation tactics. So before I know it, I'm in a group hug started by my dad. We're quickly joined by the moms and Anna, who won't stop singing "I knew before you guys did!"

With the way our mothers are wiping away tears, you'd believe we'd just had our first kiss at the altar as husband and wife.

Although their thoughts aren't far from it, as they shout and call each other suegras. Spanish translation: mother-in-law.

This is Mateo's cue to get out of Dodge, yet the small shrug and smile he gives me make me nervous for a whole other reason. "Do you not hear these cackling women? They are essentially planning our wedding, and they've known for five seconds."

He leans down, whispering in my ear. "Did you think being mine had an expiration date, tesoro? I might not be a fan of the term boyfriend, but husband? That one I can get behind. Especially if it means I get to call you my wife."

He silences my gasp with a sneaky kiss, and not a quick one.

The room erupts into cheers and whistles, and I'm sure I'm burning bright red. From the attention and that blistering kiss.

"Sorry, had to get one in before the game. Didn't think I'd be able to get one once you're out of this suite." He smiles shyly.

And guilt weighs heavily in my gut.

"Well, it's just that a lot of people are watching…"

"I know."

"And people will talk…"

"I know."

"And I—"

"Baby, you don't have to explain or worry about me, okay? We move at your pace and your pace only. I'm just the smart bastard who thought ahead and came to get what's mine before this show starts." He kisses me again, then winks as he retreats. "Have fun tonight, baby. Oh, and by the way, I love your jersey." He smirks as he backs away and slowly retreats from the suite, waving goodbye to our crew.

I laugh as I recall the jersey I found on our bed this morning. The very one I'm wearing tonight. With a big 1 in the center and *Morales* written in big block letters over my back.

Chapter Forty-Two

MATEO

THIS PAST WEEK, I've been brainstorming with Isabella and Daisy about the charity game nonstop.

Daisy's in charge of the charity event, and after I decided I was going to participate, I realized that there was so much more I could do.

I gave her free rein, including permission to use my name and promote the event however she saw fit, auctioning off signed items, and scheduling meet-and-greets with me. Something that seems so stupidly trivial, yet can bring in so much aid for those in need.

Though I did keep some things close to the vest when I decided to make a few phone calls and make some changes to the opening ceremony.

For instance, after the national anthems for both the US and Puerto Rico were sung, I let Daisy know at the last minute that Marc Anthony would be stepping up to my pitcher's mound to sing "Preciosa."

The opening notes of the Puerto Rican cuatro vibrate through the stadium, and I can see the collective gasps within the audience.

I let Marc get through the first half of the song on his own, but once he gets to that long note, I make my way onto the field. I jog with the Puerto Rican flag on a pole leaning against my left shoulder and, for the first time ever, run the bases.

The place feels like it's going to erupt with all the barely contained energy.

The flashes from professional camera bulbs look like small fireworks surrounding every corner of the field.

As a pitcher, I never get this view or the chance to run these bases, but as I do now, with a grin plastered on my face, I vow to never take this place or these people for granted.

When I round third and start to make it to home base, some of my team is waiting there, rallied around in a huddle of overexcited Hispanic men.

When I arrive, they give me a moment to step on home properly, and with a shift of the pole, I'm able to get a good grasp, and wave it proudly for all of Monarch Stadium to see.

For the entire world to see.

Because my island may be small, but it is powerful.

And it may have taken me almost thirty-three years to claim it as my own, but just like everyone I love in my life, it shall forever remain mine.

With misty eyes, I mouth, "Te quiero, Puerto Rico," I place my right hand over my heart and nod my head to those cheering up in the stands.

My team decides that they've given me enough of a moment to shine, and they promptly surround me, bouncing in place as if we've just won a big game. I'm completely put out of sight, but I make sure to prop the flagpole higher so eyes are always on my beloved Puerto Rico.

When the song is over and the pitcher's mound is now vacant, I hand the flag over to Anthony, who takes it proudly and starts to wave it enthusiastically while yelling, "¡Eso eh puñeta! De Puerto Rico pa'l mundo!"

I'm handed a mic as I settle into the spot that has been my home for many years. Where I've made my career and lost some hard games.

From the pitcher's mound, I'm able to see it all.

My team, the crowd, my family.

My Isabella.

And there's not a dry eye in the place.

I lift my wrist, making a point to jiggle it slightly, then kiss the friendship bracelet Anna made for us. Then quickly make a mental note to have a platinum and diamond one made for my girls and myself.

I guess Ace's jewelry habits are starting to rub off on me.

I clear my throat and welcome everyone to the event.

Then I ask for a round of applause for our performers, especially Marc, for agreeing to fly up and do this for us last minute.

And halfway through my speech, I realize that, once again, there is so much more that I can do, that I can say. So I forget the lines that I practiced with Isa into the late hours, and I speak from the heart.

"You know, I haven't always had the best connection to my roots." The crowd's rowdy cheers softly subside as they hear the change in my tone. "There were moments where it was tough, trying to figure out who I was as a man, as an athlete. As someone who is Puerto Rican, but not born on the island." I falter for a moment. "Sometimes, I felt like I had let my people down by not knowing or being able to relate to the lived experiences of those who grew up in Puerto Rico. Felt even worse when I struggled with not being able to speak Spanish. And I know I'm not the only one out there who has probably felt a little disconnected with their homeland." I look up into the stands and see an array of nods and mouthed *yeses*.

"Although in my own small ways, I've kept a tight hold on my love for the island." I pause as I get ready to reveal something I've kept to myself all of these years. "Early on in my career, I was asked to pick a jersey number. Many pick a year or a specific number that means something to them. I picked number thirty-five. Because Puerto Rico is one hundred miles long and thirty-five miles wide. An island so small that, in theory, shouldn't make such a big impact on the world. Yet here we are." I smile as the cheers threaten to overwhelm me.

"But recently, someone very special to me made me realize something. Something that I will never forget." I clear my throat as I prepare to say the first Spanish words I've ever spoken in front of the media. I take a moment to breathe, because I want this shit quoted correctly. "Yo soy Boricua aunque naciera en la luna."

The crowd goes wild.

Torres looks unhinged, probably yelling some amped-up profanities, making it impossible for poor Daisy to use in her hot mic'd segment. But what snags my attention is the suite housing some of the most important people in my life.

I can see my mother fully sobbing into Isabella's mother's shoulder. I spot Isabella carrying Anna in her arms and waving their friendship bracelets in the air, pointed at me.

She mouths something to me, and it might be my wishful thinking, but I'm pretty sure it's an *I love you*.

I don't chance not saying it back. Even if I'm wrong, she's going to have to get used to me saying it. So I look right at her as I speak into the microphone. "I love you, tesoro."

ISABELLA

I said *I love you* first.
Again, I have no regrets.

MATEO

THE GAME IS WRAPPED up, and I take a quick shower before changing into a maroon Monarchs button-down and black dress pants.

I barely toweled my hair long enough to dry. I'm too eager to see Isabella.

The event is officially over, but there is an after party in one of the stadium's function spaces for the biggest donors and high-profile attendees, along with the team and their families.

I saw my mother and Anna as soon as the game was over, since they were allowed in the dugout to greet me. My mother could barely keep it together long enough to tell me how proud she is of me. And I made sure she knew that the feeling was mutual.

She then stated that she was taking Anna to her apartment because the game ran later than expected and she didn't want Isa and me to miss out on the party.

With my mother and daughter safely tucked away, I'm a man on a mission.

I make it to the massive party room, one with a curved glass wall overlooking the stadium, and scan the crowd.

I spot her immediately—on the dance floor with her friends.

She's taken off her specially made Monarchs jersey, and I fully take in the silver dress and black thigh-high heels she's wearing.

She was definitely *not* wearing that under her jersey earlier.

I'm about to make my way to her when a hand lands on my chest.

"If the look on your face matches your intentions, then you should consider grabbing a drink before you maul her on the dance floor right in front of the cameras, my friend." Nick Stonehaven hands me an amber drink with a gray stone in it. "It's the good stuff from my office." He winks as he takes a sip of his own drink.

I join him, and damn, this shit is smooth. "You make it a habit to walk around with two drinks at all times?" I raise a questioning brow.

He shakes his head. "No. Just figured you were the safer target to receive a drink from me than the person I initially intended it for."

It's fast, but I see the moment his eyes flicker to the group of women dancing with Isabella. By a simple process of elimination, I figured out who he has his eye on. I pat him on the shoulder as I let out a low whistle. "Good luck with her. She's a tough cookie."

He looks at me, slightly perplexed, as I say, "Let's just say I might not be the only one with my intentions written all over my face." I tip my glass in his direction.

He sighs and clinks his glass against my own. "Fucking hell." He downs the rest of his drink and turns to leave without another comment.

I, on the other hand, laser in on Isabella again, only to see her sight already settled on me and a smirk on her face.

She's dancing sensually, running her hands down her sides until they land on her hips. She then starts to slowly spin as she grinds her ass in the air. The desire to dance behind her is causing me to white knuckle my glass so tightly that I have to put it on a passing waiter's tray in fear that I might break it.

She's teasing me. Testing my resolve.

Knowing that I will respect her wishes for us to remain under the radar until she explicitly tells me otherwise.

But the way she's dancing to this damn Sean Paul song from years ago is making me question it all. She's a siren, pulling me in. And after she slowly raises her arms and traces one hand down the other, I'm done for.

Let's see how bold her dancing gets while I'm standing only a few feet away from her.

Evan and Tony are close by, so I hope I'm not raising any alarms by joining this dancing crew.

Isabella's smirk morphs into a full-on smile by the time she's within arm's reach. And to my surprise, she gets even closer.

"Careful, tesoro," I warn lowly.

"Of what? Because I'm pretty sure I heard you say three little words loud and clear down there." She inches even closer.

"And if I'm not mistaken, you may have even said them first..." My face does nothing to hide my hopeful expression.

She simply bites down on her lip and nods, stepping right up to me along with the beat of the music.

My body vibrates with the need to get my hands on her. Feel the sway of her hips, the heat between her legs. All of it.

"Isa, a lot of people are watching," I warn gently.

"I know."

"And people will talk." I parrot her concerns from earlier.

"I know." She slips her hands around my neck, and I instinctively wrap her in my arms.

"And I'm going to kiss you anyway."

She pulls me down slightly, and my body melts the rest of the way to meet her. Our lips meet in a delicious dance, familiarity leading us to this point as she opens up for me without me asking, and I pull her impossibly closer.

I'm faintly aware of flashing lights and hollering around us, but honestly, a freight train could pass through this room, and I wouldn't be able to tear myself away from this woman.

The woman who is kissing me publicly, announcing to the world that she is mine.

The woman who has set my world upside down in the best way humanly possible.

The woman who loves me.

She pulls back slightly as I continue to rain kisses all over her cheeks and lips.

"I love you, Isabella. Eres mi luna y mi sol. Mi principio y mi final. I once thought I was a wealthy man. Little did I know that one of life's biggest treasures—you—was yet to come."

Her grin widens even farther as she pulls me in again and kisses me without the ability to wipe the smile off her face. "I love you, Mateo. Thank you for making me believe in love again. Believe in *me*, again." Her smile turns playful. "And for not firing me, because the benefits at my job are quite excellent." She erupts into giggles as I attack her neck with kisses.

My tone turns darker as I say, "I'm going to need you to work overtime tonight baby, just a heads-up."

She nods, feigning seriousness. "Yes, boss. I aim to please."

And that's enough for my sense of self-control in public. I grab her hand and turn us toward the exit, but she pulls on my arm. "Wait. I need a second." She laughs as her meek attempts to pull me back only leave her boots sliding on the smooth dance floor. I look down at her, clear desperation on my face as she rolls her eyes. I'll make her pay for that one later. "I'm serious. Wait a sec. I want to say hi to Daisy's fiancé. He must have just shown up."

I sigh deeply as I release my iron grip on her hand and slowly walk toward where Daisy is leaning by a high table with her head tilted down as her fiancé drones on about something. "... just saying that the wedding is coming up soon, and I don't think this piece of cake is going to help you fit into the dress my mother's picked out for you."

Isabella clearly catches the end of his statement, as I did, and I squeeze her hand to let her know I heard it, too.

Once Daisy realizes she has company, her head pops up, and she puts that bright smile back into place. I used to think she was a naturally chipper person. Now I see it's just a mask.

"Isa! Hey, uh, this is my fiancé, Da—"

"Senator Damien Fischer, nice to meet you, Mateo. Big fan of what you do here." He reaches out his hand for me to shake, as if he didn't just disregard the woman whose hand I'm clearly holding.

"I believe you were being introduced to my girlfriend, Isabella, here, first." I nod at his awkward outstretched hand.

His face does a terrible job of hiding his annoyance, but he tries his best regardless. "Oh, well, of course. It's just, you know, my Daisy here knows everyone in the stadium. I'd be here all night if she tried to introduce me to everyone she knows." He chuckles as he moves his hand toward Isabella's to shake, but she crosses her arms in front of her chest, and I bite back a smile.

"Sorry, can't relate," I say dryly, as if he's not in *my* stadium.

He clearly gets that this is no longer a warm welcome and pulls back his hands until they're both in his pockets. "Well, then, I've got to head out since I have to be at the capitol tomorrow." He squeezes Daisy's shoulder as he speaks. "See you next week, love." He kisses her on the cheek as he grabs the untouched dessert that sat on the table in front of her and makes his quick exit.

Daisy seems like she's on the verge of tears, even though you wouldn't be able to tell by her perfect posture and blinding smile.

"Daisy..." Isa starts, and Daisy quickly flicks her gaze toward me and back down to the empty table.

As much as I'm dying to get home and have my way with the woman I've publicly declared my love for, I know deep in my soul that Isabella is needed here by Daisy's side.

I spot a few of the guys from my team and plant a quick kiss on Isa's head. "Gonna go grab a drink with the guys. Come find me when you're ready, no rush," I whisper into her ear, then place another chaste kiss on her temple.

Appreciation floods Isabella's face, and I'm glad I made the right call. I turn to walk toward the guys, when movement catches my eye.

You would think it was a waiter discreetly placing a plate in front of a guest as he doesn't break stride passing by Daisy and Isabella's table.

But it's not.

It's Coach.

Putting two pieces of cake in front of Daisy without a single word spoken as he continues to walk out of the room and into the night.

Chapter Forty-Five

ISABELLA

I wake with a smile on my face.

Eyes closed, I stretch lazily as everything from last night's event comes flashing back.

And I moan slightly as I remember what came after Mateo and I finally made it home.

"You better be thinking about me, making sounds like that." Mateo shifts slightly to where I know he's hovering above me, yet I keep my eyes closed.

"Nah, you weren't in that dream where I was on all fours and—" My eyes fly open, and I squeal loudly as Mateo manages to flip me to where I'm on top of him, straddling his hips. His hardness, confined by his boxers, is nestled between my ass cheeks.

"Cleary, I took it too easy on you if you're still able to run your mouth first thing in the morning." He runs his hands up my thighs, bunching up my sleep shorts in the process.

I shake my head. "No, you very much did *not* take it easy on me. And therefore, I shall spend all day lounging on the couch watching Bravo until my insides rearrange themselves into their original positions."

He smiles, but it doesn't reach his eyes.

"What's wrong?" I tense above him.

"Nothing," he answers quickly. "Nothing with us, tesoro. We're perfect." He kisses both of my open palms, yet the gesture doesn't take my initial suspicions away.

"*Okay*. So what, *besides us*, is wrong?" I venture.

He sighs, then gently sets me back on the bed.

"There were pictures taken last night. Of us."

Oh, *that*.

I knew the moment that Mateo told me he loved me in front of a stadium full of people that we could no longer remain hidden.

I also knew that decision would come with the inevitable media coverage. The very thing that sent me into a dark spiral for years.

And yet, as I stood in a room with Mateo's loving eyes on me, I knew I could no longer live in the shadows.

For so many years, I kept myself hidden, kept my dreams and aspirations under wraps. In fear of what online trolls would say about me.

And now I look back at that time and wonder why.

All that time wasted, I'll never get back. Just because people who didn't know me had nothing better to do than to try and tear me down?

And while I withered away, in my own self-appointed solitary confinement, the villain in my story got to carry on and live large.

The fact that I can even think this way is because I have grown stronger from the things that promised to break me but failed. Because I had an amazing support system in my mother, Beth, and Denise—when I allowed them to be there for me.

And because now I have Mateo. And somehow, by his side, I truly feel invincible.

So yeah, I knew exactly what would happen if I kissed Mateo in public.

And I did it anyway.

"Isa—"

"I don't care." I bring my hand up to his cheek and try to wipe away the fine lines filled with worry. "Truly, I don't."

"You... don't care," he says slowly, needing to process my words out loud.

"What others think of me is none of my business." I shrug. "And as long as that outside noise doesn't interfere with our relationship, then to hell with them."

Mateo's eyebrows rise so fast it's comical. "Are you sure? Because in the article—" I put a finger over his lips.

"Don't. Care." I kiss him quickly before he gets the chance to deepen it, then bound off the bed to use the bathroom and brush my teeth.

Once I'm done and about to walk back into the room, Mateo blocks my path and hands me my phone. "You've got a text from Nick. Read it, and you might change your mind." He smirks as he walks by me, swatting my ass lightly as he moves to turn on the faucet and brush his teeth.

Curiosity gets the best of me.

I open my text and see that I received a message from an unknown number at five a.m.

Unknown:

Hey, this is Nick. Just wanted you to know that I keep my promises.

Unknown:

> Tabloids were going to go live with camera pics of you and Mateo last night. I was able to get those blocked and instead offered them something better. Our team's photographers got some pretty nice shots of you two, and I had them retouching and editing them to what I hope is your liking all night. Those are the pictures you'll see on the covers of every newspaper and magazine this morning. And I went ahead and took the liberty of planting some background info on you. Hope you don't mind my being busy, because I made sure your book cover design business was name dropped. And in regard to your ex, I made sure his name was scrubbed from any association with you, although I should give you a heads-up and say that it doesn't mean internet sleuths might not pick up on it. So just be ready if, later on, the connection is made. But I wouldn't harp on that, since I'm sure this story is going to be the main attraction for weeks to come.

Unknown:

Just realized the time and the fact that you don't have my number saved. I texted the message above to Mateo so I don't have an angry pitcher coming for me on Monday morning. Cheers -Nick Stonehaven

I spin in place, jaw dropped.

Mateo is already standing there with my brand-new iPad and the cover of the biggest magazine in the country pulled up.

And smack dab in the middle, barely making room for the headlines, are Mateo and me, wrapped up in one another as we kiss as much as our smiles will permit.

It looks like a cover of a rom-com movie.

It looks like the book cover of my dreams come to life. And somehow, it's my love story.

I make grabby hands at the device like the adult that I am. "Gimme. Hand it over."

Mateo chuckles as he lowers himself back to the bed, leaning on the soft headboard, and nudges me down to sit between his legs so he can read over my shoulder.

And within moments, I'm in tears.

Mateo silently kisses my temple as I read out loud.

"According to sources, Isabella Morales is the founder and CEO of Bella Covers, a Latina run small business that offers a multitude of services in the booming book cover design world."

It goes on to say, *"Morales, 25, seems to be the bright light in Martinez's, 33, new life in the spotlight. Last night marked his first appearance speaking in his native tongue, as well as stepping out with a love interest. It seems like Isabella and Mateo are each other's endgame, and we can't wait to see how much of their happily ever after they decide to share with us."*

"It's... they're being nice. To me." I turn, wrapping my arms around Mateo's neck as I nuzzle into his chest. "It's perfect." I smile as tears continue to fall silently.

"You're perfect." He kisses my hair. "And I owe Nick a very expensive bottle of whiskey."

CHAPTER FORTY-SIX

ISABELLA

THE NEXT TWO WEEKS are extremely busy.

Just as Nick promised.

My work email has been flooded with book cover requests. And the book box company I was able to snag a deal with before my photos with Mateo went viral is offering me an insane amount of money to be their in-house cover designer. They want to give me a set salary for giving them a certain number of exclusive covers for the next year.

Mateo hovers over my shoulder, reading as many incoming emails as I allow him, like a proud stage parent. Going as far as flagging certain emails that praise the work posted on my Instagram page and requesting I print them. Creating what he calls the "my woman is a badass" folder.

I'd be lying if I said I didn't take a peek inside every other day or so and pinch myself, since it's hard to believe that this is my life now.

A life that includes family dinners, where my mom and Bethzaida go to town in Mateo's kitchen as he and my dad get lost in deep baseball history conversations while setting the table and keeping Anna entertained. The house speakers are on most of the time now, having an array of music playing at all times. Though the moms usually take over that arena as well when they come over. "Matí, have you told Isabella how much you love Ednita Nazario yet? Oh and don't forget Luis Fonsi!" Bethzaida once shouted over her shoulder as Mateo groaned from the couch.

But the most interesting thing happened this morning in bed.

When Mateo fired me.

Yep, that's right. What was once my worst fear was now just plain rude.

"I didn't even earn a strike!" I argued as Mateo laughed.

"You'll always be there for Anna and me. I know that in my heart. But you got yourself a big girl job now that you need to focus on. I'll worry about finding your replacement, if we even need one between you, me, and my mother."

"My work schedule is flexible, and I work better early in the morning or late at night anyway. So I could still pick up and drop off Anna from school. I really don't mind."

"And if you can't, my mother or I can step in. Ever since we decided to cut back on Anna's extracurriculars, the scheduling has been easier to manage anyway."

"Or my mom. She's been glued to Anna's side since the charity game."

"Exactly. We got a nice crew going for us. So having you in a nanny position doesn't really make sense anymore, especially since the world now knows about us."

I fake gasped. "And what will they say when they find out you've been nailing the nanny instead of a 'family friend turned more'?"

"Did I already tell you that you're fired? Might want to nail the nanny one more time."

"At least I get to keep my benefits."

And now I'm home, a place that I'm getting more and more comfortable calling my own. I'm making myself a cup of coffee before getting ready to answer my overflowing emails when Mateo walks into the kitchen.

He has his practice bag in hand and a worried look on his face.

"Got a second to talk?" he asks as he drops the bag to the floor by the island.

"Yeah, what's wrong?" I put my coffee down as I round the corner and make my way to him.

He pulls me into his arms and holds me a bit too tightly.

"Breathing would be nice." My words are muffled into his chest.

"Sorry." He releases me slightly, then plants a deep kiss on my lips.

I put my hands on his cheeks and study his golden eyes, taking in the concern laced in them.

"What is it, babe?"

He sighs. "I was thinking maybe you stay home tomorrow instead of coming to my game."

I'm taken aback. I haven't missed a single home game since I've been living here, and I don't understand why he would want me to start now. "But it's the big one. We'll know tomorrow whether the Monarchs have made the World Series. Why would I miss out on that?"

He squints his eyes slightly. "How about you just take my word for it and agree nicely?" I drop my hands and cross my arms in front of my chest, my face surely giving off the annoyance radiating from my body. "Yeah. Figured." He sighs.

Without another warning, his hands find purchase on my hips, and he's setting me on the kitchen island. My legs naturally open to make room for him as he settles in.

"You know what team we're playing against, right?" he starts, and I nod.

"It's not the first time you've played against the San Diego Sparks. It wasn't a problem before." My tone is clipped at the reminder of the team he has to play against.

Jeremy's team.

Although it's hardly that, since he's been out most of the season with an injury. So Mateo hasn't had to pitch against him. He's been on medical leave and hasn't been obligated to attend away games, so it truly has been fine.

"He's cleared to play tomorrow night, baby. So I'll be playing against him for the first time since you and I..."

"Oh." My heart sinks.

Not only at the reminder of my sleazy ex, but because Mateo even has to worry about something like this during such a monumental game.

I've grown from my past. I'm not the person I used to be. But I can't deny it's a gut punch imagining my new love playing against my spineless ex.

But it's an even worse feeling imagining myself hiding back here, once again in the shadows, while Mateo sees my empty seat in the stands.

With that thought, I lean forward and kiss him. It's much deeper than I anticipated, but he welcomes the affection freely.

"I'm coming to your game, and you're gonna put on a hell of a show." I look up into his smiling eyes.

"Oh yeah? And why's that?"

"Because you've got someone you want to impress coming to the game." I shrug my shoulders. "So don't let me down, Martinez."

CHAPTER FORTY-SEVEN

MATEO

It's game day, and I'm dreading it.

I knew the day would come where I would have to pitch against Jeremy Anderson, but I truly hoped he'd be out for the rest of this season.

The fact that a few gossip websites picked up on Isabella Morales being the Izzy who was once briefly engaged to that asshole doesn't help my mood either.

The jersey-chasing accusations were quick to pop up, but between my attorneys sending cease and desist letters left and right and Nick's media company, we've been able to keep the murmurs at bay for the most part.

At least Isa hasn't read any of that crap.

Ever since she saw that we made front page news, she made a promise to never seek out information about herself on the internet. In her words: "If it's not written by me, then whatever is put out there is a brand of fiction that I'm not subscribing to. I'm the only author of my story. Everyone else's is fanfic."

And we're lucky. Without Nick's intervention, a story like ours could have spiraled in the media, especially with the little-known fact that she was my daughter's nanny.

I know many reporters who are foaming at the mouth to write something negative about me, but I never give them a reason to.

At least I hope not to, because as I gear up in the locker room, I can feel the tension in the air. The guys are amped up, knowing this is the game that decides whether we make it to our very first World Series as the New York Monarchs.

I know how important this is to everyone, especially the guys who haven't earned a ring yet. I need to keep my head in the game, but I understand that we're a team, and I need to let them know where my mind is at in order for us to perform on a higher level.

"Yo, guys. Bring it in for a second."

My teammates, in various stages of undress, walk up to where I stand by my locker, wearing looks of intrigue. "Okay, I'm gonna keep this short. We all know that this is a big game, and we're more than capable of taking home the win." Various cheers and curses erupt out of the adrenaline-pumped bodies around me. "But I need to let you all know what else is playing on my mind tonight. Number six from the Sparks is my woman's ex-fiancé. He did her dirty in the past, so you can say I'm not too keen on the guy. He's been out most of the season on an injury, and tonight, he decides to come back. The fact that a picture of me and my girl has been circulating everywhere probably hasn't made it easy on his ego, so I'm anticipating some shit talking here and there." I nod as I see the men around me take on protective stances, as if Isabella were in the room with us right now. And my heart softens a bit more for the guys I'm lucky to call family. "Now, I have no problem taking care of this the way I know best, out on the field. But I just needed you guys to know in case it gets a little hostile out there. Got it?" Grunts and a couple of *fuck yeah*s are thrown around. "Good. Now let's get our asses out there and win this damn thing."

The team starts to file out of the locker room, chanting and slapping each other's chests. I'm about to join them when I see Coach leaning against his office door, staring at me intently. A barely perceptible dip of his head is all I get. And it's all I need as I make my way out to the tunnel that'll lead me to victory.

I warm up and try my best to ignore the other team. It usually isn't a problem, but I'm on high alert today.

Anna has a cold, so she's skipping tonight and staying with my mother.

The chilly October temps have arrived, but it's still not fully coat season, so I'm able to see the sea of Monarchs jerseys in the crowd.

I look for Isabella, but she's not in her usual seat. Maybe she took my advice and decided to watch the game from my suite, away from the rowdy crowd.

Ever since her picture hit the papers, she's been stopped everywhere she goes. For pictures, autographs, or for a statement. She's handled it like a pro, and the only statements she's given are her bodega food orders. In turn, it's brought a surge of business to her local food spots.

I keep waiting for the other shoe to drop. For something to break her, or us. I feel like I'm constantly waiting on the sidelines to swoop her up and save her. Yet at every turn, she ends up saving herself, and it makes me love her a little more each day.

I'm making my way to the dugout when I hear a change in the crowd's cheers.

I can tell it isn't for me, since they're yelling into the stands. I look up, searching for who might be the cause of this circus, when I spot Charlie. He's walking closely behind my Isabella, who has taken a seat in the front row right behind home plate. In direct line of sight from the pitcher's mound.

She waves at the people seated around her graciously as Charlie mean mugs the hell out of them and reminds everyone to keep their hands to themselves.

Gotta remember to give him a raise for that.

She spots me looking at her and instantly raises a finger, indicating that I should stay and wait.

She's wearing dark jeans and a thick hoodie with an oversized Monarchs jersey over it. She pops the hood on top of her head, covering her beautiful curly hair, and slowly starts to spin.

I'm already grinning, because no matter what name she's rocking today, she knows I love our little game. And she probably knows that this is exactly what I needed to keep my mind on her and not on who I'm about to play against.

As her back fully turns to me, I let out a loud laugh.

She's wearing my damn jersey.

Fucking finally.

Not only that, but it seems like she broke into my daughter's bedazzling kit. Because this jersey reads MY MAN MARTINEZ on the back.

She turns back my way, clearly proud of her little stunt, and raises her wrist and wiggles her bracelet.

I do the same, because I refused to take it off for tonight's game.

She mouths an *I love you*, and I return it with a *te amo*.

She acts like she is swooning and starts to fan her face with her hand while batting her eyelashes. I shake my head and mouth *brat* back at her as she continues to giggle.

I blow her a kiss, which makes the throng of people around her cheer louder. She blows a quick one back and gives me a cute thumbs-up.

I can do this.

One more game, and we're in the World Series.

With Isabella's encouragement, I make it down into the dugout, fully zoning in and ready to play.

One way or another, Jeremy Anderson is going to learn a lesson tonight, and I'm much too eager to teach it to him.

CHAPTER FORTY-EIGHT

ISABELLA

I'M BOUNCING IN MY seat, and it has nothing to do with the cold.

Mateo is striking out players left and right, and it's reminding me of that first game I attended, when I wore Anthony's jersey.

It's clear that he's a man on a mission, and so far, the other team hasn't been able to get a single hit or man on first base.

This is good.

This has the potential of being another shutout game.

And then the Monarchs would make history as the first team in MLB history to make it to the World Series in their first year as a team.

During the second inning, Charlie and I got up to get some snacks. Or at least that was my excuse, because I needed a moment to walk off my lingering nerves.

I haven't seen him yet, but I know he's here.

The monster from my past waiting for me around the corner.

I ran into Luisa, and she looked more stressed than usual. I know that this is a big game for her as well, since it's her first season as the general manager, and I'm sure she feels like she has something to prove.

Nick spared us no mind as he stalked past us, speaking threateningly into his phone that seemed seconds away from snapping in his hold.

Luisa tracked him like a hawk, and I took pleasure in the slight distraction of the game happening below me.

We make it back to our seats by the third inning. The score is 2-0 in favor of the Monarchs.

Mateo spots me immediately as I take my seat, and the tension in his shoulders subsides slightly.

I lift the hot cocoa in my hand and give him another thumbs-up, letting him know I was on a snack run and that I'm doing okay.

His face remains unreadable for the camera, but I see the slight crinkle around his eyes as he blows out a breath and starts swinging his arm around for the next batter.

But in the next second, the temperatures seem to drop, and the air from Mateo's nostrils comes out in a puff of white smoke, like a bull who's just spotted a red flag.

And in my bones, I know the moment has come.

Jeremy Anderson, number six for the San Diego Sparks, starts to make his way to the plate, waving at the Monarchs fans who are clearly booing him.

A petty part of me wants to join in, but I know I have eyes, and probably cameras, on me now.

Shit. I probably should have stayed up in the suite for this part. It's too late now.

I watch Anthony lift his catcher's helmet and exchange some words with Jeremy. He keeps his fake smile in place as Anthony's body language clearly screams to anyone watching that he does not fuck with this guy. Jeremy takes a moment to comb back his longish dirty-blond hair and puts his helmet into place. He grins from ear to ear as he searches the crowd intently.

Eventually, Anthony squats down and takes his position, bouncing his weight from his left foot to his right as he waits for Mateo's call.

Mateo switches gloves and prepares to pitch with his right arm. Yet he takes his time when he moves the friendship bracelet from his right wrist to his left.

The action makes me release the breath I hadn't realized I was holding.

He's got this. He's got me.

After a single nod, Anthony settles into place, and Mateo pitches a fastball at Jeremy. But it went high, too high for it to have been an accident.

Jeremy dodges the fastball aimed at his face at the very last second, and the umpire calls out that it's a ball. The first of the game.

The horde of fans is shocked. A collective low *ooh* rumbles through the crowd, like they just realized they're experiencing much more than what they had bargained for. They all lean forward on the edge of their seats to see what Mateo does next.

Only then do I realize that I've done the same.

Charlie clears his throat next to me. "Isa, do me a favor." His eyes never stop scanning the area around us as he speaks.

"Uh, sure." My eyes flick between him and the field.

Mateo pitches again, this time the ball aimed right at Jeremy's lower body. He hops back quickly, but it causes him to fall on one hand as the other clutches the bat.

"Ball!" the umpire yells once more.

I see Coach Weston walk out of the dugout and give Mateo a slow head shake.

"Listen." Charlie grabs my attention once more. "If, for whatever reason, I believe there is a safety risk, I'm going to hold you by the upper arm and walk us out of here quickly. You got that?"

My brows furrow. "This place is crawling with security. Why would you think there'd be a safety risk?"

Charlie looks down at the field. "Call it a hunch." His tense body is coiled like a snake that's about to strike.

I look back down at the field and hold my breath when I realize Jeremy is staring right at me while standing a few yards away.

He then shouts, loud enough for everyone around us to hear. "Oh, hey, Izzy. Long time no see. Miss me?" He winks, then lifts his gloved batting hand to blow a kiss my way.

The action forces me back into my seat.

I feel a hand on my arm. "Now, Isa. Get ready to move before this thing gets even worse."

I'm still having a hard time catching my breath when I realize what Charlie is trying to warn me about.

Because the threat was never on me.

But on Jeremy.

Because Mateo has abandoned his spot on the pitcher's mound and is making his way straight toward my ex.

Chapter Forty-Nine

MATEO

AND TO THINK I was doing so well.

I've stayed focused and on task, pitching at the top of my abilities.

I thought I'd had enough practice during the first two innings.

And then *he* stepped up to the plate.

I want to say I tried, but I really didn't. Because when the opportunity to throw a fastball at his infuriating face arose, I couldn't let it pass me by.

Thought it'd give myself that one petty pass, and then I remembered how he also had the audacity to cheat on my girl. So yeah, that second pitch was aimed at his junk.

After that second pitch and watching both looks of slight terror on his face, I thought I had calmed the beast inside me. The one that's bloodthirsty for revenge on Isabella's behalf.

But I'm here to do my job, and although I didn't show it just now, I know how to be a professional.

That is until the fucker steps out of line.

The moment I see him face Isabella, I want to physically turn his neck around myself and have him face me, the person who would happily be the star of his nightmares.

But when he shouts something to make her face go ghost white, followed by blowing her a kiss? Yeah. He's officially done for.

I toss my glove on the ground and flip my hat backward as I make my way toward him, my long strides eating up the distance fast.

At the sight of me leaving my spot on the field, the crowd starts to go absolutely mental. Because something that sports fans like to see almost as much as their home team win is a fight.

And I'm about to give them a good one.

Jeremy turns and almost seems amused that I'm walking toward him. His survival skills are clearly lacking, among other things.

He shouts as he drops the bat and takes off his helmet. "Oh, I'm sorry. Are you here to tell me that I've been very bad, Mr. Golden Boy?" He laughs. But that laughter slowly dies the closer I get.

The look on my face gives anything but wholesome.

Gone is the passive face of the player who takes pictures with fans with his hands behind his back so there is never an accusation thrown his way.

Gone is the made-for-TV smile, the one usually on display when promoting toothpaste or whatever other shit I've sold under the guise of being America's Sweetheart.

In that man's place is the one who has promised to forever protect his woman.

As well as an exceptionally pissed off Puerto Rican man.

So I don't give him a warning.

Fucking with what's mine sealed his fate anyway.

So when I grab the neck of his jersey and pull him close to me, close enough to finally see the fear of God in his eyes, I put the power behind all my years of training in my swing. And the satisfying crunch that vibrates under my knuckles as he starts to bleed profusely from his nose brings me an intense amount of gratification.

So I do it twice more before I'm pulled back and engulfed by my team.

ISABELLA

BY THE TIME MATEO reaches Jeremy, Charlie and I are on our feet.

By the time he lands the first punch, we're rushing up the steps.

And by the time the fight is over, we're long gone.

MATEO

I'M EJECTED FROM THE game.

Coach is busy breaking up all the smaller fights that formed around me, so Luisa jumped in and escorted me down the tunnel and to the locker room.

We're quiet as we bypass all the stadium cameras, keeping our heads down as we make it past the checkpoint where no media is allowed.

And that's where she goes off.

"What in the actual fuck were you thinking back there, Martinez? You think tanking your career on one good hit during a career-defining game was worth it?"

"Three hits. And yes." I start to unbutton my jersey and notice my swollen, bloody knuckles.

She sighs loudly. "Trust me, if I could get that asshole in a room for five minutes, I would have caused some serious damage myself. But on the field? In a world where instant replay exists?"

"You didn't see her face. He said something to her." I turn angrily and point in the direction of the field. "And if you think I would reel in any sense of control when I saw it happen right in front of my eyes, then I'm sorry to learn that you think so poorly of me as a man."

She takes a step back, hands on her stomach, eyes wide. She starts to nod as she looks off to the side. "Wash up, get dressed, and get the fuck out of here before the mob gets you. I've already got your driver in the car and two police escorts waiting to get you home safely." She starts to walk out when she suddenly stops and says over her shoulder. "Coach had a message for you, by the way." She laughs humorlessly. "Said, 'first tell him to fuck off for screwing us this early in the game. Then second, tell him that if it had been me, I would have done worse.'"

She turns to leave, muttering Spanish curses under her breath.

Chapter Fifty-Two

ISABELLA

Monarchs lose.

And it's all my fault.

After Charlie got me home safely, I turned on the TV to see what happened. Which was a bad idea. Because all I could see was the rage on Mateo's face as his fist pummeled into Jeremy's face.

I did this to him. A man whose reputation has been pristine for almost fifteen years has been officially tarnished because he felt like he had to jump in and protect my honor.

I shut the TV off and make my way upstairs to shower. But then it suddenly feels wrong to do so in the shower I've shared countless times with Mateo.

This home was built on his baseball legacy. And tonight, I played a part in tearing it down.

So I grab the few things I need and head downstairs to my old room. I shower and quickly get into my old bed. I have no idea when Mateo will get home. Shit, will he be arrested? I start to panic, the incessant alerts of people trying to reach me on my phone tipping me over the edge. So I shut it off and lower myself under the covers, hoping like I did when I was a child that the nightmares can't reach me if I bundle myself tightly.

With barely controlled sobs and a mind-numbing headache, exhaustion eventually takes pity on me, and I fall into a restless sleep.

Chapter Fifty-Three

MATEO

She's not answering my calls, and I'm starting to panic.

I know she made it home safely and that she's still there based on the updates I got from Charlie.

I called my mother after I saw all of her missed calls, bracing for how this has impacted Anna when she saw what I did on TV.

Silver lining from her being sick is that she had taken her cold medicine and was fast asleep before the game even started. I'll still have to sit her down and tell her about what happened, since I'm sure she'll see or hear about it eventually, but at least I get to do it myself.

Now all I can focus on is Isabella.

And the daunting feeling that the other shoe has finally dropped.

As the elevator makes its way up to my home, I'm racking my brain as to how I can fix whatever pain that is consuming Isa.

I want it handled, I want it gone, and I want to do it myself.

Nothing has ever made me feel so powerless than seeing the woman I love get hurt right before my eyes. If I wasn't so hell-bent on getting to her as soon as possible, I would probably be finding my way back to Monarch Stadium to get another round in with Anderson.

The elevator doors barely open before I'm barreling through, shouting Isabella's name.

Our home is silent, and I wonder if she's already asleep. Except when I search our room, she's not there, and her shower gel is missing from our shower.

Fuck, fuck, fuck.

It's worse than I thought.

I run down the stairs, barely keeping upright as I make my way back to the first floor. I force myself to gently open her old bedroom door instead of ripping it off the hinges like I want to.

When I do, I find her waking up, rubbing at her tear-streaked face.

I force myself to keep hold of the doorknob and to quiet tonight's inner rage at the sight of her.

She seems so small and fragile in this bed, and I don't want to be the thing that breaks her.

But to my surprise, she gently lifts the comforter on the empty side of the bed and nods at me to get it.

I quickly step out of the sneakers and socks I didn't bother taking off when I got home and slip into the bed beside her.

If she needs more space, she's going to have to use her words, because I simply wrap my arm around her middle and pull her into me.

Her arms go around my neck as my face nuzzles into hers.

There. I can breathe again.

"I'm so sorry," we say at the same time.

I rear back, because what the hell does she have to be sorry about?

"The team lost. Because of me," she hiccups.

Oh, fuck that.

I lift her quivering chin with my knuckles. "Escúchame, Isabella." Her eyes widen as I speak Spanish. "Esto no es tu culpa. ¿Entiendes, mi amor?" If I tell her that this isn't her fault in Spanish, then it might start to sink in after I repeat it a million more times in English.

"I can't take away all the pain he caused you in the past, although I hope you know I'll try. But I could not, and would not, let whatever move he pulled tonight slide. Never on my watch, Isa. Never."

She sighs against my chest, then notices my messed-up knuckles.

"This looks like it hurts." She reaches for my hand and kisses each knuckle softly.

"Trust me, I'm not the one that is hurting tonight." I kiss her forehead. "On the bright side, it looks like my season is over, so I don't need to pitch with it any time soon," I try to joke.

She groans and leans her head back on my chest. "Not funny."

"Maybe just a little. You're gonna have to get used to the fact that I have no more games and, therefore, will be around all the time to annoy you while you try to get your work done." I kiss her head. The scent of her floral shampoo puts my soul at ease.

She's in my arms. Everything else will be all right.

"And why are you down here instead of our bed?" I chastise lightly.

She shrugs. "Didn't feel right being upstairs. Felt guilty of my role in it all." She raises her voice when she sees me ready to cut in. "Even if it wasn't my fault, it still didn't settle well with me."

"And now?" I shift so some of my weight is on top of her, but not all.

She looks up at me, wet lashes clumping together as she searches for something she must find, because she smiles. "Yeah. Now I'm feeling much better." She nudges me slightly, and I eagerly take the hint.

I finally kiss her and feel her soften under me.

Her legs open, allowing me the space to get closer to her.

Our bodies know this dance well. Our hands travel, and we start to pull at each other, trying to find ways to get even closer.

Isabella breaks the kiss, only for a moment, to take her tank top off and throw it across the bed.

I look down hungrily at her breasts but pause. "Are you sure, baby?" I know it's been an emotional night, and I want to make sure her mind is in the right place.

She takes my moment of hesitation and shimmies herself out of her panties and sleep shorts. "Yes, please. I need to feel you. Feel us. Right now."

The urgency in her voice has me snapping into action, pulling down my sweats along with my boxers and tossing them aside. Before I have the chance, she's ripping the T-shirt over my head and pulling me back down to kiss her.

My hand goes to her breast, pinching and teasing like I know she likes.

As much as I try to hover, my hard cock leaks precum onto her stomach, and I'm doing everything in my power to keep it from touching her pussy.

Which reminds me. I let out an agonizing groan. "Fuck, baby. Condoms are upstairs." I run my fingers through her wetness and curse my past self for not thinking ahead and stocking this room with condoms as well. "Let me eat you out down here, and then we'll head up to our bed for round two. How does that sound?" I easily slide a finger into her, causing her back to arch and her breasts to inch closer to my face. My favorite.

I suck a nipple into my mouth and bite down lightly.

She moans. "I have a better idea." She reaches down and finds my hardness. I slide my finger out of her so I can get a better look at what she has planned.

When she rubs the tip of my cock on her needy clit, I almost lose it.

When she lines me up bare into her opening, I think I see heaven.

"Please," she pleads softly.

I don't need to be told twice.

With my thumb firmly planted on her clit, I start to rock, giving her an extra inch of me each time I thrust into her.

We both release animalistic sounds at the feel of fucking each other without anything between us.

Her tight heat threatens to be my undoing, and I do everything possible to focus on her and hold off my looming orgasm.

I start toying with her pretty little clit, teasing, rubbing, and pinching, causing her to clench that beautiful pussy around my throbbing cock.

At times like these, as I play her like an instrument, I'm glad I'm ambidextrous. One hand squeezes and plucks her nipples while the other rubs her clit, all while keeping my thrusts deep and evenly paced.

I feel my own orgasm on the rise, so I know it's time to make my woman scream. I shift slightly, hitting that spot that usually sends her flying off the bed. I push down on her lower stomach, forcing her to stay put as I watch her face morph into ecstasy. Her pussy starts to flutter around my cock, and I pick up the unrelenting pace, now wanting my own orgasm to meet with hers.

She starts screaming my name, and there's no holding back.

We come together. Kissing and moaning against each other's lips.

I slow my pace, catching my breath, as I continue to fill her up, leaning over her, making sure not to spill a single drop.

The way she continues to suck me in long after the orgasm has overtaken her leads me to believe that she just had another. As I swipe my thumb over her clit one last time, my suspicions are confirmed as she hisses at the contact.

After I've recovered a bit of my strength, I allow myself to slip out of her.

I lean back on my knees to take in the view I've never had before.

My cum starts to slowly seep out of her, and an immense sense of satisfaction threatens to consume me. Isabella tries to close her legs and says something about the sheets, but I keep her legs wide open for me by keeping one hand on each knee and take it all in.

Eventually, I can't help myself.

I release her legs. They helplessly fall open as I let my thumbs open her up farther, smearing our collective arousal and making an absolute mess.

She half chuckles as she rises up on her elbows. "You almost done down there, big guy?"

I look up at her, my smile predatory. "Water and ibuprofen. Right now." She quirks an eyebrow at me. "If you thought you were getting any sleep after you let me fuck this pussy raw, you're sorely mistaken, tesoro."

ISABELLA

SORELY WAS THE OPERATIVE word.
And once more:
Not. One. Single. Regret.

ISABELLA

The next twenty-four hours were pure media mayhem.

Or at least that's what I've been told.

Because I've kept strong and stayed off the internet, especially when I can only assume side-by-side pictures of Mateo, Jeremy, and me are being posted.

I did ask the group chat to give me a simple heads-up as to how bad we're talking here, and they advised me to stay off the internet until the story dies down. After I explicitly asked, Denise did say that the link between Izzy and Isabella has been fully confirmed, and those old articles are unfortunately circulating again, although no leaked pictures have reemerged anywhere. A part of me believes Nick had a hand in blocking them.

Beth decided to keep Anna at her place for the day, since she's still under the weather and because we have media camped outside our building.

My mom is joining them and making Anna some sancocho, along with some other Dominican food, since, apparently, Beth's cooking isn't "doing the job properly" to heal Anna's simple cold quick enough.

I know Anna loves making Beth jealous when she mentions how good my mom's cooking is, and a part of me believes she gets real pleasure out of her real grandmother and now surrogate grandma duking it out for her affection.

I'm burrowed cozily on the couch with a fluffy blanket as Mateo comes over and offers me a glass of wine.

I narrow my gaze and eye him suspiciously.

He laughs as he leaves the glass on the coffee table. "I come in peace... and with my penis in my pants. I promise. I'm pretty sure we almost broke it last night," he jokes.

I drop the act, because who am I kidding? I was riding that bull like it wasn't my first rodeo last night. But it's always nice to give him a little attitude. It's who I am, after all.

He looks at my open notes app and asks, "What are you up to?"

I've toyed around with the idea all morning, but just wanted to run it by Mateo first. "I was thinking about putting out a statement." His expression seems shocked, but he urges me to continue. "When everything happened last time around, I felt so helpless, voiceless. But now, I feel like I have the power to use my own words, tell my own story, what I feel comfortable sharing about it, on my terms." I shake my head. "When I said 'statement,' I meant posting screenshots of my notes app on my Instagram. I'd turn off the comments so that I'm not tempted to read them and just let my voice be finally introduced into the conversation."

Mateo nods, his large hand rubbing along his short beard. "Do you know what you want to say?"

I pick up my phone and hand it to him. He reads it out loud.

Hi everyone, it's me, Isabella.

I'm sure the internet is working overtime in light of last night's events.

And although I have many thoughts on the matter, I'm not here to speak about the actions of two grown men.

I'm here to speak about myself and publicly use my voice for the very first time.

It'd be very easy to fall into the trap of he said, she said and speak of the headlines that plagued me five years ago.

But I'm not interested in speaking about things like my heartbreak or the feeling of betrayal that comes with infidelity, because I can promise you, that is something we can all survive, even if it takes some of us a little longer.

No, what almost broke me were words.

Words spoken of and about me on the internet.

Painful untruths that followed me long after the headlines faded in your memories.

Because while I was tending to a broken heart and public humiliation over leaked photos, it felt as though the world was sitting back and watching every tabloid write scathing articles about me.

While I sat in abandoned silence, picking up the tattered remains of my stolen girlhood, the media moved on to the next story, not caring that I was collateral damage.

But I've learned from that young girl who once felt helpless, and I am no longer in the place I once was, even if the gossip blogs tempt to pull me back in.

I'm here to say that we are all allowed the space to grow and evolve.

To not be ashamed of our past or our journey to find a place of healing.

Because we are more than our circumstances, more than the titles bestowed upon us.

We are worthy, we are loved, and we are strong women who don't cower to man children who have no power over us.

And maybe some of us have a Monarch with a mean right hook in our corner that you shouldn't mess with.

Love,

Isabella

"Yeah, I probably should take out that last part before your PR people come for my head," I mumble into my wineglass as I take a sip.

I almost spill it all over my chest as Mateo pulls me by my ankles and manhandles me into straddling him.

"I swear to God if you have a boner, I'm getting you institutionalized."

He laughs as he takes the glass out of my hand and puts it on the coffee table.

As soon as the glassware is safe, his hands are on my face and he's pulling me down for a kiss. "I love you so much, Isabella. Promise you'll be mine forever."

I smile against his lips. "Careful, Martinez. You don't want to go around making a girl think you're proposing to her or something."

He hums. "I wouldn't dare. Although, tell me. If this were your favorite romance book, how would I propose to a woman like you?"

I smirk as I whisper into his lips. "You know where we keep the Post-its. I'm sure you'll figure it out."

MATEO

I'm about to scramble off this couch and scribble the quickest marriage proposal known to man when my phone vibrates next to me.

It's a text message from Nick.

Shit.

On my way out of the stadium, I saw him stalking furiously into his office with Luisa hot on his heels.

He probably wants to have my head on a pike.

I open the text and am taken aback by the fact that it's a group text for the entire Monarchs team.

Nick:

> Hi all, I know last night was a disappointing loss for all of us, but today is a new day. I am hosting a dinner party at my home tonight, and your attendance is mandatory. Plus-ones are encouraged, although no children, please.

Nick:

> Make sure to wear your finer clothes and arrive ready for a celebration.

What in the actual fuck?

Isabella's phone starts to go off, and I see it's Daisy. By the way they're texting back and forth, they too are at a loss.

Either way, after the stunt I pulled last night, I don't have much of a leg to stand on when it comes to blowing this party off, so I guess we're going out tonight.

ISABELLA

The sidewalk leading up to Nick Stonehaven's brownstone looks like it was secured by the same people who work the MET Gala. Valets and security keep the long line of cars moving smoothly.

When it's our turn, Mateo steps out first, looking handsome in a black suit, then reaches out for me.

There are only two steps before the privacy screen on the street blocks us from the view of the awaiting paparazzi. Still, it's more than enough for them to get a shot of Mateo smiling down at me as I give a little shimmy in my low-cut maroon dress.

After I posted my statement this morning, the group chat has kept me in the loop with how it's been perceived by the media.

If the four million likes are any indication, it's going over pretty fucking well.

It felt good to take control of a situation that once felt impossible. Put my own words out there for the world.

Although the best feeling was simply not caring if I got ripped to shreds again. Because I no longer put my value in the hands of strangers on the internet.

And the hunky man next to me sure isn't a bad consolation prize.

We make it into Nick's impressive home. The entryway opens into two wide staircases, curving around on each side of the room.

Staff take our coats, and our hands are quickly filled with glasses of champagne.

Seems like everyone is huddled under the staircase, waiting for Nick to make some sort of grand entrance.

As if my thoughts have summoned him, he strides onto the second-floor landing, with his own glass of champagne in hand and looking quite dapper.

He's sporting a white tuxedo jacket, with a black shirt, bow tie, and pants.

"Welcome, everyone. Welcome to my home," he starts as the crowd around us starts to quiet at his arrival. "I want to thank you all for coming on short notice, even though I didn't give you much of a choice." He chuckles, then turns serious. "I know last night was a tough loss, and I myself probably didn't handle it in the best way, and for that, I apologize." He nods. "But tonight, we are here for a celebration. Because while most of you were home, licking your wounds, I was busy... getting married." After a collective gasp from all of us, the room is so quiet, you could hear a pin drop.

Nick is no stranger to having a beautiful woman on his arm, but I had no idea he was seeing anyone seriously or even engaged.

"Yes, yes, it was a spur-of-the-moment decision, but as they say, when you know, you know." He smiles, then looks off to the side of the staircase, making a gesture to someone I can't see. "So tonight, you are all actually at our wedding reception. Thought it'd be fitting, given my bride... hold on just a moment, seems like my bride has gotten cold feet, even though we've already signed the marriage certificate," he jokes awkwardly as he moves to the side of the stairs.

After some hushed whispers, he finally walks back out, hand in hand with someone I can't see yet. "Ah, here she is, my blushing bride."

My champagne glass threatens to slip from my hands as Luisa steps out in a shimmering white pantsuit and a large diamond wedding band visible on her finger.

"To the bride and groom!" Nick lifts his glass as he slips a hand around her hip and squeezes.

She discreetly lifts her heel and steps on his foot. Hard.

His smile only broadens.

Something isn't right here.

There's no chance in hell.

The crowd starts chanting, "Kiss, kiss, kiss."

He raises his brow as he slowly turns to kiss her.

And when their lips meet, Jesus Christ, there's no faking *that*.

Holy shit. My mind is reeling.

My friend married a fucking billionaire.

NICK

TWENTY-FOUR HOURS BEFORE

I storm into my office, tugging off my tie as I do.

I was stupid. For a moment, I believed this team would win, and I would walk away clean, having accomplished one of the proposed terms of my dead grandfather's will and getting back what I so carelessly lost.

Fuck. I was so fucking close.

I'm granted only a moment of serenity before Luisa bursts through my office door, having no problem bull dozing in here, since it seems to be the only way she knows how to enter my work space.

"What the hell is wrong with you? Stepping out on the team as they were just handed their loss. For what? So you can drink your expensive booze and sulk in silence?"

"Silence, in my office? I would never dream of such a delight," I snark as I get up to pour myself some of the alcohol that Luisa helpfully reminded me of. Even though my guest wasn't invited and can currently be described as hostile at best, my manners ensure that I pour her a glass as well.

Looks like we both need it.

"Those men down there have put their absolute blood, sweat, and tears into this game. Their families deal with not having a family member for most of the year. Did you even know that baseball has the longest season of all professional sports?"

I eye her over my glass as she continues to spew sports facts that have no hope of being retained.

The way her chest heaves as she tries to prove her point makes it quite hard to pay attention, in my defense.

While I've thoroughly enjoyed this season, with Luisa ready to rip me a new one at every turn, it seems our perverse form of foreplay has abruptly come to an end.

Because it's all coming to an end.

As in the New York Monarchs.

All because I didn't satisfy the terms of the living will that haunts me daily.

"Love, hate to interrupt, but your breath is being wasted, unfortunately."

"Love? You think 'cause you own this team, you can go ahead and avoid HR complaints? Because I'll let you know—"

"It's over, Luisa. All of it. The New York Monarchs just played their first and final season as a team. And there's nothing we can do about it. So yes, scurry off to HR, and while you're there, let them know that a severance package is coming their way."

Her face drops. And so does her body—into the chair in front of my desk.

Feels like she's docile enough to slide the glass in front of her without having it boomerang back to my head.

She takes it without a fuss and throws half of it back in one go.

Rookie mistake.

But to my surprise, she doesn't flinch. Nor does she have an exaggerated coughing fit.

The woman is a whiskey drinker. Another thing to add to the list of reasons why she intrigues me so much.

But not even the slit in her fitted skirt can get a rise out of me at a time like this.

"Explain," she says warily.

I stand and close the doors that Luisa so unhelpfully left open.

Instead of walking back to my chair, I move to stand in front of my desk, forcing Luisa to sit back unless she prefers to sit with my crotch in her face.

Pity.

I cross my arms and pin her with an unyielding stare as I start. "What I'm about to tell you cannot leave this office, understood?"

She nods.

"Use your words. We both know you know how to cut me with them," I push.

"Yes, understood," she grits out.

I smile condescendingly. "Good. I'd usually have someone sign an NDA, but if there is anyone else who has just as much to lose by this going public, it'd be you."

"Get to the point where I have to clean up a rich man's mess. Go on, I know it's coming. What is it? Found yourself in a sex scandal? No, too boring for a guy like you. Has to do with money. Maybe a little embezzling or money laundering?

What's your poison, Stonehaven?" She pushes back, and my God, now is not the time to admire the woman.

"Trust me, Luisa. If I had a poison, it would be you. Since I can't seem to help myself from drowning in it." I pause as I watch her take a smaller sip this time, her eyes never leaving mine. "Very well. I'll save you the sob story and get to the point. My father and I have never gotten along. A few years back, after I made my money on my own, a true thorn in my father's side, by the way, he bet he could acquire a company quicker and more efficiently than I could."

"You said this story would be quick, but all I'm hearing is that you have daddy issues. If the next sentence out of your mouth is close to 'I'm self-made, but I took a one-million-dollar loan from my dad to do it,' I'm out of here."

"Retract your claws unless you plan on leaving marks down my back, Luisa." Her jaw drops slightly, and I take it as my cue to continue. "I was foolish, and in my haste, I didn't do my due diligence. What I put up for the bet wasn't mine to give. And to ensure my father wouldn't play dirty, I made sure to move that asset into my grandfather's name, another man I no longer had a relationship with, although he seemed like the lesser evil at the time. Needless to say, I had no idea my father was sleeping with the wife of the CEO of the very company we were vying for and therefore had insider information. The asset has remained in my grandfather's name since then. Once he passed, I went to the reading of his will to see if he would give it back. First, he gave me this team, which I had no interest in keeping and was planning on immediately selling off to whoever wanted to bore themselves with this sport. But then the asset was offered back, but only as long as I accomplished at least one of the two proposed terms."

She waves me on. "Well, what are they?"

"One, I keep the team and lead them to a World Series game in their first season. They didn't have to win the World Series, just make it. Something they would have accomplished had they won tonight."

I can see the wheels start turning in her pretty little head, and I know she's connecting the dots as to why I was so furious earlier.

Not my brightest moment, but we all have flaws, don't we?

"This team can't be over." She stands abruptly, not bothering to step back and leave appropriate space between us. "This is my first season as a general manager. Hell, I'm the first woman general manager ever. If this team goes down the drain, so does my career." She digs her hands into the tight bun on her head, and my hand twitches to let her hair down once and for all. "It'll fuck my career and that of any other woman who's working her ass off to get a respectable position in the sports industry. Me going down is a clear message that I've failed and that there is no space for women in professional sports." She shakes her head, her spine straightening, resolve in her voice. "No. Not an option. What was the second term?"

Well, this one's the real kicker.

"I get married."

"*Excuse me*?"

"For a year, I have to be a married man. With no public scandals and no claims of infidelity made against me."

She huffs out a laugh. "Perfect. Call up one of your brainless bimbos and give them an offer they can't refuse. Have them sign an NDA, and you're golden."

I take a sip of my drink as she starts to pace back and forth. "You see, that's where things get dicey. Because I thought about it immediately after I heard the will. But I'm not allowed to get any prenuptial agreements. Meaning, that once our one year is up, if my dashing bride decided to take half of my entire net worth, she'd be well within her rights to do so. And I'm sorry to say that I'm not keen on giving away five billion dollars to a, what did you call it? Ah, yes, brainless bimbo."

Her eyes widen. "You're worth five billion dollars?"

"No, that's the half I'd have to part with. Please keep up, sweetheart."

Her mouth snaps shut as her mind spins, her eyes looking like the slot machines in Vegas, spinning to land on the winning solution.

She goes rigid, and for a moment, I worry that she's going to pass out.

"What is it?" I ask.

"I'll do it."

"And what exactly are you offering to do, Luisa? You don't leave a man with a mind like mine to go off and assume."

She comes to stand in front of me, face stoic as she says, "I'll do it. I'll marry you."

I roll my eyes. "Yeah, that five billion sounded nice enough to sweeten the deal, I bet."

She scoffs. "Is it a stupid amount of money? Yes. Should there even be a singular human walking around the Earth with that kind of cash at their disposal? No. But that's not what I'm after." She takes a step closer, and I drop my arms. "This might look a little different from your point of view with all the zeros in your bank account, but I am self-made too. I have worked tirelessly to carve a path not only for myself, but for the women coming up behind me. So believe me when I say I'll marry you, and when the clock runs out on our sham marriage, I'll happily walk away without a cent of your money, because I'd get to keep what I brought into it."

"Hmm, and what's that?"

"My integrity."

Silence.

We stare at each other for what feels like an eternity.

I'm well versed in reading people, and Luisa isn't bullshitting me.

This is stupid.

A much too rash decision.

I can clearly hear my accountant screaming in my ear to reconsider.

But it doesn't stop me from goading her. "I retrieve my lost asset and keep my money, and you keep your position not only on this team, but as the beacon of light for all women everywhere."

She glares at me, and I smile. "Oh, and that integrity. Let's not forget that."

"So, Stonehaven. What do you say? We getting married or what?" She holds out her hand as if to shake on a simple deal.

I take it and quickly pull her into my chest. Her soft gasp does something to me, and I make a mental note to make sure I get to hear it again.

"I recover my asset, and you keep your job. Sounds like a fair trade to me."

THE END

FAIR TRADE
COMING 2025

Tesoro

ACKNOWLEDGMENTS

I'M EIGHT MONTHS PREGNANT as I write this, so bear with me.

Thank you to all the badass moms out there who have shown me that I can do hard things, even while parenting a toddler and heavily pregnant.

This book would not exist if not for my amazing husband, Hugh, and his unwavering support. Whether that be words of affirmation or white knuckling a few hours at the children's library in Mount Dora, FL with our son as I type my little heart away a few aisles over. Thank you for always championing my dreams and for being the best dad to our children. I love you deeply.

My beta readers (but you're all alphas to me) Carla, Lela, Esther, Sam, Brenda, E, Marietere, Maria, and Andrea, thank you for all you do. From sensitivity reading to adding the acentos to my Spanish dialogue. Writing this book wouldn't be half as fun without your unhinged commentary on the Google doc.

Sandra, my incredible book cover designer, who held strong while I couldn't figure out what the color "lavender" was, because first trimester Millie was clearly lacking brain cells. Thank you for not only being a true professional, but now someone I consider a friend (and since we live in the same city in Spain, I apologize in advance for being clingy).

Beth, my editor who not only makes me sound way smarter by lending me her editing talents, but is also the most supportive mama bear who let me push back my deadline twice because she was one of the first people I told I was expecting, and she made sure I was able to do this book justice. And Nyla, for agreeing to jump in last minute to proofread. I wasn't joking when I said you're stuck with me for life, friend!

Hannah and Taylor, I gotta love my girls for holding me down as I bombarded the group chat with a million meaningless questions. Thank you for rooting for these characters before you even read a word of my first draft. If I walk away from publishing today, I walk away a winner knowing I gained friends for life with you two.

And finally, to my readers. To the ones who immediately picked up on the possibility of Mateo's story being the next book I wrote while reading *You Never Forget Your Worst*, and the newcomers, who decided to give this Latina author a chance. Thank you for believing in me and my stories. Can't wait to bring you Nick and Luisa's story next. And after that... yes, they get a book as well.

* 9 7 9 8 9 8 8 6 5 1 5 1 2 *